IN MEMORY OF A LOST WORLD

ROBERT W CELY

In Memory of a Lost World

BY
Robert W Cely

ATHANATOS
PUBLISHING GROUP

In Memory of a Lost World
By Robert W Cely

Published by Athanatos Publishing Group

ISBN: 978-1-64594-041-8

Prologue
Written by the Finder of this Journal

This book was found sitting atop a piece of crumbling wall in the old section of our city. I am not the author of its contents. Nor do I wish to have been the one to behold all the awful things the book recounts.

I happened upon the book as I wandered the city one night. One of those listless moods had overtaken me without cause or explanation. The grimy walls of my miserable apartment grew too close and I longed for some freer, fresher air.

Outside, the grip of winter still seemed to hold fast. It was a cold though that had a weakness to it that heralded the coming spring. It had been a long, hard winter. Now I know why it was so.

The cold air refreshed me. I took to the city glad of the open sky and atmosphere. Even though I could see no stars through the glare of the city lights, I felt the grandness of the heavens above me nevertheless.

As I wandered, I came upon an old wall, only about as high as my knee, crumbling and covered in mossy growth. It surrounded a mostly empty lot. The only things I could see were scattered remains of detritus and trash, some long, brown scraggles of last summer's grass, patches of unmelted snow, and oddly, a mass of raven feathers that must have been dropped from at least 100 birds. Only one other thing stood in the otherwise empty lot - a magnificent and unusually large, green ash tree.

The tree looked hard-battered by the long winter, but still thrived. I could see premature buds forming on the ends of the branches, as if the tree knew somehow that the end of winter was closer than anyone expected. Something deep and powerful had me fixated on the tree, something I could not see that held my attention. So fixated was I on the magnificent tree that I almost didn't see this little book laying atop the wall.

I looked around to see if anyone else was nearby, if the owner might be hurrying back to retrieve his lost book. Satisfied I was alone I thumbed through it quickly, admiring the precise script in which it was written. I pocketed the book and hurried home.

You should judge for yourself the contents of this book. It outlines the discovery of a most fantastic conspiracy, that if true, would be a conspiracy to pale all other cover-ups, and whispers of a worldwide, shadow government. It tells of a hidden war that rages all around us, one we don't even know we are fighting. Or rather, that we are losing. It is impossible to win a war that you don't even know you're involved in. But such is the strategy of our powerful and deceitful enemy.

It is a war for the heart and soul of humanity, for the future of every nation and race alive today. And while there are some of our very own people who conspire with the enemy, very few of us even know that there is even a war at all. Even fewer know how miserably we are losing, and how close we are, not to oblivion, but to a fate far worse. For if we lose, our slavery to these dark forces will be complete, and every semblance of hope and joy will be blotted from our earth.

I will say no more except explain the order of the work before you.

Whoever has written this, and I have no idea who he is, wrote some of this looking back into the past, as a narrative of what had already happened to him. The rest is more a journal of what was occurring day by day. I have separated these two sections to help make their division clear.

I made further divisions based on visions that seem to be central to the narrative. Whether these visions were truly prophetic or merely hallucinations is for you to decide. However, it was these visions that drove whoever wrote this to his discoveries.

My only request for you is that you read with an open mind. Afterwards, search your heart and open your eyes. Observe the world around you. Tell me then that this story is far-fetched. Tell me if it is not true. Tell me if you can, that there is not a war, and we, our very souls and selves, are both the battlefield, and the spoils for the victor.

Part I

The First Vision

It began with a fever. A summer flu struck me, the nasty kind with chills and aches and a feeling that reality is slipping away from right underneath me. When I came out on the other side I was...different, changed. It's hard to say how, even harder to say what happened. I just know I'm not the same man I was.

It began with a fever, and it ends with my death. I know it is near. Perhaps in a week, a month, I can't say exactly when. Whatever that fever started led me directly to this moment here, on a collision course with vast and powerful forces - forces I could never have believed existed - that want me dead.

I do not regret the events that led me to this moment, even though they kill me. These last few months contained more purpose and fulfillment than all my previous forty-five years. I feel like...what is the word for this sensation? I feel like for the first time I have substance. I feel real.

Not real in the sense of genuine. I feel real in the sense that I know I have true existence. Whereas before I had been a mere phantom in life, though made of flesh and blood. Now I have weight. Before I could not even leave ripples on the water of life, now I break the surface and plunge deep into its depths.

So few exhibit this quality, I can see it clearly now. Our crowds are so weightless and pale, hardly impacting the world around them. Even our admired stars and supposedly influential politicians are some of the most insignificant among us. They all tread but on the surface of the water. They lack the realness, the substance, to even leave a trace of their passage.

Do not mistake me, this is not arrogance. This is simple truth. Very few people have any weight at all. Not that the potential is absent. There is not a man or woman alive that lacks the ability to be profoundly real. Yet they hardly use the opportunity.

1

I have only been real for a short time, perhaps a few months. The difference cannot be mistaken. This is what life was meant to be like. When you feel like this there is no existential doubts about your reality, no anxieties about whether your life matters or if there is even a point to living.

When you finally become real you know, and everything changes by consequence.

Before this change, I was probably less real than most. My life had followed the pattern of so many American men, living a life automatically, with hardly a moment's reflection. I never questioned where life took me. It looked like everyone else's life so I assumed I did things right.

To dispel a common rumor, yes, that many people can be wrong. In fact, they usually are. The wisdom of the masses is no wisdom at all. It is merely the shared assumptions of life and has nothing to do with truth.

After graduating college with an immanently practical degree in business, I took up the field and entered into a large firm that oversees sales, distribution and marketing for smaller companies that have outsourced to us. Somehow, I lodged myself into middle management and became stuck fast.

A few years after college it became clear that the time had come for marriage. This was mostly due to the fact that most of my friends were getting married and the girl I had dated since college grew impatient to have the spotlight of a bridal day.

Looking back I see the folly in what I did. Laura and I had so little in common. Perhaps at one point we enjoyed each other's company, shared the same vision of life, which is the vision that society had cast upon all of us. After a time, lacking any major relationship issues, we allowed ourselves to be carried by the tide of life. We married, and a few years later children followed, a girl and a boy.

My life was such a sham it is a constant shock to me that I did not recognize it earlier. It wasn't just the pointless job that

I hated. And I truly hated it. It wasn't just my marriage and family either. All of my life I lived automatically. We vacationed twice a year, made love three times a week, dined at seven PM and ate out every Friday. I couldn't tell you anything really personal about my wife or kids. They all remained a part of the background. Except there was no foreground. I did what life required of me, but I did it without thought or feeling.

I did everything like that, automatically. Although I was aware of what was going on around me and can still remember everything, I did things without any deep thought or feeling or awareness. How can I explain it? It was like I was walking around in a fog. Except I didn't realize I walked in a fog until I first came out of it. I could have been a robot save for a few moments of true passion.

This is how I found myself, forty-five years old and abandoned by everything I had invested my life in.

Perhaps for the hundredth time I had been passed over for a promotion. I saw younger men enter the company and quickly climb past me. Almost all of my superiors had been below me at one point. Twenty years of work for the same firm and I had hardly moved at all.

Two weeks from our anniversary Laura took the kids and left. She said she had finally fallen in love and moved in with a man she had dated in high school. The finally part hurt worst of all. She made it clear with those words that she never really loved me. The hurt was as dim and distant as the rest of my life. It happened, and I moved along accordingly.

The children didn't seem to notice my absence. The weekends they were supposed to spend with me they usually found excuses not to come. When they did, most of their time was spent on their phones, interacting with me as little as possible.

Any friends I had were also friends of Laura, and none showed interest in me after the divorce. Even the church acted indifferent to my plight. I attended a divorce support group until they changed the time without telling me. The shame-faced elder apologized for the oversight when I saw him next, but I didn't bother to return. Eventually, I stopped attending church altogether. No one noticed.

Our house was sold and I moved into another, this one much closer to the city. Unlike most urban plots, this one boasted a large yard. The neighborhood was semi-historic, full of turn of the century houses with small plots and drafty hallways. Mine was just as old and musty, an imposing Romanesque structure, quite out of character for me as a buy. Something about it attracted me, and though I questioned my sanity once the sale had gone through, knowing it would tax my moderate resources, I found myself unexpectedly enjoying the old house.

Most of the rooms stood empty but I felt at home there. The old, wood paneling, the twisting floor plan, the rough stone exterior covered in arches and turrets, the memory held in its walls, the tower, with its circular room at the top overlooking the vast front yard; all of it created a special place for me in an otherwise grinding and ordinary life.

The property stood on a vast yard full of old oaks that put ample space between the house and the rest of the neighborhood. A crumbling stone wall and iron gates completed the distance. Sometimes the separation was too complete. At night the front yard fell dark and imposing beneath the shadow of the trees. Not a single visitor rang my doorbell on Halloween.

In the back yard, almost as vast as the front, an old forest butted up to the edge of the property. As anyone who has lived in old, urban neighborhoods will know, a piece of land like this is most unusual. And these were no ordinary woods. The trees grew up huge and ancient, sprawling a thick, green canopy on top, and bulging with massive, twisted roots on the ground. A little path wound from the backyard and into the depths of the trees. I kept meaning to explore it one day. In the two years I have lived in the house I have yet to follow up with the intention.

Admittedly, it is quite sad as a life goes. If ever I had the thought to write a biography it would be the most dismal piece of confessional literature ever written. Anything worthy of mention has been noted in these few pages.

That is, until now.

One night everything changed. I can hardly explain what happened. In a few words, after sleepwalking through forty-five years of life, I finally woke up.

It was the fever. A particularly nasty strain of flu hit me late in August. I thought it odd, but the doctor explained that summer offers many of its own cases of influenza.

I spent several days alone suffering with aches and fever. There was no one to take care of me. More than once I wondered how long it would take my body to be discovered if I died. Weeks? Months? Would work even notice I was gone?

Through the sickness I wallowed in self-pity. It was the first time I had probably engaged in any serious reflection of my life. And even though I was only feeling sorry for myself, at least I felt something.

Early one Saturday my fever peaked. I huddled beneath blankets inside my massive and empty house. Aches wracked every corner of my body and chills seeped into the marrow of my bones. Warmth wouldn't come to me no matter what I did. I trembled uncontrollably.

The creaks and groans of the old house began to sound like voices. Dark things growled at me from the shadowy corners. Then they laughed. Far away screams echoed in my ears. Whispers floated up from the musty hallways.

I shivered almost as much from fear as from the cold. My fevered imagination conjured demons stalking around my bed, hungry to devour my soul. I laughed, thinking what a meager meal I would make. Yet I still feared to die.

It was at that moment that I found a resolve deep within me. A passion, buried long ago, perhaps even before my memory; a passion burned strong, stronger than anything I had ever felt before. I wanted to live. I wanted to be alive. I wanted my life, even my pathetic, lost and useless life. Life was not something I possessed, I discovered. I was life. I am life. At least this weak and pitiful incarnation of it.

More than that I wanted something more than just mere existence. I wanted to matter. I didn't want to be another face passing by on the sidewalk, another car on the interstate, another suit idling away in a cubicle on the seventh floor. I didn't want to be a consumer, an employee, a citizen, or even a member of anything. I wanted...what was it?

I wanted to be.

I wanted to bend the grass and send ripples across the water. I wanted the wind to have to blow around me. I wanted to make some sort of impression on time. Not just leave a trace or footprint, but an indelible mark that says, "This is me and no hand may undo what I have done."

I wanted to be.

No sooner than I desired this than a deep sleep fell over me. I dreamt furious and ravaged fever dreams. Strange creatures swam around me, things out of myth and other things surely unimagined. Faces out of my past appeared and drifted by me. A song played in the distance, an oddly familiar tune by a lone voice and guitar.

Suddenly, I found myself in a swamp, standing knee deep in muddy water. After struggling and fighting my way out of the mire I came to a desert. Through long tracks in the sand I walked under burning heat until I made my way to the mountains. There I climbed and climbed over higher and higher peaks until I reached the vault of heaven.

When I reached the top of the world I found a cave leading deep into the bowels of the earth. The same voices that whispered and growled about my house echoed from out of the cave. This time, instead of frightening me, they sounded afraid of me.

I stepped into the cave. Darkness closed all around but somehow I could still find my way through the tunnels. For days I walked through the dark with voices whispering and growling. Finally, the tunnel ended at a door.

I pulled and pushed at the door with all my might. It wouldn't budge in the slightest. The voices laughed at me from the dark. I looked and found no lock on the door, only a heavy, iron ring for a handle. I tugged at this too and the door still didn't move.

"You cannot force your way in," an old man said, sitting on the floor beside me. It didn't surprise me in the least that an old man sat there where no one had sat a moment before.

"How do I open the door?" I asked.

"You don't," the old man answered. "You must knock."

Strange that it had not occurred before that I must knock. So I knocked.

The door creaked open, revealing a bright light behind it. Everything in the dream grew sharp and vivid, as real as life. I could feel the grain of the wood beneath my hand as I pushed the door open. I could smell the wet stench of the cave. The light burned clearer than anything I had ever experienced before.

"Be warned," the old man said beside me. "Once you go through that door you may never go back. What's done there will not be undone."

The door pushed open and I stepped through, and then....

Something happened.

I don't know what. For the life of me I cannot remember what I saw or what happened behind that door. All I know is that something deep and powerful happened. I know because everything in my life changed after that moment.

I awoke covered in sweat.

The fever had broken and the ache of sickness had left my body. I sprang up from the soaked sheets with a new burst of energy and life, and walked out onto my upstairs balcony. The night was charged with cool energy and I felt its invigoration flow into me.

Something was very different, apart from my sudden recovery. I thought it might be the world around me at first. Almost immediately I realized that it was not the world that was different. I was different.

I was awake.

And it wasn't just sleep I had awoken from. I had stirred from that slumber that I had mistaken for an existence and had awoken to life.

For the first time ever things around me seemed real, seemed of substance. And because the world felt more real, I felt more real. I noticed a power infused in all things that had been previously absent.

The wind on my face felt cool and benevolent. The trees swayed gently in the breeze and I saw it for the dance that it really was. I could smell something deep and rich on that wind, an earthiness that reminded me of fertile ground broken by the plow.

I looked up at the stars winking down from the darkness. They seemed so bright and wonderful. I could feel them pull at me, as if they were trying to say something. Or rather, they screamed something, though somehow I couldn't hear.

That's what it was more than anything else. The whole world- the ground, the sky, wind and trees, even the stone of my house along with the stars,- they appeared to hold a deep and marvelous secret. Only I couldn't see it.

Perhaps the word that makes the most sense is, awareness. I was aware for the first time in my life. I was acutely aware, almost hypersensitive, to everything around me and within me. I could almost feel the world turn beneath me as sure as I felt my own heartbeat.

To be filled with sudden and wild energy you would think I would not be a able to sleep. Instead, as I sat down to admire this new world around me, I fell into a deep and dreamless sleep.

When I woke up this time I found myself, inexplicably, back in my own bed. That sense of acute awareness still thrummed in me along with an accompanying vigor. I had never felt so alive.

Feeling new, but following the same rituals of life, I dressed and made my way to work. The office looked different too. I had never noticed before how ugly the building looked, how offensive it appeared.

The tower, all of glass and metal, seemed just a rectangular eyesore in the blue sky. Inside it smelled of plastic and chemical cleaner. The attempt to appear modern and clean succeeded. Everything shined, elevators, floors, windows. The expensive lobby furniture screamed success to the world.

It seemed wrong to me. It seemed dead. For all it's efficiency and marks of splendor it was just a pile of glass and metal. There was no artistry involved, no depth, no life.

On the floor where I worked things felt even worse. The massive space was divided by cubicles, boxing workers into a few, bare feet of space while dividing them from others at the same time. A fortunate few actually got a window office. How I used to aspire to one of those coveted places. Strange, man used to always work outside. Now he labors endlessly to just work in a place where he can see the outside.

I saw the office through newer, more truthful eyes. What I saw was an insect colony. It wasn't a place for living men to work, it was a hive where he became part of an unfeeling machine of raw production. It buzzed with efficiency but made nothing of value or true worth. Here man reduced himself to a mere unit of labor, like so many gears in a large machine. And he even prided himself for this lost humanity.

9

That day plodded on unbearably. I stood sometimes looking at the complex of cubicles, not wanting to move. Nobody else seemed to notice me. They moved around, oblivious, uncaring. To my vision they hardly appeared alive. The unfocused, empty eyes, the blank expressions, the subservient, unthinking way they moved about marked them for who they were. These people were sleepwalkers and little else.

Had it always been this way? It must have. Only I never noticed it before, being a sleepwalker like the others. The thought made me sick that I could have been like that too. But when one sleeps it is impossible to tell who wakes and who slumbers.

How could I bear that place another moment? I wanted to flee. My lungs contracted, burned, begged me for fresh air.

After only half an hour there I bolted for the outside. The city street felt hardly more tolerable. The empty faces appeared there too, marching by unreflective and unfeeling. The towers of grey solemnity, reached their ugly fingers at the perfect, blue sky.

What had happened to me? Or rather, what had happened to the city? Had human civilization always been this grim? If not, when did it sell it's soul, and for what price? Could we even get back whatever it is we have lost?

As I looked around the city, seeing it for what it really was, I saw *him* for the first time.

He stood amid the rushing crowd, staring at me with icy blue eyes that sent a chill and tremble though my bones. He wore a grey suit that hung off his deathly pale frame. A thin hand reached towards me, fingers curled to beckon me towards him.

For a moment I mistook him for a madman, one of the semi-sane vagrants that wander thick through the city. Yet there was a clearness in his eyes that spoke of only a keen and marvelous intellect. And the people didn't treat him like a vagrant. The people walking around him passed close by on the sidewalk, some almost brushing his arm.

They cannot see him, a thought came to me. Only you can see him, only you see those terrifying blue eyes. It is for you that the pale, thin hand stretches out.

The one, clear thought that pounded in me was that this man was death. He looked every bit the part of an undertaker and I almost expected to see a hearse parked nearby. That cold stare promised death, fixed unwaveringly on me among all the passing figures.

I remained unable to move despite a primal fear screaming at me to run with all my might. I couldn't move. Then he mouthed my name and stretched his hand further toward me. Something fierce inside broke and I darted back into the building, back to the safety of my cubicle.

Never had I felt terror so acute as then. Every fear I had ever felt before seemed petty in comparison. Whatever power this pale man possessed could crush any meager efforts I could raise. He wouldn't even have to try.

For the moment, my cubicle felt warm and comfortable. Memories of the encounter kept me from desiring the outside again, at least for a while. By the end of the day feelings of suffocation returned, locking me between fear of the pale man and spite for the drudgery of the office.

I did not yet associate the pale man with the visions that would follow. Later I would learn. For now, I hurried home, glancing all around to make sure he did not appear among the blank faces, fixing his icy stare on me.

Later that night, the door appeared for the first time.

On my walk home I forgot the pale man for a moment as the cool, night air refreshed me. Pensiveness took over as I trudged down the sidewalk, stepping over the cracks and bulges in the cement caused by the roots of old oak trees. Sparse moonlight fell down through the leaves and branches, painting the ground at my feet with eerie shadows.

With eyes on the ground I pushed through the iron gates of my drive and made my way up to the house. As I passed by the shadows of my own oaks I noticed something that didn't belong.

The thin moonlight and shadows made it impossible to make out clearly, so I stepped closer for a better look. As impossible as it seemed, it soon became unmistakable. A door stood in the shadow of the trees.

Confusion washed over me, and more than a little disorientation. No door had been there before. Certainly I would have noticed.

I approached the door cautiously, more than a little frightened and unsure. As strange as it seemed I couldn't deny its reality. In the poor light and shadows I could discern figures carved into the wooden surface. Otherwise, it looked like any ordinary door except for its odd location, and the fact that it wasn't attached to anything.

A quick circuit around revealed nothing. It looked the same on both sides. I knelt down at the keyhole where a shaft of orange light streamed through. Peering in I saw not the other end of the grove but flames burning in a fireplace. By all appearances the door led somewhere other than my own yard.

Strangely, I felt no confusion at this. I almost expected it, or something like it. With my new awareness had come the anticipation of great wonders. Or perhaps it was just an eagerness to see something other than the banal world I lived in.

With no more hesitation I opened the door and stepped through.

I looked around to find myself in a study, or someone's personal library. The fire on the far wall gave off the only light, but I could make out the rows of books that lined every wall except for where a bay window allowed the moonlight to stream in.

A figure stirred by the fire where an old man curled up in a chair. He moaned and shifted in his sleep. He looked pitiful, thin and wasting. Liver spots dotted his bald head.

A coldness entered the room. Heat from the fire retreated and dark corners crept in upon the light. The old man seemed to sense the change too. He groaned and stirred again in his sleep.

A flutter of wings drew my attention to the bay window. Outside, in snow I knew wasn't there a moment ago, a raven perched on the sill. He tapped the glass with his beak and stared curiously at me.

The chill in the room grew deeper. The shadows fell darker. A whisper rose up from all directions at once.

"The Keeper is dying," it hissed. "The last Keeper is dying."

Another raven landed on the sill and tapped at the glass. Malice glared at me from their yellow eyes. The old man moaned again, his face contorted by unseen nightmares.

More ravens landed on the sill, tapping at the glass and glaring hate at me. With each bird that landed the chill leaked deeper into the room and the shadows darkened. The window filled with birds until they blacked out the world outside and all I could see was the fire and the old man writhing in nightmare.

"The Keeper is dying," I heard as the ravens tapped on the glass.

It sounded like pelts of hail battering the bay window. Hundreds of ravens bunched outside, tapping on the glass.

"The Keeper is dying," the voice hissed. "The Raven King comes."

With a burst of black feathers the window exploded. My hands jerked up as glass shards flew around me. I lurched back, through the doorway again, falling, endlessly falling.

With a jolt I hit the ground. The door was gone. I was alone in the grove. And the vision, though burned into my mind, began to fade like a dream.

For a moment I wondered how real it had been. Perhaps I would have disbelieved. But the cuts on my hands and arms told me differently. And broken glass shimmered around me amid the scatter of raven feathers at my feet.

The vision of the old man in the library continued to terrify me. A part of me thrilled at what had happened, something beyond the drudgery of ordinary life. At the same time I felt as if the foundations of my world had crumbled, and I, by consequence, had become moorless. What could I trust as real? What was certain anymore? If doors could appear in my front yard that led to some dying man's library, then what else could happen?

Anything, I had to conclude. Anything was possible now.

After seeing the door I began to look for them everywhere. On my way to work, on walks through the city, everywhere I kept looking for the strange portals. I even tested out doors in my office building, just to see.

Life returned to normal, that grating, insistent normal. I grew increasingly restless, wandering with no destination in mind. My steps took me from bar to bar, searching the faces of the people for someone who knew what I knew. All I found were the blank stares of incomprehension, and the insatiable look of those searching for the next opiate to numb their senses. Strange, I never recognized the oblivion and desperation on the faces of the people all around me. Then again, I never looked.

Things would have continued this way, perhaps for the rest of my life. But then I met a woman who changed all that.

I had settled in an out of the way place, a bar underneath one of the older towers, the kind with small windows at the top of the low ceiling. The place filled frequently with disillusioned businessmen, lonely divorcees and women long past the prime but unaware of the fact. I too should be counted among these weary masses, an exile in my own country.

When she first walked in a silence fell over the place, conversations dropping suddenly quiet, eyes drifting over to the door where she stood gazing over the crowd. It was like a flash of radiant color entering a black and white world, and we saw something that took forceful hold of our attention. She seemed not to notice that everyone stared, waiting. It seemed to her the most normal thing in the world.

Then her eyes met mine, and just as quickly the noise resumed. Like a spell breaking, the normal world came crashing back in. Heads turned back to their companions, conversations picked up their abandoned threads. I still stared at her, helpless to do anything else. I couldn't tear my gaze away if I wanted to.

How could I tear it away? I was not used to seeing such total beauty. Her dark eyes held my stare boldly, even drawing me in. I somewhat noticed her flowing, dark hair and the olive complexion of her skin. She possessed vaguely oriental features, something middle-eastern perhaps, not anything I could readily recognize. Whatever people she descended from, they must be renown for their legendary beauty.

I had never before been so taken by a woman, unable to pull my eyes away. More than that, there was something else in her face, her eyes, even the way she held her head and slightly parted her lips. She looked as if she understood. I could swear, in that one glance, that she could see as I did, recognizing the world we have created for what it was. She too could see that our vaunted civilization amounted to nothing more than a pile of steel and glass waiting to be abandoned.

After holding my stare like that she moved across the bar towards me. I watched, paralyzed and fascinated as she came closer and closer, unbelieving that such a gorgeous woman would hold even the slightest interest in me, convinced she would walk past. But she didn't walk past. She stopped, a slight frown on her face, and took the empty seat beside me.

"You're supposed to offer to buy me a drink, right?" she spoke, her voice reaching all the way into my spine.

"Yeah, I guess so," was all I managed to spit out. Still, I didn't move to comply.

Somehow, I tore my eyes away from her face only to have them move over her body. I gazed over the athletic, but decidedly feminine figure beneath the short black dress she wore. She leaned on the bar and stretched out her legs to rest her feet on the legs of my stool. I dimly noticed she wore nothing on her feet. This hardly registered as bizarre, that a beautiful woman would walk barefoot into a downtown bar, for my attention stayed fixed on the shapely legs that reclined towards me.

"Then buy me something," she whispered.

"What do you want?" I asked, prepared to empty my savings to get her whatever she desired.

"You tell me."

I had no idea what a woman like this would drink. Surely something expensive and fine. An aged wine perhaps, a rare brandy? What could be as exotic as her?

An image rose up in my mind. I saw wagons of barley unloaded beneath an autumn dusk. A chorus of celebration rose up while bearded men mashed dark grains with juniper berries and heather flowers. A fire flared to life as night fell. Women danced half drunk around the flames, toasting the moon and stars. All around them the joy of a younger age rose up like smoke from the festal fire.

"Stout," I turned to the bartender and said. "The lady will have a stout. The darkest one you have."

The lady smiled when she lifted the black, foamy liquid to her mouth. She licked the foam slowly from her lips, her eyes still on mine.

"Maybe it's true," she mused mysteriously.

It didn't cross my mind to wonder what she might mean.

A hand rolled cigarette appeared in the woman's hand, held just away from her mouth.

"You can't smoke in here," the bartender said.

She turned and fixed her eyes upon him. He looked every bit as transfixed as I felt.

"Would you light it for me?" she asked the bartender.

Unbelievably, he complied, lifting one of the accent candles on the bar to her cigarette. As it lit I could smell incense and some strange mix of spices on the smoke. Other patrons looked her way with disapproving glances, but none objected to her bold flouting of the law.

"So," she said, turning her attention back to me. "How did you know I wanted stout?"

"Just a guess." I shrugged, not wanting to reveal the vision that had informed me.

"Really?" she asked with a skeptical twist to her mouth. "So tell me then, have you gone into the woods behind your house?"

"No... How did you know there were woods behind my house?" I asked. A realization dawned on me that this woman was of the same world as the door and the old dying man and the new awareness that had come over me.

"There are no woods behind your house," she answered cryptically.

"What does that supposed to mean? Who are you?"

"I am Eladora," she breathed in a cloud of sweet, spicy smoke that enveloped me.

Either the name or the cloud of smoke did something to me. Or maybe both bled into my brain. A slight intoxication came on with a pounding vision, more vivid than the other.

Moonlight streamed in through old, bending oak trees. A longboat, like the kind the Vikings used to ride, lay wrecked on an abandoned shore. A crumbling castle straddled the rocky coast, silhouetted by the stars. Then I saw Eladora, but younger somehow as she wept on the broken battlements,

17

looking with sadness across the dark and howling ocean.

"Are you... like me?" I asked hesitantly.

Eladora laughed at the suggestion. It was a sound at once more and less than any laughter I had ever heard.

"I am nothing like you," she said. "But you aren't like other people, are you?"

"I guess," I said with a shrug. "I don't know. I've changed."

As much as I wanted to tell this woman everything, I held back. She seemed to know I held back, as she also seemed to know how badly I wanted to tell her everything.

"Something has definitely changed," she said, making me think she knew much more about it than I did. "That is what has made you so interesting to us."

"Us? Did someone send you to find me?"

"Only my own curiosity," she said. "I have always been fascinated in men like you. Of course, everyone is interested in you right now. They want to know which side you're on, where you stand."

"I don't have the slightest clue as to what you're talking about," I admitted. "I'm not on any side."

She looked at me curiously and leaned close.

"But you started the dweomer," she whispered. Her breath in my ear sent shivers through me.

A strange power reached from her and pulled on me from a place so deep inside I didn't know it existed. All this talk of sides and dweomers sounded crazy, but in that deep part it somehow made sense. I couldn't tell if she was putting the idea there or pulling it out. Either way I turned my face from hers, desperate to get out of whatever spell she cast on me.

"I have no idea what you're talking about," I told her.

"Maybe," she shrugged. "But you have made yourself a part of things whether you like it or not."

"And how did I do that?" I asked.

"The dweomer," she repeated that strange word.

18

"You're going to have to help me here," I said. "What exactly is a... dweomer." The word didn't sound near as melodious coming out of my mouth.

"It is... what would you call it?" she searched for the right words. "You have a new recognition. A new way of looking at life."

"Yes," I answered excitedly, for a moment forgetting my caution. "That's exactly what happened to me. I have this new awareness, like I'm seeing things for the first time. Yes, that's what it is. How did you know? Can you see it on my face?"

"It's much more than a new awareness," she told me. "More comes with a dweoomer than that, especially the kind you started."

She leaned in close again to whisper. It was a conspiratorial gesture, like she was afraid we would be overheard.

"It put you in the middle of something much, much bigger than your are, son of Man."

Something about the way she said it set off alarms in my head. There was no mistaking the warning in her voice.

"What am I in the middle of?" I asked.

"Something like a war," she said, leaning back against the bar. "It's more like a conquest than a war though. It's an ancient struggle, and the victor has long been decided, unfortunately for you."

"I don't understand."

"I know," she said as smoke absently drifted from her mouth.

She puffed out a cloud and for a second it looked like it split apart into dozens of pieces, forming into a swirl of feathers. The feathers fell and billowed, dissipating into a cloud of smoke again.

"Maybe you never will," she told me. "Be careful though."

She crushed her cigarette out on the bar and turned to leave. As if in afterthought, she stopped and faced me again.

"Has anyone else tried to contact you?" she asked.

"Anyone that seems strange? Not entirely normal?"

"An old man," I said before I had time to think better of it.

"What did he look like?"

"Old and pale, with a gray pallor" I told her. "He was thin and had icy blue eyes. His stare made me cold all over."

The radiant color from Eladora's face drained at my description. Her eyes widened and her face took on a grave cast telling me she was terrified of that man. Perhaps more so than me.

"Is he dangerous?" I asked, already knowing the answer.

"More than you will know," she said grimly.

She tilted her head to the side and stared intently at me, into me. It looked as if she were evaluating some vastly important matter and wondering if she should tell me. I felt naked under the searching glance.

"Listen carefully to me," she said, gripping my arm, her eyes intent and serious. "You will be summoned very soon to meet with some powerful people. The summons will come from a person of authority in your life, one whom you will not be able to deny. You will have to go to this meeting. But remember this, if you remember nothing else. When you go before these people they will offer you a drink. It would be devastating for you to refuse, for the laws of guest and host forbid it. But you must take only one sip, the smallest one you can. You will want to drink it all, to drain the glass and have it filled again. You must not do this. Must not. Do you understand? Only the smallest sip. Everything may depend on it. Do you understand?"

She had gripped my arm in her intensity. I winced at the surprising strength and tried to pulled back.

"Yes, I understand," I answered, not really understanding at all.

"Say it, tell me what I told you," she demanded. "What did I tell you to do?"

"Only take a sip," I echoed for her.

"The smallest sip," she insisted.

"Yes, the smallest."

Apparently satisfied, Eladora's features relaxed and she released my arm.

"That old man, he will have his way with you," she told me, smoothing the arm of my shirt. "It's better to give in now rather than later."

"I plan to stay as far from him as possible," I told her, meaning every word.

She laughed again, that sound of music and desperation. I felt sure there was a time, a very long time ago, when that laugh was only music.

"Maybe it will be different this time," she mused sadly.

She reached out and touched my hand. The tenderness surprised me, almost sent a palpable shock through my arm. In it's own way it seemed more powerful than her seduction and beauty.

Eladora smiled again, warmly this time, then turned and left. After a moment the sounds and sights around me came back to my senses. Until then, I hadn't noticed how they had all faded into the background while Eladora sat with me. It made the whole encounter surreal, dream-like. After a while I wondered if she was even real or just a phantom of my mind. The only proof I had of her being there was the smell of spice and smoke on the air, and a cigarette crushed out on the bar.

The Second Vision

For days after I could think of nothing but Eladora. Either her face danced before my memory or her scent lingered in my nostrils. Unexpectedly I would catch the smell of exotic flowers and spices, and turn, expecting to see her. I only saw the mill of empty faces about me on the street.

Her cryptic warning played over and over again in my mind. For the better part of a week I sat at my desk and wondered at her words, of this supposed war, this summoning I was to receive, the dweomer I had begun and the pale, old man who had frightened me so.

It was the pale man I saw again first.

Late night restlessness had driven me outside. At that hour the street around me was dark and quiet. For a moment the stillness and cool air relieved the anxiety that had haunted me the last few days. I drew into my own thoughts and became lost in them.

A chill went through me that had nothing to do with the cold. I felt eyes boring into me. A palpable presence drew near, unmistakable in its approach. Looking up, I saw the pale man standing on the edge of my driveway.

He wore the same dark, gray suit that had reminded me of an undertaker. The shadows cast by the streetlights hid his face, though there was no doubting who he was. The reek of base fear emanated from him as if he embodied that primitive essence.

I froze in panic, not knowing what to do. Eladaora's words echoed in my head, that he would have his way with me in the end. I had no idea what that meant, only that I wanted to have no part of it.

The pale man stretched his hand out towards me, as if beckoning me to come. As before, it was this gesture that stirred my limbs to action.

I turned and hurled myself into my house, slamming the door behind me and throwing the bolt in place. Still not feeling safe I ran up the stairs, across the hallway, and up

25

another flight to the third floor tower. It was the furthest I could think to get from the horrible man. As soon as I reached the door I threw myself inside.

I fell into darkness.

A rush of wind and a dizzy sensation enveloped me. I flailed my arms out for something, for the wall, the floor that should be there. My reaching hands touched only the emptiness of air and the pit of darkness that had swallowed me whole.

Slowly, my senses returned, and I found that I was not falling at all. Instead, I lay prone, the feel of carpet beneath my fingers.

My face pressed up hard against cool glass. Outside I could see a high-rise office building across the street. A cleaning lady vacuumed an empty office, illuminated against the night by the steady glow of fluorescent lights. A murmur of voices sounded somewhere close.

"I don't know why we let him do this to us," a man's voice said.

"What choice do we have?" another countered.

"What choice? He needs us as much as we need him. He couldn't do any of this without us."

The disorientation faded completely and I picked myself up. I was definitely not in my tower room, but I was not in an altogether unfamiliar place.

A large conference room opened up on either side of me, one that could be found in thousands of business buildings across the world. This one showed more prestige than most. The long, center table shined in polished mahogany. Thick, leather chairs, at least twenty of them, were occupied by dark-suited men. They all held themselves with the unmistakable bearing of power.

The men around the table seemed not to notice me, or at least they gave no indication. Still, I stepped back closer to the window to render myself as inconspicuous as possible.

"Perhaps, but that's because he is the one in charge of all of this" a dark-skinned man spoke up with a thick, foreign accent.

At that moment I noticed the immense diversity seated around the table. Almost every nationality seemed to be represented. I saw two Asian men, a few who looked Hispanic, three of African descent, and the rest either white or of indeterminate race. An Arab in traditional garb stood out noticeably.

"Because we allow him to be," the first voice answered, coming from an older white man seated at one of the table's heads. He spoke with an English accent.

"He lifts a finger and we go scurrying in a thousand directions. He tells us to come to these secret meetings and we drop everything and come to wait on him to arrive. Why we're hardly better than slaves."

"What would you have us do?" one of the Africans asked.

"We stand together," the British man said. "I think it's reasonable to make a few demands of our own. Look around here. You are all men of power. Who do you answer to back home? No one. We don't even answer to each other. But we are Lord Daniel's lap dogs. We sit at his feet waiting for him to scratch our ears or throw us scraps from his table. We should be partners, not employees, all of us equal."

"But we do not even know where this is all going," a Japanese man spoke up. "We each have our parts, but none of us knows how it fits together. How can we be partners in that?"

"That's what we need to demand," the British man said, pounding his fist on the table. "We have a right to know what this is all up to instead of stumbling around in the dark. We need to know who is in charge, I mean really in charge. We're captains of industry, damn it, not some pitiful band of foot soldiers.

"I for one want to know some things. And what I want to

know more than anything else is....."

The elevator on the far side of the room rang and the British man fell silent. Every head at the table turned to watch as the doors slid open. A man stepped out with fluid grace. Thoughts of Eladora immediately came to mind. Not because the man looked like Eladora, yet they shared the same dark features. His face, though, was austere and sharp where hers was soft and open. His thin figure showed signs of a well-muscled frame beneath his black suit.

He seemed delicate and powerful all at once, strong and fragile, a bull and a hummingbird. And oddly, like Eladora, he too wore no shoes on his feet, but strode into the conference room barefooted.

"Is what?" the newcomer asked as he slid into the empty chair at the other head of the table.

"Lord Daniels," the British man greeted with a conciliatory nod. "We've been eagerly awaiting your arrival."

"I see," Lord Daniels nodded. "And I eagerly await to hear what you were about to say."

"I...I don't rightly recall," the British man answered. He licked his lips nervously.

"I'll remind you then," Lord Daniels said. "Just before I walked in here you were complaining about your place in the organization. And you were about to tell everyone what you wanted to know more than anything else. Now you have to finish such a pregnant statement. We can bear the suspense no longer. So please tell us, what is it you want to know more than anything else? Keep us in suspense no longer. Please, continue."

The British man seemed to wrestle within himself. He looked around the table for support, and finding none, slammed his fist on the table.

"Damn it, we have a right to know what's going on," he blurted out. "We do everything you ask us to. Much of it we could get in a lot of trouble for, but we do it anyway. And now, all these resources you're taking to build something and we don't even know what. The cost is astronomical. It's outrageous. Nothing should cost that much. But still, we do everything we can to give you what you ask of us, no matter what laws we have to break to do it. I think it's only fair that we know what's going on, what's really going on. What is it you're building? What's the purpose of all this?"

Lord Daniels leaned back in his chair and propped his bare feet on the table. "Fair enough," he said without any sign of consternation. "I will show you exactly what this is all about.

"Do you mind, though, if we take care of a bit of business first?"

The British man nodded, breathing a heavy sigh of relief and falling back into his chair.

"Splendid! Pasha, the oil situation?"

"Production is still contracted," the Arab answered in a thick accent. "Prices stay in the ideal range."

"Let them drop," Daniels said. "Just for a month or two, very slowly. Then, right before it gets to our lower threshold send it up sharply, almost overnight, up to our maximum. Then let it come down to mid range and hold there.

"Connors, Mitchell, Ernst, I think it's time for a conservative demagogue. Start pulling support away from the liberal agenda for a while. Not too noticeable, just get a little lukewarm. I have several good candidates I'm deciding between for the next U.S. President. Let's make sure our liberal outlets seem a little complacent and charge our right-wing agenda up."

"We may need a little help," one of the men spoke up. "We may have been too successful in promoting the current administration. Irrational loyalty runs high with him, especially among our journalists."

"Yes, you were a little heavy-handed there," Daniels remarked. "See that you don't make that same mistake.

"Connelly, how is our progress?"

A red haired man cleared his throat. "The new additive is almost ready," he said in a thick Midwest accent. "We could have it in food by next March. We submit to the FDA in a few months."

"Sebron, see we get no surprises there."

"Sure thing. Forward me the formula and I'll make sure it happens."

"Excellent gentlemen," Daniels said, rising from his chair and walking the room in graceful strength, like the walk of a predator who knows there is no danger to him.

"You have all done well, much better than even I expected. Events are ahead of schedule, and you have my gratitude for that. Not only have you performed well, you did so without any idea where all this is going, as Geoffrey so rightly observed. And now you ask, what exactly have we been up to this whole time.

"I came to all of you at one time and made you a promise, did I not? Chon-Lee, what did I promise you?"

"You promised me I would be rich and powerful," a thick, Asian man responded. "Beyond my wildest dreams. And that I would live longer than any man in memory."

"And how long ago did I make that promise to you?" Daniels asked.

"Eighty years ago," Chon-Lee answered.

"And that would make you how old?"

"127."

"Amazing!" Daniels said, placing his hands gently on Chon-Lee's shoulders. "127 years old, and if not for that nasty habit of calamari and chocolate cake you would have the body of twenty-year old."

The room echoed with subdued laughter. Nervous restraint edged the sound. Geoffrey alone did not crack a smile.

"Who among you is not one of the world's elites? Who among you is not among the most powerful men on the planet? Who has not lived a life of unbridled pleasure? The youngest among you is seventy years old, yet you all enjoy the vigor of youth. Sure, you may have had to do some things not considered moral by traditional standards, but have you not also enjoyed my protection?

"Mitchell, twice you have committed murder and not once have you had even a whiff of suspicion upon you. Connelly strangles a prostitute now and again and enjoys that pursuit freely. And Geoffrey... Geoffrey loves the taste of young flesh."

Daniels stood behind the British man. He leaned in close so his mouth hovered near Geoffrey's ear.

"Boy flesh if I'm not mistaken," Daniels whispered loud enough for everyone to hear. "And have you ever feared the punishment of the law for that harem of orphans you keep locked away? Or for what you do with them when they grow too old for you to enjoy?"

Geoffrey grew pale and ashen. He shook his head slowly, a slight tremor to the movement. Beads of sweat rolled down his forehead.

"Everything promised has been given you and more," Daniels said, straightening up to address the whole table again. "I have made you lords of creation. And you ask me now where this is all going. You ask why I make you do all these things that seemingly make no sense. A perfectly reasonable question to ask. So tell me, who else besides Geoffrey would like to know the answer?"

No one at the table looked up. All eyes fixed themselves firmly on the spot in front of them. They all sat stiff and tense, stifling even their breath as they waited.

"C'mon, no one?" Daniels asked. "Geoffrey is the only one who wants to know?"

Only Geoffrey looked up. His eyes darted desperately from face to face, searching for support.

"Damn it all, don't do this to me!" he said in a quivering voice. "Edgar, don't hang me out like this. Pasha? After all

31

I've done for you. Musashi? Grow some balls you pack of cowards."

"Geoffrey, Geoffrey," Daniels said in a dangerously soothing voice. "This is what you want, after all. And like you said, it's only fair. Let me give you what it is you want. Let me show you where all this is taking us."

"That....that won't be necessary," Geoffrey stammered. "I don't really need to know. Just idle curiosity is all."

"Nonsense. Curiosity is never idle. It eats and eats at the heart. It preys on the consciousness. It fills the mind with no end to wonder and speculation. It's an itch you can't scratch, a lust you cannot sate. Like a woman who has you infatuated...or a boy in some cases, it will keep you up at night and occupy all your thoughts. No, curiosity is never idle. It will gnaw at you until it is satisfied."

Daniels approached Geoffrey again and leaned in close. He whispered something only the British man could hear. By the widening of his eyes and the color that drained from his face I could tell the secret horrified even him.

"Why.....that's impossible," Geoffrey breathed. He looked up at Daniels with incredulity spread across his face.

"Really? After all you've seen?" Daniels said, crossing the room. "No worry. I'll show you. But in order to see, and see that I am telling you the truth, you will have to cross the veil for yourself and gaze upon what lies beyond."

Two women walked past Daniels towards the gaping Geoffrey. I couldn't tell from where they appeared, so fixed was I on Daniels. They stood out immediately being impossibly tall and thin, black as the pit of night and dressed in the same kind of black suit Daniels wore. Two slits for eyes stared out of cat-like faces. The stride of their walk and the long, swinging arms furthered the feline appearance.

Geoffrey appeared not to notice as they approached him. His eyes still fixed their unbelieving stare on Daniels. It wasn't until one of the women sat down on the table in front of him that he finally looked up. The cat-like woman took his hand gently in her own while the other one knelt down beside him.

The woman who held Geoffrey's hand smiled, revealing a row of tiny, sharp teeth, accented by needle-like canines. Geoffrey gasped in fear and tried to pull away. The kneeling woman pushed him down, stroking his thighs with her hands, her eyes fixed firmly on him. Her sister - or who I assumed had to be her sister they appeared so alike - took Geoffrey's finger to her lips. She kissed it lovingly and rubbed the palm against her cheek. A sound between a moan and purr came from her, expressing her bizarre satisfaction.

Slowly, the feline woman took Geoffrey's finger into her mouth. She pursed her lips around it and pulled on it slowly as Geoffrey watched in a horror that suffused into arousal. Seeing his expression the woman smiled, flaring white teeth. Then she bit down.

I heard the sickening crack of bone as Geoffrey's face spasmed in pain. He opened his mouth to scream, but no sound came out. The other feline woman lunged forward and buried her mouth in his neck stifling the latent cry. Geoffrey fell back, his face a mask of silent terror and pain.

"Now, to other business," Daniels said as the cat women pulled Geoffrey to the floor and leaned into him.

The sound of soft flesh being torn away and chewed echoed through the room. My stomach churned in knots. Dread settled like thick fog in my limbs. The other men felt the same I could tell. Their eyes darted back to the far end of the table where the heads of the women bobbed up and down in their macabre feast. Every face had drained of color.

"I'm talking to you!" Daniels leapt up and yelled. Everyone in the room, myself included, jumped at the sound.

"This enterprise we are on requires men of focus!" Daniels said firmly. "If any of you are not up to the task then let me know now. If this mild chastisement of an ungrateful lackey has you so unsettled that you can't pay attention then I will find men who can!"

Mild chastisement. I had never witnessed anything so horrific in my life. I shuddered to think what his moderate displeasure looked like.

"That's better," Daniels said to a table that held it's composure with visible effort. He seemed to relish their effort. A bone crunched and more than one face spasmed involuntarily.

"To more pressing matters at hand," Daniels continued. "There is a man I need found with all haste. He works for one of our local operations, no one of apparent significance. But as of late he has become a possible threat to our operations in a most unexpected way. His name is...."

My heart, already pounding with terror as I listened to the feline women consume a man not fifteen feet from me, stopped for a beat at what I heard next. Daniels said my name.

I heard it, dimly recognized the sounds that made up my name, but I couldn't believe it. Eladora's cryptic words came crashing back to me. Still, what could these men, powerful beyond my imaginings, want with me? What could Lord Daniels want with me? What had I unwittingly involved myself in?

Daniels had moved on to other business, talk of a building project somewhere. Beneath me, the floor gave way and darkness rushed in from the corners of my eyes. I screamed and felt myself falling as the blackness folded over me and buried me in its embrace. The last thing I remembered before unconsciousness took me was my name drawling smoothly from Lord Daniel's lips.

Within a week the summons came to me. I had been so dreading it for days, when it finally arrived I actually felt relief.

The call came from work. One Thursday as I sat at my desk, struggling to get through the day, my manager arrived. I remember training the snarky young man, and called him Tom then. Soon after he was promoted he insisted on being called Mr. Jensen. For appearances, he said.

"Mr. Calloway wants to see you," he told me with a befuddled expression on his face.

"The Mr. Calloway?" I asked incredulously. "CEO Mr. Calloway?"

"That's the one," Jensen shrugged. "Any idea what he wants?"

I shrugged too though I knew what he wanted. Visions of the cat women jumped out in my mind to frighten me. I could still hear the crunch of bone beneath their teeth and the squish of Geoffrey's flesh as they tore it from his body.

Strangely, Mr. Calloway looked nervous when I sat down across from him. A vast space separated us by the volume of his monstrous desk. The large, oak surface was empty, oddly empty. The desk calendar, I noticed, had nothing written in it. The CEO leaned forward, stroking his mustache over and over again. His eyes darted from side to side like he was expecting an intruder to burst through it any moment.

"You've impressed some people, young man," Mr. Calloway told me. "I don't know who, but they are very impressed with you."

"I've impressed people?" I asked.

"Men high up," Mr. Calloway answered. "All the higher-ups."

"You're the CEO," I pointed out. "It doesn't go any higher than you does it?"

Calloway laughed loud and brashly. It sounded artificial. He forced the sound out and slapped the desk.

"It goes no higher than me," he echoed. "That's right. That's right. But you know how things go these days. Subsidiaries, mother companies, offshore owners, silent partners. Very complicated stuff."

"And I've impressed someone," I said, careful to keep the incredulity in my voice.

Mr. Calloway laughed uproariously again. Out of context as it was, it sounded a bit mad.

"You have, you have," he said. He began to twitch nervously. I could feel his leg shake and he pawed at the desk calendar.

"You've been marked for big things," he continued. "We have a new title for you, a new office."

"Off we go, into the wild blue yonder," he sang off key.

A whimpering sound came from him, something like a stifled cry. Sweat poured down his forehead. His twitching sped up. His lips curled back in a smile-sneer hybrid. I could feel the pressure building up in him that was somehow connected to me. He looked like a man who was barely keeping it together.

"All very proud of you of course," he stammered. "All very proud, very proud. Ha ha ha ha."

"Maybe I should go now," I said softly.

"Yes!" He yelled out. "You have to go. Big things to do. Very busy man. Janice, talk to Janice. She will show you to your new office. Janice! Janice!"

Janice turned out more helpful than Calloway. I gratefully left our CEO to stew in his own spasms. There was nothing of the man I had experienced in the brief walk-throughs and company speeches he had given on earlier occasions.

"Is he okay?" I asked Janice. "He seemed a little... off."

"Oh it's Thursday is all," she said by way of explanation as if that made perfect sense. "Shall we?"

Janice led me down a hallway to the opposite end of the building. Unlike the frazzled Calloway, she appeared the very picture of efficiency and order. It helped that she was older, too old to put up with any trifling nonsense. And she looked the part. Gray hair was pulled back into a bun to tighten her already pinched face. She had that librarian aura, the kind that lived to keep young boys from hunting the nude pictures in the art books.

She pushed open a set of double doors that opened into a large corner office. Half the space was covered in windows that offered a commanding view of the city. A fully stocked bar stood on one end, a fish tank the opposite. A pool table and small putting green completed the decor along with the usual desk and bookcases.

"Do you know who exactly wanted me here?" I asked, impressed but unable to relax knowing the true source of my new fortune.

"Didn't Mr. Calloway explain it all to you?" Janice asked impatiently.

"He didn't explain much of anything."

"Well, you're being promoted." She pursed her lips.

"I can see that," I said.

"Do you not want the promotion?"

"Of course I do. I just want to know who gave it to me."

She paused for a moment, as if considering whether or not to tell me anything.

"The executives," she finally answered.

"The ones above Calloway?"

"Yes," she said.

"I don't suppose they have names," I said.

"You can find out for yourself when you meet them tonight."

In my head I heard bone crack under feline teeth. My heart dropped and I could feel the blood drain from my face.

"Don't be nervous," she said, misinterpreting my stricken features. "They are quite kind. You will see. The driver will pick you up at eight."

She smiled. If it was supposed to be a comforting gesture it failed miserably. She reached out and squeezed my arm, then turned to leave.

"So what's my new title?" I asked her retreating figure.

"Chief Coordinating Officer," she answered.

"And what does a Coordinating Officer do?"

"Coordinate."

Of course.

A few minutes after Janice left I met my new assistant. A stunningly beautiful and far too young girl walked into my new office with a dress bag over her shoulder. Her blouse was cut too low, the skirt too high, and her body moved unabashedly seductive in high-heeled boots. Blonde hair braided across the top of her forehead.

"Sir, your suit for tonight," she said, laying the bag across the pool table.

I had to ask for her name. She told me it was Sierra as she crossed her legs and leaned on my desk. She did it in a casual way, as if she belonged there more than I did. Which was probably true.

Later I unzipped the bag and pulled out the black suit. White shirt and black tie made it all look exactly like the one Daniels had worn. The bag even included Celtic knot cufflinks, a white handkerchief, a golden pin of a creature I did not recognize, and a black belt.

There were no shoes in the bag.

At eight o'clock a limousine pulled into my drive. Up until that point I hadn't made up my mind whether or not to go. Part of me was naturally frightened. Memories of Geoffrey consumed by the cat women still rattled my brain. The sound haunted me. I was certain the same fate awaited me.

Another part of me said that this was important. This was bigger than me, bigger than whether I lived or died. Whatever happened to me that night with the fever, the dream, it had changed me for good. What had Eladora called it? The dweomer?

Whatever it was called, I was not the same. Some fundamental change had taken place in my being. My concerns no longer settled on conventional worries. I didn't care about my car, or house, or having saved money for retirement, or even if I had money anymore. At least not the way I used to.

Something bigger, deeper, moved in this new universe I found myself in. And I was a part of it. That meant, I decided, doing irrational things like meeting the men who govern the world in secret. Even if their mysterious leader may want to kill me in a horrible and gruesome way. These are the sorts of things that felt right to me at that moment. Not to mention, if I were to be a part of things, I at least wanted some idea as to what these things were.

So that is why, adding shoes to the ensemble given me, I followed the limo driver into the black car. He held the door for me as I slid inside. Sierra waited for me there.

Not surprising, she wore black. The long, silken dress hugged her curves, splitting at the bottom to reveal a shapely leg, one crossed over the other. Blonde hair spilled over her shoulders and she leaned to the side, champagne glass dangling in her hand.

"Good evening boss," she smiled.

I returned the smile weakly. In any other situation I would have thanked all the blessed fates for putting such a young and beautiful creature in my path, especially considering how eager she seemed to seduce me. Sexuality clothed her, emanated from her. She smiled invitation. Even the way she leaned to the side seemed like an opening, like she was opening herself to me. The casual way she held herself, taut yet submissive, promised that anything I chose to do she would allow.

Such an opportunity rarely presents itself to a man. Yet, for all her beauty and seductiveness, I withheld. If anything, she took her role as a temptress to such an extreme that it began to have the opposite effect. It went too far, like watching an actress over dramatize her role. For many, it would be too much to resist. For me, it gave me the opportunity to resist.

"So where are we going?" I asked as I took the glass of champagne she offered me.

"To meet your benefactors," she answered. "You have made quite an impression on some powerful people."

She looked me up and down and smiled to herself. I could sense danger in that smile. If a wolf found himself sharing a cage with a lamb I'm sure he would've smiled the same way.

"Can't imagine how that happened," I honestly remarked.

"I'm sure," she laughed. "There is much about this world beyond what you can imagine."

Wanting to get out from beneath her unsettling gaze I turned to the window. The tint was so dark I could only see my own reflection staring back at me. I could also see her eyes still fixed on me.

"So, does this benefactor of mine have a name?" I asked, desperate to break the uneasiness.

"No one you would know," she answered.

"So he is no one famous?"

"Truly powerful men keep themselves out of the public eye," she said. "Your celebrities and politicians who are always parading themselves in front of the camera are little puppets on a string. If you want to find true power, look in the shadows, look behind the curtain, not the limelight."

Satisfaction filled her voice. Despite all of her sensual beauty I loathed her at that moment. I wanted badly to shake her obvious sense of superiority. That new attitude of mine, the one of warrior rather than victim, railed at being dealt with in such a trifling way.

"Did Lord Daniels tell you to say that?" I asked, stabbing in the dark.

My blind aim proved true. The smug, predatorial look on her face fell away instantly. Her mouth tightened and her whole body tensed. And if I was not mistaken, her color even paled slightly.

"Who told you that name?" She asked.

"There is much about me beyond what you could imagine," I answered.

She scowled at my reply. From that moment she dropped all of her seductive posturing and regarded me with suspicion. We didn't speak for the rest of the journey. I couldn't tell where we were going due to the dark interior tint of the windows, but I looked out nonetheless. Sierra sipped her champagne and studied her crimson nails.

When we finally stopped, the door opened and Sierra leapt to get out. She hesitated for a moment and leaned in close to me, so close that I could feel her warmth.

"There are two types of creatures in the universe," she said to me with surprising earnestness. "Some are predators, the rest are food. Most people fancy themselves predators. That is until they get eaten. But by then it's too late."

She disappeared out of the limousine. I waited alone for a moment, contemplating the strange words. They seem to be directed at me, but I couldn't help but think that she also spoke of herself.

After a moment I too stepped out of the limousine and found myself in front of an old, ivy-covered mansion. The dark night prevented me from discerning all its features, for the only light around flickered out of its windows. The stone structure rose at least three stories high and I could make out various wings on either end. Large, oak doors creaked open and a pale butler stepped up to beckon me in.

I followed the butler by candlelight through rooms cold and dark. Within the small aura light appeared the trappings of old money: molding tapestries, wood paneling, Persian carpets over the creaking hardwood floors. Portraits of ancestral figures decorated the walls alongside dusty weapons and iron sconces draped in deformed mounds of candle wax.

Strange things flitted by the brief passage of light, too quick to make out. Some grotesque statue of a horned creature stood just outside my vision. A coiled thing appeared overhead, gone as soon as I took note. Other things moved within the encircling shadows, always to the sides of my anxious eye. No matter how quickly I jerked my head to see, the unknown spectors had disappeared by the time my eyes searched them out.

The butler seemed to notice none of these things. Impassively and without a word he guided me down the empty halls until it led to a large, iron door set into a stone wall. It looked as if it had not been opened in years with rust flaking off of the rivets and hinges.

"I'll have to ask you that you remove your shoes before we proceed to the grotto," the butler said to me in a rumbling voice.

Wondering what he meant by grotto I kicked off my shoes. The heavy iron door swung open with surprising ease and the butler indicated for me to step through.

The grotto looked much like what I would expect it to, though it felt strange attached like it was to the mansion. A large area opened up before me, the walls of which were the roughhewn rocks of a cave. Wall niches appeared sporadically, some with only candles, others decorated with busts or large statues. I recognize none of the figures.

Like everywhere else in the mansion, the grotto was lit only by fire. Candles and torches offered more than enough illumination to make out reasonable details of where I stood. Around me yawned a large space, supported all around by pillars. Across from me waited a gathering of the most beautiful people I've ever seen in my life.

About thirty in all they seemed to have come from every race the world contains, and some I have never heard of or laid eyes on. I saw the dark skins of Africans lounging next to the olive tones of Mediterranean people. Women of Arab descent mixed with men of decidedly oriental features. Brown, almond shaped eyes stared back at me as well as wide, blue eyes. Hair that was white as summer clouds mingled with hair dark as midnight. I saw every skin tone there from deep black to others so pale it was almost opaque. Some of them stood, some sat in plush chairs while others reclined on couches. They all wore black suits or dresses, of different styles but of the same dolorous color. None of them wore anything on their feet.

"Welcome," Lord Daniels called from a throne carved of the same cave rock as the grotto. The rest of the beautiful people gathered around him.

A shot of fear rocketed through me at seeing Lord Daniels. I forced my feet to walk and to my surprise they obeyed quite readily. A thrum passed through my feet as they touched the warm cave floor, as if a generator whirred beneath or some source of great power lurked under the grotto.

As I approached I let my eyes scan the people who watched me. That they were all beautiful is an understatement. They were radiant. They were glorious. Normal human beings, I couldn't help but think to myself, just don't look like this. And it wasn't even their perfect proportion, or the finely shaped features of their faces and bodies that had me so enamored.

They all possessed that quality, that undefinable essence that can only be described as beauty. These people were beautiful because they possessed beauty, and to a high degree. Even though I feared them, I could not help but admire them. I tread dangerously close to that adoration we call worship.

Above Lord Daniels another group lounged in the balcony. Some sat with their legs dangling over the edge, and others crowded behind them looking curiously at me. These people seemed different somehow. By all appearances they looked as handsome as the group below. I could pick up no physical trait that distinguished them. Yet all at once they seemed less somehow, and felt more real. They reminded me of Sierra.

"I am told you already know who I am," Daniels said with a feral smile. "I feel the advantage is all yours."

"Any advantage I may possess," I said in a voice steadier than it should have been. "Is due only to a stroke of fortune that I did nothing to deserve."

Daniels nodded, satisfied by my answer. Movement from behind the group of people grabbed my attention. A shadow appeared from a side hallway, followed by another beautiful figure who stepped out and padded with soft confidence to stand beside Daniels.

My breath froze as her eyes fixed upon mine. I could smell the exotic spices from her cigarette, the rich aroma stirring my memory. As if I could ever forget such a face.

Eladora.

"Look sister, the guest of honor has arrived," Daniels said.

Sister? I felt a ridiculous sort of pleasure to know she was not his wife.

Eladora looked bored. She passed an indifferent glance over me and puffed at her cigarette. The grotto filled with the smell of her strange smoke. I felt giddy seeing her there, like a boy seeing his crush from across the room.

"What would we want with him?" Eladora asked. She gave no indication at all that she knew me, so I thought it best to do the same.

"This is one of the bright new stars in the Corporation," Daniels answered, looking at me. "He is a man of great talent I'm told."

"Looks like an ordinary man to me," Eladora said with a shrug.

"Yes, and you know how difficult they can be," Daniels said.

Feeling like a child being discussed in front of his parents, I stepped forward to interject.

"So what is it exactly you want with me?" I asked.

"Ah, look at me, I have forgotten my manners," Daniels gushed. "Come, you must drink first. It is the law of hospitality."

A girl came forward carrying a silver tray and presented a goblet to me. She was bare chested, wearing only a white tunic

44

that wrapped around her waist and fell down to her knees. Her cool, blue eyes fixed upon mine without the slightest hint of shame at her nakedness. By the juvenile swell of her breasts I estimated she could be no more than sixteen.

I took the tarnished, silver goblet and began to raise it to my lips. Eladora's words came back to me. Only a sip, she said. Take only the smallest of sips.

A musty, sweet smell crept up my nose as I placed the cup to my lips. The liquid touched my tongue and a drop slowly trickled down my throat. It tasted horrible, but I found myself wanting more. It tasted like wine that had long gone to vinegar with sugar mixed in to hide the rancid flavor.

But I wanted more.

My body ached with thirst, a thirst only for that mixture. Just a sip she had said, yet how could I? My hands trembled. Drink deep, something whispered. Paradise waits within. Open your mouth and pour it down.

Strange eyes stared at me, from Lord Daniels and all the beautiful people around him, from the shadows and flickering lights of the grotto. They all urged me to drink. Without opening their mouths I could hear them, feel them. Drink. Drink. They all told me to drink.

All their eyes, wide and insistent.

Except Eladora's.

Her stare, still indifferent, fixed on me too. Something else was there. Stifled hope maybe?

She pursed her lips and blew a cloud of smoke towards me. My whole body shook and sweat had begun to pour out of me like the sweat of a breaking fever. My hand, shaking as it held the goblet, crept closer and closer to my mouth. Vaguely, I thought I wasn't supposed to do this. It didn't matter. The goblet drew closer and closer.

The cloud of Eladora's smoke enveloped me. I inhaled the drifting billow of spice and green earth, of smells undefinable. I felt the smoke pass into me and something broke. Or rather, it shook my mind awake again.

Then there was only the taste of sour wine. A vague flitter of temptation remained to drink deep. This time it was easily overcome. I put the goblet back on the tray and nodded a thanks to Lord Daniels.

Disappointment stood out plainly on his face. Quickly, he put away the scowl with a broad grin.

"No more than that?" He asked. "You can have all you want."

"No more," I assured him.

The girl took away the goblet and we were left to stare at one another again. Daniels tapped his lips with a finger, obviously considering within himself.

"Do you know who I am?" He finally asked.

"No idea," I answered with total honesty.

He considered me again for a moment. "Me and my brothers and sisters," he indicated the group around him. "Are, what shall we say? Overseers of a large empire. We have a considerable investment that we must protect at all costs. Do you understand?"

I nodded, though unsure I understood a thing except in the vaguest terms.

"So you see why someone like you would pique our interests, do you not?"

"I'm afraid I don't have the slightest idea what you're talking about," I confessed.

"Don't lie to me!" Daniel screamed, banging the arm of his chair. Everyone in the chamber jumped as his voice echoed off the stone, and the arm of his chair crumbled into flakes of rock.

I felt my own insides lurch at the burst of anger. He stared at me hard for a moment, and the cat women smiled devilishly in my mind, before he masked his emotions again.

"Come now, be honest," he said in a voice of forced pleasantness.

I dare not answer for risk of provoking his wrath. Eladora leaned in and stroked her brothers hair.

"Look at the poor thing," she said. "I really don't think he knows."

Daniel studied me for a minute more. The whole cavern waited in silence. Tension hovered in the air like thick fog.

"How can he not know?"

"He probably just knows something is different," Eladora answered. "He is oblivious to the rest."

"Can they really be that stupid?"

"Naïve," Eladora corrected. "The poor thing is naïve. The world he occupies is so small and timid. It has been so stripped bare of wonders that they have forgotten there's even such a thing. How could he even imagine the truth when what is real has been hidden from him?"

Daniels nodded thoughtfully.

"Possibly," he said. "But can we risk it?"

"We can make it one of ours," Eladora suggested as she looked over me herself. Once again, I felt like a child whose fate was being decided in front of him.

"He's been marked."

"So he has. What does that have to do with anything?"

Daniels finally addressed me. "Have you gone into the woods behind your house?" he asked. The same strange query Eladora had asked me.

I shook my head.

"There are no woods behind your house," he said. The whole company laughed, the sound of their scorn bounced surreally off the rock walls.

Hadn't Eladora said the exact same thing? I couldn't get a read on her at all. She betrayed nothing on her face of good or ill intentions towards me.

"Perhaps we can be friends then?" Daniels said.

"You know how useful they can be," Eladora told her brother. "The potential that is there."

47

Daniel stood up decisively. "Off to the Grove!" He announced to a chorus of cheers.

The company bustled out of the cavern through different hallways until only Daniels, Eladora and myself were left. Eladora allowed only the briefest of smiles to cross her face before she too turned away. My eyes followed her as she left, unable to turn away from her sensuous form.

"She is a delightful creature, is she not?" Daniels observed of my gawking.

"I've never seen her equal," I confessed. It would have been foolish to lie.

"Of that I have no doubt," Daniels said. "So tell me, do you wish to be friends in these matters? Will you help us? Or at least stand out of our way?"

I laughed and spread my hands wide. "I can hardly say as I have no idea whatsoever as to what any of this is about."

"Fair enough," Daniels conceded. "Come then, let me show you."

He turned and indicated me to follow. We stepped through a tunnel carved out of rock, then giving way to worn stone. The hallway twisted and curved, lit only by the flickering light of torches. We went through the hall and up a winding staircase, the narrow kind you see in castle towers, with stairs barely wide enough for the foot to gain safe traction.

Daniels flew up the stairs without apparent effort. I labored behind, losing more breath by the second. The climb finally ended at an access door set into the stone roof of the tower. Daniels pushed it open and pulled himself up. I followed him and stepped out under the night sky, the stars above me blazing brighter than I ever remembered.

On top of the tower the city spread out before us, blazing with a million electric lights. A thought occurred to me that a tower at this height would be an easily distinguished landmark. Yet I could not remember seeing it for as long as I have lived in the city.

Another glance at the sky increased the odd quality of the tower. Not only did the stars seem brighter, they felt closer, much closer. I checked through familiar constellations, noting how large they appeared. In Orion I could see the dark clouds of the nebula. The swirl of the Andromeda galaxy was small but easily noticed. I could even make out the rings of Saturn and the bands of the faint color on Jupiter. Likewise, in the stretch of the Milky Way I could clearly discern the individual stars instead of the haze that usually appeared.

"Where are we?" I asked, breathless and amazed.

"Behold, the Kingdoms of the World," Daniels answered, stretching his hand to indicate the sprawl beneath us.

Disorientation washed over me and I held out a hand to steady myself on the crenelations. It wasn't just a city beneath us, but cities. And mountains and deserts and jungles. The noise that rose up was the garbled tongues of a thousand languages. How, it is impossible to say, but on top of that tower I was certain that I really could see the whole world.

"What is this place?" I managed to ask, desperate for some sense of equilibrium.

"This is my perspective," Lord Daniels answered. He looked out over the vast landscape in a satisfied way, much like the way a prince would survey his domain.

"This is my business, our business."

"What? Do you rule the world?"

My senses slowly balanced out again. I could stand without the world spinning. There remained a sense, though, that either I, or the world around me, was moving very quickly.

"Not rulers, keepers," Daniels clarified. "We are the keepers of the world. The watchers."

"The whole world? How is that possible?" I asked, amazed.

"Just the parts that matter. You can't really make people do anything. Unfortunately, all you can do is influence them, try to exercise authority over them."

"Like rig elections?"

Daniels laughed. "Oh, such petty imaginations you have. No, we have no need to rig elections. Those puny creatures you call politicians, the ones you think wield so much power and influence are actually the most weak-minded, easily manipulated people on the face of the earth. It doesn't really matter who is elected. They all fall into their place pretty easily. There was a time when things were different, when men had more mettle and steel and will."

Daniel stared off, almost wistfully. A cold wind ruffled his hair.

"Not so today," he said softly. "The men of this age are like little robots. Put in the right commands and they do whatever you want."

That wistful feeling settled over Daniels again. I felt his mood change. It almost seemed as though he lamented that men today were so easily manipulated.

"Why?" I asked, unable to fully grasp what I heard. Had it not been for the strange things that had happened to me, including the fact that I stood on a tower that could see all the kingdoms of the world at once, I would hardly believe what I was hearing. As it was, that Lord Daniels and his siblings were behind the true power of the world was not only plausible, it made perfect sense.

"It's what we do," Daniels answered with a shrug. "Left on its own, life is all mayhem and chaos, a fire that rages and burns indiscriminately. It must be focused, tempered. Only then can it be put to great use. In fact, nothing is impossible for man if he would but work as one. We offer man direction. We offer him the possibility of reaching his true potential."

"And where are you taking us?"

Daniels turned and his eyes bore into me. I thought of that poor Englishman who had asked a similar question just before the cat women devoured him. Too late to take the question back I forced myself to meet his gaze.

"Let's just say we are doing what is best for mankind,"

Daniels answered. "We are restoring an ancient glory that was lost long, long ago. And since then the world has run amok. We can do great things, you and I. We truly can. Man has such incredible potential within him. He only lacks direction, order. Someone to tell him what he needs to do."

"And you offer him that?"

"I do. That and so much more."

"Well tell me this then," I said. "Why me? What do I have to do with all this? How could I even help, or hurt for that matter?"

"Look at this, all around you," Daniels indicated strange environs outside the tower.

I looked up, awash in dizziness again. Somehow, I managed to keep a hold of my spinning mind. The scenery bombarded me, flooded into me. I could hold a direct look only briefly.

"A normal man cannot do that," Daniels explained. "But something is different about you. No?"

I nodded. "What is it?"

"It's called a dweomer," Daniels said. He pulled out an old piece of cloth. In the dark, I could barely make a pattern sewn into it.

"Some men are born with it. Not many, but a few. Even fewer come across it in their age, men such as yourself."

"What is it? How did it happen?"

"It is a heightened sense of awareness, an opening in the mind. Think of it as a new state of the soul wherein your potential has suddenly increased exponentially. Imagination, memory, senses, your grasp of things normally hidden has all increased. You have opened doors in yourself that most men are not even aware exist, except those born with the innate capacity.

"As to how it happened. You can answer that better than I."

Memories of the dream immediately sprang to mind; the

51

cavern beneath the mountain, the old man by the door, the door opening...

I shook myself out of the reverie. The memory had come back so strong as to almost take me out of the tower.

"Are you like me?" I asked. "Are you not aware also?"

"I'm nothing like you," he said coldly. I could feel the venom in his voice, the unmasked contempt.

"But we still can be friends," he said as he slapped my shoulder. I could still see revulsion in his eyes, in the sneer that crept up to his lips.

I nodded, feeling very small beside him. If he had wanted to throw me off that tower he could have done so without any effort, and I gather he would suffer no consequences either.

"Let's join the others," he suggested instead. "The Grove awaits."

He turned and made his way downstairs. I followed down the spiral staircase, through another series of fire lit corridors. We passed through a small doorway that opened to the outside. The air was clean and cool, and the stars above back to their normal height above my head. Daniels pointed to a footpath that wound through gardens in front of us.

In the middle of the garden we came to an old stone pool. Actually, it looked more like a decorative garden pond than a pool. The water, though, was clean despite its greenish hue, and steam rose from the surface. Statues graced the perimeter and a bathhouse stood on either side.

"First, we bathe," Daniels said, stripping off his clothes.

Adonis-like features appeared as he undressed, the supple body of the young and strong. Like everything else about him, his body was perfect. The proportion, the muscle, the tone of the skin; the pure artistry of all his features made it seem as if I were looking at a classical sculpture rather than a flesh and blood creature.

Next to him I couldn't help but feel insecure. My thin limbs, my middling pudge, pale and splotchy skin compared to his flawlessness was nothing short of comic. If he had any of these thoughts he betrayed none of them.

I dove into the pool after Daniels. Warm water enveloped me and caressed me in womb–like comfort. A palpable vigor enveloped my limbs and suffused into the pores of my skin. When I broke from the surface of the water, steam rising from my face in the cool evening air, I was filled with an almost intoxicating energy. Undoubtedly, the pool possessed some strong mineral content, fed by underground springs to account for its warmth. But there had to be something else, something to explain the giddiness I felt in the pit of my stomach. By the smile on Daniels' face I could tell he felt the same.

"What's in there?" I asked wide-eyed and amazed.

"Oh, just an old world mix," he said as he pulled himself out the other side.

I clambered up beside him. Immediately, the chilled air sprouted goosebumps over my wet skin. A young boy ran forward with towels. Like the girl who had served me the goblet, he was young and handsome and clad only in a sheet wrapped around his waist.

After we had dried, the boy wrapped Daniels in a purple tunic that ran over one shoulder. Then he stepped up to clothe me in a similar one, but of a dark, crimson color. I stood like a lord being dressed by his servants as the boy wrapped the cloth around my waist and combed back my hair.

"Now we're ready for the Grove," Daniel said approvingly.

We walked down from the pool into a forest path at the foot of the sloping lawn. I looked back, hoping to see the tower silhouetted against the stars. I could only make out the dim lights flickering in the mansion windows. A figure shadowed one of those windows, staring down at us crossing the lawn.

As soon as we stepped into the Grove a surreal sensation washed over me that makes it nearly impossible to remember

53

what all happened there. I recall stepping into a large clearing. A bonfire blazed in its midst. Massive, orange flames licked at the sky. All the beautiful people from the grotto were there. Like me and Daniels they had dressed in different colored tunics. Somewhere on the edge the Grove I saw musicians playing on drum and fiddle and some form of old guitar. Singers added their own music to the strange and haunting tune, something ancient and achingly beautiful.

Tuniced figures danced around the fire. Young, bare-chested servants walked among the crowd passing out goblets of red wine and refilling empty ones out of long, clay vessels. I vaguely remember staring at one of the servant girls as she refilled my cup. She was offered to me at one point. I became aroused and cautious, for she couldn't have been of legal consenting age. But I remember no more of her for the rest of my broken memory of the Grove.

I recall the sensation of dancing. Jumping, twirling, laughing around the fire, and rich wine being poured down my mouth. I remember warm lips, tongues hot like fire. Hands grabbing me and pulling me forward. Sweating bodies pressed close to mine while we danced. The fire danced too, as well as the stars above the trees. There was ecstasy there, unbridled and free like we have never known. I felt the ground rejoice with us. I remember thinking, this is what a celebration should be like. How can we have forgotten how to do this?

I remember no more.

The Third Vision

When I awoke I was at home again with no recollection of how I had gotten there. Strangely, I felt no hangover from all I'd consumed the night before. Instead I sprang out of bed revived and clearheaded as ever.

Thinking it was Friday I prepared for work and stepped out the front door only to find three newspapers piled on my porch. On top waited the thick Sunday edition. Had I slept that long? That certainly explained my rested feeling. Perhaps I had spent more time at the Grove than I thought.

Seeing as it was Sunday, I had the day to myself and confronted the arduous task of finding something to do. It was a new problem.

Ever since my recent awareness, what Daniels had called a dweomer, I had become consumed by an incredible boredom. None of my former pastimes held the same interest for me. The little work around the yard and house could be completed quickly enough. I tried to take an interest in sports, but to watch others play a game grew quickly boring. On some nights I would go into the city and frequent the local bars. Being alone, I mostly watched others.

At first, the people seemed fascinating. So much drama went on right beneath me I had never noticed before. So much variety to human nature had gone unacknowledged. I drank it all in eagerly.

Then, I began to notice patterns. The same people had the same arguments at the same table with the same conclusions. The disheveled divorcee with the blonde, thinning hair would hit on any girl half his age, no matter how many times his advances were rebuffed. Somehow, he seemed oblivious to the looks of disgust on their faces. Either oblivious or he didn't care.

There was a woman his own age who always tried to talk with him. He would acknowledge her politely and she would watch, sipping an old-fashioned, as he crashed and burned over and over again.

There was that group of older women, not old, but far from young, who came in every other day. Most had fine wrinkles around the corners of their mouths from years of smoking along with a husky voice. After three drinks they would forget their age, or perhaps they regressed on purpose, and act like the college girls they had once been.

If you came on Thursday you could join in Music Mike's Karaoke. The divorcee would sing "Here's a Quarter, Call Someone Who Cares." The girls would spend forty-five minutes flipping through the song selection before deciding on "I Will Survive." The fighting couple never sang, nor did the woman who watched the divorcee, but she always told him how well he sang. One could fairly rely on hearing "Annie's Song," "Honky Tonk Woman," "Sweet Caroline" and "Hotel California" from the other regulars. On at least a monthly basis the middle-aged member of a local cover band would belt out "When a Man Loves a Woman," with all the sentiment he could muster.

The people quickly went from fascinating to pathetic. To see parades of women long past their prime dressing as if they enjoyed the bloom of youth, grind and strut like misguided teenagers, men who leered at every pathetic show of skin, young girls so plucked and bleached they seemed more plastic than flesh; Botox lips, saline breasts, rub on tans, bleary-eyed men staring transfixed at the television, the same people making the same mistakes, telling the same jokes, laughing the same tired laughter. I still watched. Fascination grew into horror. I watched and waited for something to change. I waited for something different to happen.

For a time nothing of note happened in my life after the night at the Grove. I didn't see Daniels or Eladora or any of the other people from the grotto. Their look was so distinguished I could pick any them out in a crowd of thousands.

Instead, I was faced with the irksome task of finding

something meaningful to do. Work had become effortless. In my new position I was bothered by no one nor ever asked to do anything. I could sit in my office and play pool or walk through the building and not a single person had anything to say to me or ask of me.

At one point I confronted the CEO about my lack of productivity. He immediately grew so nervous and fidgety I let the matter drop. Whenever I approached Janice about the matter she would return with a stack of papers and reports that she said needed my approval. Their subject matter ranged from the trifling to the economic. I would initial each paper and turn them back into Janice. If I didn't ask she wouldn't bring me any of them. It became clear that I was only given that meaningless task if I went searching for something to do. I quit asking and wasn't bothered any further.

Sierra didn't return. Instead, she was replaced by a young girl fresh out of college named Erin. At first glance I could tell she was a singularly unique person. On the surface she was decidedly pretty in a conventional way; straight brown hair, a small, athletic frame, dressed in proper business attire for a young woman. But the almost unnoticeable stud she wore in her nose betrayed a subtle contempt for convention. You could hardly see it, as well as hardly miss it. There was brightness in her eyes that usually accompanied a keen intellect, one that could see a bit deeper than most.

Erin introduced herself as my personal assistant, so she quickly grew as bored as I was. A few times a day I would peek my head out of my office and she would put her phone down and ask if I needed anything. I never did.

Inexplicably, my pay increased about four times what I made before. With nothing to do, and plenty of time and money on my hands, I was forced to reevaluate the miserable state of my life. I had no real friends. The group of people I always called friends belonged to that circle that included my wife. When she left, the friends left with her.

Hobbies were another thing noticeably missing. Life before had always been dictated by my wife. Whatever she wanted to do, the family did. Now, left on my own, I was forced to find something to do with all this spare time.

This proved more difficult than one would think. Oddly, I had no idea what I liked or what I was good at. I think this is a feature of my generation. So many of us are raised having to do nothing but entertain ourselves that we have no opportunity to find out what we have talent for.

For a while I picked up whatever seemed a good idea for the time. I did yard work, but quickly found I had neither the talent nor the desire for gardening. I tried my hand at hunting and fishing, and though I enjoyed the peace of the outdoors immensely, I proved a poor hunter as well.

One bored afternoon, when perusing my memory for something in my childhood that might give me any indication as to what I might like to do, I remembered my grandfather. He died when I was a boy, but I remember him being a man of tenderness and affection. His hands were large and worn from work, his serious eyes full of warmth. He always held a mouthful of tobacco and the front pocket of his shirt was always stained with the dark juice.

What I remembered most about my grandfather, though, was his truck. He spent countless hours working on his beloved '64 Ford. Not that it was ever broken, he just loved to do what he called tinkering. My fondest memories of him were watching while he leaned under the open hood. I usually held a glass bottle of Coke in my hand. The garage smelled of tobacco and oil. The sound of the ratchet cranking mixed with his deep and soothing voice. He spun out stories of his childhood during the Depression, his time as a fighter pilot on a P-38 during the war. He sprinkled in golden nuggets of wisdom here and there, a gift I only now began to realize and appreciate.

"I gotta tell you slick, people are a funny thing," he said to me one day. He always called me slick.

"Most of the time they're pretty ordinary. Hell, they're damn sheep if you ask me. They follow the herd this way, then that way. Hardly an original thought within a thousand heads. Then one day, ka-pow, out of nowhere they do something that totally surprises you. I've seen men I had figured for pretty worthless step in front of bullets or dive hellbound for glory into a cloud of Messerschmitt's. Just goes to show we got it in us all along. We do, slick, don't never believe otherwise. We all have the potential to be great, or at least to do great things. Imagine if we tried all the time. Imagine what we could do."

Inspired by the memory I hunted for the better part of three weeks until I found a rusted and battered 1964 Ford F-150. Instead of cherry red like my grandfather's, this one had been white some time ago. But with time and money I was determined to make it every bit like the one I remembered.

A second hobby cropped up purely by chance around the same time. This one turned out to be the more time-consuming and productive. In fact, you could say the second pursuit changed everything.

It began one day at work. I stood at the window of my office, looking out at my ridiculously great view of the city. Thoughts of Eladora haunted my memory. Not only her, but the whole strange company I met in the grotto still occupied my thoughts. I wanted to know who they were, though I had not the slightest clue as to where to start looking for them.

While lost in these thoughts a soft knock sounded at my door. I heard it open and without turning knew it was Erin. It was her daily inquiry about what she should do.

"Need anything?" She asked.

It had become a bit of a ritual over the last weeks. Even though we shared few words I felt our mutual boredom gave us at least a tenuous connection.

I shook my head and shrugged my shoulders as I always did. She smiled and rolled her eyes in commiseration. As she began to close the door a thought occurred to me.

"Erin," I called to stop her. "You went to college, right?"

"Yeah," she said with a self-conscious shrug.

"What was your major?"

She pivoted one foot on a high heel shoe. This was by far the longest conversation we had engaged in.

"English," she answered. "Not that it did me a whole lot of good. But I'm certainly not the only English major who answers phones all day."

"Except you don't really answer phones all day," I pointed out. This won me a smile.

"Right, I'm an English major who sits at a desk all day waiting for the phone to ring."

"You've done research though, right?" I asked. "I mean research beyond a Google search?"

Her mouth fell open in either mock or real offense.

"I didn't mean it like that," I tried to backtrack.

"Well yes, if you must know, I have done research that didn't involve the Internet at all. In a real library with real books."

"How would you like to do some research for me?" I asked.

"You mean something besides staring at my phone all day?" she asked with palpable relief.

"No Internet," I told her. "Keep this off the grid if you can. It probably won't get anywhere, but I want you to look up a name for me. Anywhere in literature or history it might show up. Any significant mention of the name at all. Doesn't matter how bizarre or outlandish the reference is."

"Okay, you're the boss. What name am I looking up?"

I thought about it for a second, feeling that once I opened this box whatever came out wouldn't easily go back in. Did I want that kind of trouble? Then again, answers weren't going to fall into my lap. More importantly, if I was unwillingly thrust into the middle of something, I wanted to be an active agent in whatever was going on.

This is the way it would be. I heard the name roll like music off my tongue.

"Eladora."

During this time my personal life had undergone a type of upheaval. I thought about my wife and children more than ever. She treated me with an indifference that had become characteristic. Before, I am not sure if it actually hurt. Now it was quite painful.

The difference may be that now I felt more. Everything felt more. Happiness was happier, anger more aggravating, lust more consuming, and loneliness more poignant than it had ever been in my life.

It was the loneliness more than the lust that drove me into the arms of women. In my defense, they were lonely too. It was like we put out some sort of beacon to one another, and finding each other in the night, agreed to share loneliness and expect nothing else. Or at least, that's what I told myself.

Sometimes they were older than me, sometimes younger. We took no time to discover if we shared anything in common besides our loneliness. I don't brag as a lothario would, though I could feel an innate ability to draw women to myself. Something stirred in my new expansion of being that made me larger than most men. Women could feel it. It had nothing to do with physical traits, for I am average looking on my best days. This was something that ran deeper. This was primeval.

Perhaps I took advantage of these women. Perhaps they took advantage of me. But for a moment we were not lonely. And I can promise I wasn't driven by lust. You can probably not even imagine what its like to be the only one that's aware, at least of all the people around you. It is so lonely it physically hurts. I needed relief from it from time to time. I needed to feel as if I still belonged to the wider world, even as I felt more distant from it.

My children proved only slightly less distant than my wife. On their required weekends with me they tried to stay glued to the TV or phone. My constant attempts to engage them met with mixed results.

Progress was slow. After a time I began to notice the walls of their resistance weakening. One night we even managed to play board games together and went hours without a single electronic device. The next weekend they came over my son helped me with the truck, and my daughter asked me how my job was going! To you it may sound minor, but for me it was history in the making.

They still remained distant, occasional parts of my life. Loneliness stood out as the dominant feature of my days. It wasn't until the call from Erin that things began to really change.

I had not seen her for at least three weeks. This came as no surprise. I had put her on a research project and insisted she work in the library. The idea sounded paranoid from time to time, until I remembered the people I was looking into. Considering their strange powers I do not think I could be too careful.

She called one afternoon and asked to meet me at the university library on the third floor. I found her working in a private carrel.

"Oh, there you are," she said in greeting. She looked uncomfortable. At first I thought it was because of the isolated setting. Then she stuck her head out and looked down both ends of the aisle.

"Do you have your phone?" She asked.

I nodded and she held out her hand. Curious, I handed her my phone. She put it in the carrel, closed the door and motioned me to follow her through the stacks.

After we had arrived at an isolated corner she stopped and turned to me. That troubled look reappeared, as well as a sense of indecision. She twisted a ring nervously on her finger. Her lips pursed to one side.

"Look, you seem like a really nice guy," she finally said. Odd words, I thought. She made it sound as if she were breaking up with me.

"Okay, did I do something wrong?" I asked.

"No, nothing. I just need to feel like I can trust you. You seem like someone I can trust." The tension in her voice rose as she spoke.

"I'd like to think so," I said. "What exactly is this about?"

"Because Janice doesn't seem like someone I can trust. She gives me the creeps and I'm scared to death of her."

"Erin, please. What is this about?"

"Sorry, I'm just kind of freaked out," she said. "This whole thing has been bizarre."

"What? What things?"

"Everything!" she almost yelled. Then she seemed to remember herself and looked around to make sure no one else heard.

"Everything about this job is weird," she said. "Starting with how they hired me."

"How did they hire you? Didn't you apply?"

"No, that's just it. I didn't. They called me, out of the blue. I'm working as a waitress, two months behind on every bill and all of a sudden I get this phone call offering me a job at your company making a hell of a lot more money than I ever have."

"That is a bit strange," I had to admit. "Did they tell you why?"

"They said someone came in the restaurant one day and thought I would be perfect for the job," she told me.

"That's possible," I argued, though I knew there must be more.

"That's not all," she pressed on. "The interview was super creepy. Janice never asked me anything about my qualifications. She asked me about my family, a lot about my dad who I never knew. Then she asked a lot of random questions about my childhood, very strange things. Then she just went on and on about how they used to torture traitors in the dark ages and how you need order for the world to survive. She was kind of obsessed with it. We must have order. Order is the pulse of the world. Life is chaos without it, or some crap like that.

"I couldn't wait for it to be over so I could get out of there."

"I don't blame you," I said. "Why did you come back?"

"She offered me the job right there," Erin explained. "Attached to a lot of money. I mean a lot. I figured I could take a little weirdness for a few months to get me out of debt.

"But it just keeps getting weirder. I just sit at a desk all day with nothing to do. I see the CEO wandering around muttering to himself. And at least once a day Janice comes over and glares at your door. I mean glares like she wishes she could shoot lasers out of her eyes and burn you up. That whole floor has a funky vibe. They're handing out pills or something. I don't know, I'm scared to drink the water. I keep thinking they're going to come after me and put me through the brainwashing too."

Erin had become visibly upset. She began to pace in a tight formation, her movements hampered by the narrow space. Her hands gestured wildly as she spoke.

"Look, it's okay," I tried to assure her. "If you can't stay don't feel obligated. Especially on my behalf."

"That's not all," she said, stopping for a moment to face me. She tugged on her lip and wore that indecisive expression again.

"There's more," she said. "Please don't be mad at me."

"What?" I asked, troubled by her obvious anxiety.

"She wanted me to spy on you."

"Who? Janice?"

Erin nodded.

"Not much to spy on, is there?" I chuckled.

Erin wore a sheepish expression. Before the words were out of her mouth I knew what she was going to say.

"Well, I did tell her about this research," she confessed. "I'm sorry, but I had to. It was part of my job."

"And what did Janice say?" I asked.

"Once again, weird," she said. "I told her you were sending me out to research a name, the name Eladora. She kind of sneered and laughed at the same time, a horrible look really. Then she said, the bastard thinks he's clever. Go ahead and look. You won't find anything."

I guess I should've been upset about Erin spying on me. Instead, I was flattered she told me about it. No one had ever shown me that kind of loyalty. I'm not sure I have ever shown that kind of loyalty myself.

"Well, I can see how all this seems a bit odd," I told her.

"We're not done with weird yet," Erin said, turning on her heels. "Follow me."

"Don't tell me you found something," I said to her retreating figure.

"I told you, I don't like Janice," Erin stopped and said. She flashed me a smile. "And I certainly won't have that old bag tell me I can't find something."

Picking up her contagious smile I continued to follow Erin as she plunged into the aisle of books. We were deep in the stacks when she stopped and thumbed through the worn spines of some obviously older books. She pulled out a green, tattered volume and turned back to me.

"I have to say, it was daunting at first," she told me. "The name sounded Hebrew so I looked through an index of sacred writings with no luck. Same thing with Greek, Latin, Celtic, Persian, Egyptian, Norse and Minoan. It didn't sound like anything from the Far East, so I decided to go a little unconventional."

"Unconventional?"

"I told you, I was determined to prove that bitch wrong."

She stopped and crooked her mouth at the impropriety. My nod of agreement seemed to reassure her. A conspiratorial smile crept over her face as she continued. That, alongside the passion that overtook her when she spoke of her work filled her with an energy that was nothing short of beautiful. I had not noticed it until then.

"Yes, I went unconventional and started to look into fairy literature."

"Fairies?" I interrupted. "You're talking about the little fellows with wings that live in flowers?"

"I'm not talking about the Disney creatures," she said, pointing at me with the book. "Those are the glowing little Tinkerbell's with glitter falling off their wings. If you look into the old stories, the original stories, fairies were dark and powerful creatures."

"So how did they turn into the butterfly people?" I asked.

"Victorian children's stories most likely," Erin answered, leaning on the bookshelf. "The Victorians were notorious for cleaning up stories for children, taking out the violence and sex. They thought the real fairies were too scary for kids, so they made them cuter and kinder, creatures that granted wishes and watched over children as they slept.

"But the original fairies were nothing like that. They get their name because they were once called the Fair Folk, named for their beauty and grace. There also known as the Sidhe, Fae, Tuatha De Danaan, Daoine Sidhe, Dannae, Dagda, Children of Dannae, the Blessed Ones, the Good Folk, Nephilim, Lios Alfar and Children of Light, among others. It cuts across culture and time. But whatever they were called, the Fair Folk were all beautiful, powerful and very dangerous."

"Dangerous how?" I asked. "Kill people, stuff like that?"

"Usually nothing so blatant," Erin said flipping open the book in her hand. "They were regarded mostly as tricksters, though sometimes the tricks would get malicious, or even deadly. Sometimes they would enchant people and take them as prisoners to the fairy kingdom. Children and beautiful women are particularly vulnerable. More than a few child disappearances were attributed to the Fair Folk.

"Most of them are known for being mercurial and capricious. They can go from joy to anger without warning, love and hate, favor and outright spite at a moments notice. That's what really makes them dangerous. When it comes to the Fair Folk, you never know what you're going to get."

"Okay, the Fair Folk," I said. "Any luck there?"

Erin's face lit up. The eager giddiness was catching. I found myself getting as excited as she was.

"No luck, just talent," she said. "I had done lots of work in school on romantic literature, especially Keats. I remembered reading one scholar, William Libscomb, while doing a paper on *La Belle Dame Sans Merci.*"

"What's that?" I asked.

"A poem by Keats. Roughly translated, The Beautiful Woman Without Mercy."

I remembered the work. What can ail thee knight at arms alone and palely loitering?

"It tells the story of the knight who meets with a fairy woman and spends an incredible night with her, only to wake up the next day and find her gone. The rest of his life he wanders the forest looking for his Dame Sans Merci, full of longing and heartache. Typical fairy behavior. Seduce a man, allow them to experience unearthly and blissful love, then leave him never to be heard from again."

"Or just female behavior," I suggested, trying to interject humor.

"That's where we learned it from," Erin answered.

"But I searched through Lipscomb again since he was particularly interested in the names of the Fae. Names are a big deal to them."

"Big deal? How so?"

"Names are power. If you know someone's name, their true name, you have power over them. This is especially true of the Fair Folk. Their nature makes them vulnerable to bindings and such.

"At any rate, Lipscomb had looked at a rare and obscure author named Telerus, a ninth century Irish monk. He recounted the story of a boy and girl, twins with a rare birthmark between the eyes known as a fairy saddle. One day, they go into the forest, and only the girl returns. She tells the frightened village how she and her brother stopped at a pond where beautiful women beckon them from the other side. The boy follows them, and the girl runs in terror. The local villagers search the woods up and down and find nary a trace of the boy.

"Fifty years later a young man, no more than sixteen years old, wanders out of the woods claiming to be the lost boy. No one is inclined to believe him, except for the striking resemblance he has to the girl's children who are all older than he is, and the rare birthmark across the bridge of his nose. He recounts this marvelous tale of living in the fairy kingdom, taken in at first as a guest, then kept as a servant. According to the story, he escaped only after a particularly spirited night of drinking and fighting left the gateway unguarded.

"Now the townspeople have no idea what to do with the boy, so they send him to live at a monastery. There he meets the monk Telerus, whom he befriends and eventually tells all the stories to, including – get this – the names of the Fae."

"And we have a copy of that?" I asked.

"Not likely," Erin shook her head. "The Telerus manuscript is notoriously hard to track down, and a translation of it is even more rare. However, Lipscomb inspected a copy and used it to analyze Keats's poem."

She turned the green book to me. Her finger pointed at the title of a scholarly article, "The Identity of Keat's Dame Sans

Merci."

"Lipscomb pores over the Telerus text and analyzes the character of the different Fair Folk and comes to a decided conclusion as to who the mysterious woman is who drove our knight at arms lovesick."

She paused for what had to be dramatic effect.

"And?" I asked on cue.

"According to Lipscomb, our beautiful lady without mercy was one particularly gorgeous and temperamental creature, known for falling in love with mortal men, who went by the name of Eladora."

Eladora. One of the Fair Folk. We were talking mythology, but who else could she be? It explained everything: her beauty, her enchanting nature, the aura of magic that surrounded her. In fact, the more I thought about the recent events in my life the more it sounded like I had indeed stepped into a fairytale.

I nodded thoughtfully but said nothing. What could I say? Looking down at Erin who waited expectantly I realized the awkward situation I placed myself in.

"So... these Fair Folk," I said, trying to think of something that made my interest in the name seem rational. "Who exactly are they? Where do they come from?"

"Not sure," Erin shrugged. "They're Fae. They're just there, I guess."

"Would you mind doing a little more hunting? See what you can find out about them?"

"Sure thing boss," Erin answered, slapping the book closed and sliding it back into its place. "Anything beats sitting in that office all day waiting for the phone to ring. Anything else?"

"Yeah. Try to find out more of their names. Maybe get a hold of this Telerus guy."

"No promise there. I'll try though."

I turned to go, my mind buzzing with latent thoughts. Something else struck me. I quickly scribbled some names down on a scrap of paper and the little bit I knew of them.

"These men," I said, handing the paper to Erin. "See if you can find out who they are and what, if anything, connects them. Especially look to see if they have any connection to our company."

"These are only first names," she said holding up the slip of paper.

"I know. But they are all associated with a particular industry. It's right beside their name. They'll be very high up. CEOs or something like that."

"Hey boss," she said to my retreating figure.

I stopped, waiting for her to speak.

"What's this all about?" She asked.

A host of possible answers flashed in my mind. None of them sounded particularly sane.

"Nothing, I'm sure," I muttered instead. "But if you can, keep it between the two of us."

Leaving the library I was so lost in thought I noticed nothing around me. My thoughts were all insubstantial. They swirled and swirled upon the window of possibility with nowhere to land. Where they would finally end up I couldn't guess. What I did know was that when the thoughts finally did settle, nothing would ever be the same.

A chill settled on me without warning, a feeling that grew all-too-familiar. I looked up, knowing what I would see.

The pale man stood with his arms stretched out to me, his mouth silently calling my name. Those ghastly, spectral eyes, pale blue and terrible, bore into me and froze the depths of my soul. A cold sweat trickled out from my pores. The whole world seemed to slow down. Somewhere I heard a drone, like the distant buzzing of an insect swarm.

I fled.

I ran to the old section of the University, shaded by rows of oak trees. A student stepped out of one of the brick buildings and I grabbed the door before it could close and ran inside. Wooden boards creaked beneath my running feet. Peeling white radiators lined the wall under the windows. One look out showed no signs of the pale man's pursuit.

I still ran. There was no distance too great to put between the two of us. I barreled through a door I hoped led to a stairwell.

It opened to darkness.

That odd sense of disorientation washed over me, the feeling of motion without moving. I spun head over heels, twirled around. All sense of reference disappeared, no up or down existed. Darkness hurled in a thousand different directions.

Light slowly returned. Gray light.

Except it was not gray. It was shadow.

The smell of fresh earth and engine oil permeated, with the aroma of gasoline. The grit of black dirt crusted beneath my hands.

As my eyes adjusted to the dim light, I found myself in what appeared to be a vast and deep hole. The mouth of the pit gaped above me no more than thirty feet, opening into a gray and featureless sky.

An orange light glowed and flickered from somewhere beneath me. Echoes of unknown voices rose and fell, resonating out of the formless depths.

When a sense of orientation began to seep back into me, I picked myself up. My unsteady feet stood upon a terraced path, a shelf that wound down the edge of a pit. Even though it's width seemed more than adequate, I felt the need to brace myself against the earthen walls.

When I finally peered over the edge I discovered the source of the orange light and the voices. Just below me, a shelf of rock jutted out, stretching out over the black pit. It reminded me of a diving board, but instead of hovering over water, this long outcropping of rock hovered over the rim of impenetrable blackness. All over the rock shelf a multitude of red candles flickered. Wax dripped down and pooled like seeping blood. The eerie light cast in the primal darkness made shadows writhe like tortured ghosts.

Standing amidst this strange light stood thirteen figures draped in black cloaks, hoods pulled down to cast their faces in shadow. At each of their feet lay a bundle covered in black, silk cloth. By the dim outline the bundle looked vaguely human, though small. I shuddered to think what may be wrapped in them. Revulsion quickly replaced fear.

A chant, which could only have come from those hooded figures, thrummed through the cavern. It rose in volume, dropped low in pitch until I could feel it vibrate in my own chest. The words spilled out undecipherable. The rhythm of an old and lost language fell like song. And though I couldn't translate a single word I knew it for a deep and rich language. It was a language so close to the original nature of things that its expression was near-perfect.

The robed figures stretched out their hands in unison. Images flared in my mind as the chant rose.

A dead tree in winter.

A pool of rancid water.

Ravens gathering on an ash tree.

Blood spilling from a cracked egg.

Rain on ash.

Ravens.

Black clouds covering the city like fog.

A dark tower rising to the moon.

Ravens.

Parchment burning in fire.

Ravens.

The white, glassy eye of a bloated corpse.

Ravens.

Ravens.

Ravens.

A scream struggled to escape my lips as terror rode on the

descending nightmare.

Insanity.

Confusion.

Despair.

Despair so deep my guts turned to ice.

I fell over and clutched the edge of the path. My other hand clapped over my mouth to keep me from yelling out. Sweat drenched me, dripped from my nose, stung my eyes.

Swirling.

Chaos.

Confusion.

Despair.

Ravens.

The chant rose louder. The cavern echoed and shook. It pulled and stretched, and I felt pulled and stretched. And just when I was certain I would be rent from limb to limb the chanting stopped.

A silence settled dead and calm. A wind from a deep and cold place blew up from the bowels of the pit. Decay and rot rode in its wake. The robed figures waited, gripped in silence, their hands outstretched to the chasm.

From down in the shadows, a figure rose up. A bare image outlined in the darkness at first, materializing as it came closer. Higher up it rose, swirling on an unseen wind.

I watched breathless as this thing emerged from the pit, rising and rising until it floated in front of the robed ones. This figure was noticeably larger, and instead of black, his robes were a dark crimson. Tatters flowed from the edges of the cloth, long tendrils that moved like living creatures, tasting and touching the air.

"Lord of the Deep!" The black robed figures cried out in unison.

"Behold, the Lord of the Deep! Behold, the Lord of the Dragon! We hail thee King of all that lies beyond the gates of creation! May we be found worthy in your sight!"

When the thing inside the crimson robes spoke it trembled the very fabric of the world. It reeked of something awful that I can only describe as wrongness. Its voice was the sound of distorted nature, corruption, perversion.

"What have you brought that you might be found worthy?" the thing croaked.

"We bring these gifts," the voices answered in unison. "The most treasured fruits of all the world's harvest. What is loved most dearly."

The first cloaked man picked up the bundle at his feet. Against the draped cloth the outline showed unmistakably. It was an image that will forever bring me horror and despair. I can only pray that God will wipe it from me when at last I have finished with this life. Otherwise, eternity will be hell.

The shape of a small nose rose up from the black satin, tender lips, even the curl of hair. It must have been a thin sheet like liquid draped over the small form. I could even make out the fingernails on the little hand.

Robed arms held out the bundle and dropped it over the edge. Then another figure did the same, then another. Tears pooled in my eyes and a raging sadness wracked my heart as I watched all thirteen figures drop their bundles into the darkness below the floating crimson abomination.

"I am pleased," the awful thing hummed in its broken voice when all the bundles had been dropped.

"You have found favor in my sight. Ask, and I will give it to you."

"We ask your power be in the bones of what we raise," a voice from the black robes cried out. "Let this tower rise tall and its foundations run deep. May it rise to the glory of heaven, and plunge deep to touch the walls of Tartarus. Fill it with your power and may it tremble in your might."

A silence waited on the dark borders of the pit. I waited along with the robed figures to hear what the answer may be.

"Will you welcome my servant?" the crimson figure asked.

The robed figures hesitated. They looked to one another. One of the hoods nodded in agreement, then the others followed suit.

"We welcome your servant," they chanted in unison.

"Receive then my power!" the crimson figure cried out in grotesque fury. "Receive my servant!"

He stretched his arms out to the sky. The flutter of a thousand wings rumbled in the pit.

A hoard of black ravens rose up in a tornado of feathers. I fell back from the edge and covered my head. The beating continued endlessly. From somewhere far off I heard the cry of agony and triumph.

I stumbled to my feet and ran up the terraced edge, out of the pit. Ravens poured out like belching clouds of black smoke. I ran, not caring where my feet took me. Vaguely, I noticed that I ran through the city, though my mind hardly registered the fact. The familiar streets felt ominous.

A shower of feathers fell down on me. They choked and blinded and stuck to me. I fell to the ground, enveloped in darkness. From out of the pit I heard one last rumbling cry.

"The Raven King comes!"

I started awake in the stairwell. Still expecting to be blanketed I frantically brushed off nonexistent raven feathers. Panic still shook me and it took several deep breaths to still my pounding heart.

When I felt together enough to move I made my way back home. The events in the pit replayed over and again in my mind. They made no sense except for terror. That was the only thing I could be certain of. Whatever had happened with the awful robed figures, their intent could only be terrible and frightening.

I realized two things later that night. The first is that I must keep a record of all that had begun to happen to me, the record that I am writing now. The better part of the last three days were spent making sure I had it all down as best as I can remember. Whatever happens next, I hope to have time to write about it.

Time.

That was my second realization; how little time I have left.

As soon as I fled the pit I became certain, as certain as I am that the sun will rise tomorrow, that as these events play out to their inevitable conclusion, I will not live to see the end of them.

Part II

The Fourth Vision

It is strange, I know with certainty that I am to die soon. How soon I couldn't possibly say. It doesn't seem to matter.

At the same time I know that if I were to let matters alone I would be okay. I would live a reasonably happy and prosperous life. Except I know something awful is brewing, something that is worse than the destruction of humanity. It is like watching an approaching storm. The thunder and lightning have not yet begun but I know they're coming. The clouds gather inevitably.

Worst of all, there is no one I can tell about this. What could I possibly say? Would I tell them that there is some sort of evil scheme going on? I don't know what it is but I know it's terrible. It involves more than human creatures that have some association with ancient fairies.

It makes me question my own sanity. Why wouldn't others? Just to read it over again sounds like madness. Except I've seen things with my own eyes. And the more I see, the more I observe the mass of humanity, the more convinced I become that I am acquiring sanity instead of madness. I'm becoming more, not less, sane.

Of course, that's what all mad men say. Such is the uncertainty of life.

I dream of raven feathers. Almost every night.

They swirl and flutter all around me. I try to bat them away but there are too many. They stick to me and crawl over me like each one is a living creature.

Somewhere below me I hear the voice of the crimson figure. He rumbles and croaks out awful noise.

"We come for you, Watcher," I hear him groan. "We come for you."

Erin called and said she had more information for me. This time she wanted to meet at a downtown café. She said she needed the sun.

I silently agreed when I sat across from her. She looked a bit pale. Dark rings were beginning to form under her eyes. Her glance darted from side to side. More than once she looked behind her and around the café, like she was expecting someone else to be there. A nervous leg of hers shook, vibrating the cups of coffee on the table so little ripples spread out over the black liquid.

"Is everything okay?" I asked with genuine concern. "You seem nervous."

"I'm fine," she dismissed my concern. "Just too much coffee and not enough sleep. I get this way when I'm knee-deep in research."

I didn't buy it but I let the matter pass.

"So, any great new finds?"

"Yes and no," she answered. "I've got a big nada on the Telerus Manuscript. There's a possibility Oxford might have a translation buried somewhere in their catacombs. I sweet-talked a guy who fancied my accent. Said he would dig through it a bit and see if he found something, maybe send it over on interlibrary loan."

"Not bad."

"It's a good lead," she shrugged.

Erin opened her mouth to speak again. She stopped, her brow furrowed and she turned around, looking for the faces in the café.

"Did you hear that?" she asked, still scanning the other patrons.

"Hear what?" I asked in return. "There's a lot of people talking."

"Did you hear a whisper? It sounded like somebody whispering."

I sat silent and strained my hearing. Nothing except the incessant buzz of a busy café, the mingle of voices and the hiss of the espresso machine. I shook my head.

"Oh it's nothing. Too much time in the stacks," she said,

pinching the bridge of her nose.

"Anyway, I did find something interesting about those names you gave me," she continued. "Even though they were just first names, each one matched a leader in the industry you said they were involved in. And when I say leader I mean top dog, as in the most influential person in that area of business. Your list was a who's who in the civilized world. If you would get these guys together I would say you would control most of the world's resources."

"What about association?" I asked, relieved to hear the names meant something. Maybe I'm not crazy after all. "Are they all part of a group together or something?"

"Not that I could see," Erin told me with a shrug. "I didn't see any of them associated with the same company at all. Now I had to dig pretty deep but I did find that all of these men owned shares in a particular investment group."

She took a careful sip of her coffee and pulled away when the liquid burned her lips. She blew on it and gently stared into the cup. I waited for her to continue. Her eyes remained fixed on the steaming liquid. A lost, languid look rose in her eyes. They stared for a moment, vacant and empty, the muscles of her face slack.

"Erin," I said gently.

"Orpheus," she said, the light coming back into her eyes.

"Orpheus?" I echoed.

"Yes, that's the name of the investment group. It's called Orpheus."

"And all these men are members? Is that significant?"

"Hard to tell," she said, tentatively testing her coffee again. "There's a lot of others that are also members, but these guys are obviously the biggest players. I wouldn't have thought it was significant except for the fact that Orpheus seems to have strange stuff going on with it."

"Strange how?"

"A lot of their investments are in companies that don't

seem to do anything."

"What do you mean? What kind of company doesn't do anything?"

"Your guess is as good as mine," she said. "But there are a lot of them. They have a name, a tax ID number, and most of them even have websites. But you go to them and they have nothing more than a homepage. Nothing to show that they actually do any work. Some of the websites are strange too. But that is quickly becoming the norm."

I nodded thoughtfully with no clear way to answer. Erin went back staring into her coffee.

"One of them is here in town," she mumbled into her cup. "The Rip Starr Agency. No idea what they do."

"Never heard of them."

"Their website won't help you. There's no information on it at all. It's just covered in raven feathers. Like from a Poe story or something."

At the mention of ravens my blood ran cold. It couldn't be coincidence. I swallowed hard and tried to hide my dismay.

"Why don't you get some rest," I told Erin, not having to feign my concern. "You look really tired. Take a few days off."

She nodded distantly, still fixed on her cup. Then her head jerked up and she looked around the café.

"Are you certain you don't hear whispering?"

I worry about Erin now. Perhaps it is just the lack of sleep. Maybe I should get her to stop the research altogether. Though she seems to me to be the type that will push on until she finds what she is looking for. Still, I would not forgive myself if something happened to her because of whatever it is I have involved myself in.

My daughter called today and invited me to a fundraiser this weekend. It's for the Debate Club at her school. They are raising money to go on a competition out of town.

Not sure if this was my daughter's or my wife's idea. I like to think it wasn't because of the new money I've come into. It may well be. I'll go regardless, glad to be a part of her life in any way I can. The evening will be insufferable for sure. There will be loads of preening and pretension on display. I can hardly stomach that now. But I will go.

Maybe I will ask Erin if she will go with me. Some time out will certainly do her good. I guess I should be clear that the matter is purely social and not romantic. Although I would not be adverse to her romantic attention. It would be nice to have some companionship that goes deeper than one night of relieved loneliness.

We shall see.

It appears more and more evident to me that civilization is founded on fear. Almost everything we have built is built because we are afraid.

Was it fear that led men to settle down and farm? Fear that the game would no longer be plentiful? Did we start storing and hoarding grains for this reason?

We most likely huddled into the first cities and built the first walls out of fear of those who had not given up their wandering ways.

Empire goes to war against their neighbor for fear that that neighbor will one day grow too strong. Gold is stored for fear of the uncertain tomorrow. Law strictly enforced for fear of an uncontrolled society.

What politician doesn't use fear to mold the masses to his will? Vote for me or the sky will fall.

Locked doors. Alarms. Police. All products of fear.

Insurance. Only bought out of fear.

Is there a law passed that isn't done so out of fear? Is there a government agency not fashioned from some sort of national fear?

It makes me wonder then, what would civilization have

looked like if we weren't afraid. Every man is afraid from time to time. Fear is natural to any living organism and can even be beneficial. But we are always afraid. And we allow fear to make our decisions for us. I'm not sure I can even imagine what our world would look like if we allowed something other than fear to make our decisions. I can't imagine how that would have affected the course of human history.

It's not too late. We could stop right now if we wanted. Stop acting out of fear and act out of...what?

What should motivate us? What should truly motivate us?

Love is the answer that first comes to mind. Love and not fear. Except so much of what we call love is actually fear disguised. Fear makes the lover jealous though he says it is love. Fear makes the mother overbearing, though she too says it is love.

I wonder if we even know the difference?

The fundraiser went much better than expected. Erin agreed readily to go with me, and when I picked her up she looked quite radiant. No trace of her exhaustion from the other day remained.

More importantly, my daughter seemed genuinely glad to see me. She hugged me tight and let her arms linger around my neck. I imagine this is what a father–daughter relationship should be like. To think of the years I have wasted makes my heart break.

I received no such pleasant reaction from my wife. She greeted me coolly and her new husband gave me a curt nod. Most of her attention was on Erin, whom she looked up and down disapprovingly. It took no intuition to tell my wife thought her too young.

There was plenty of pretension to go around. I suffered through dozens of dull conversations about the state of the market, how much could be made in this or that industry, and plenty of feigned interest over what I did.

Erin and I would exchange knowing glances during the most intolerable of these conversations. The brightness of her eyes and her quaint smile put everything else in the background. Warmth from the champagne combined with these to make me feel closer to her than I have felt with any other human being.

There was another one there as well.

About my fourth trip for refills of champagne I locked eyes with the bartender. Something vaguely recognizable flashed in his eyes, something that set him apart from the others.

"Reload there mate?" he asked with an Irish accent.

I nodded pushed out mine and Erin's empty glasses. He took the glasses and looked me up and down. Coming to some decision within himself he put those away and reached under the bar to produce two highball glasses. A crisp, amber liquid splashed from a decanter, filling the glasses a fourth full. He lifted one and inhaled deeply.

"Now that there's a drink," he said, handing me the glass.

I raised up a toast in thanks and sipped at the drink. At once I could tell it was an extraordinary draught. Not only did the liquor heat me up going down, I felt the sensation through my bones. A taste of something deep and peaty passed over my tongue. An image of night during full moon flashed in my head, a mist gathering around green hills and old standing stones arranged in a broken circle, glowing in starlight.

" That's a little more than whiskey," I remarked in a voice just over a whisper.

"That it is my friend," the bartender replied. "You won't find it in any liquor store."

"What is it?" I asked. The liquor made me feel better than any other drink I had ever tried. There was, I daresay, something magical about it.

"A little something I save for those who can appreciate it," the barkeep answered.

I nodded, wanting to know more, but didn't ask.

"Name's Gareth," the bartender said, stretching out a hand.

I took it in my own, admiring the warm strength of his grip. He smiled at me, the look touching his green eyes.

"Thank you," I said with all sincerity. "I will enjoy this."

"I know you will," he answered. And then, cryptically he said, "It's good to see men like you come around."

I have grown sensitive to such statements. So I pressed him.

"What do you mean by men like me?" I asked.

He smiled knowingly and let the question hang out there before answering.

"A man of taste," he answered.

"How did you know I'm a man of taste?"

"You've got a good eye for women," Gareth said, gesturing to Erin with his head.

I turned to see her standing alone in the mill of people. Gareth was right. I lifted my glass in thanks and took the other.

Erin enjoyed the whiskey more than I. After one sip her eyes took on a glassy, distant look. Her lips moved like she was mumbling to herself. Her cheeks reddened and color suffused into her face.

"This is...wonderful," she said after savoring. "Where did you get it?"

"Just Gareth there," I said pointing back to the bar.

Gareth was no longer there. I can only assume he had moved on to other business. But I can't trust my assumptions anymore.

"I hear people whispering," Erin said to me last night as I took her home from the party.

She was pretty well drunk. Though I doubt she was making it up. I got the feeling she would not have told me this sober.

"What kind of whispering?" I asked.

"I don't know," she said, closing her eyes. "Not always, just sometimes. It's like someone whispering right next to me. But I can never see who it is."

An irresistible urge overcame me to return to church. It must be the fear. Nightmares haunt my sleep, visions of ravens and the crimson–cloaked figure hovering over the dark pit. During the day I feel skittish, like something awful is about to happen. I'm almost surprised when it doesn't.

Going back to my old church is out of the question. It is not so much my wife and the rest my old life keeping me away, more the impotent and empty feeling I get there. The few times I have been since my new awareness, I was dumbly struck by the weakness of the service. It's hard to explain, to really put into words.

The service feels bland, insipid. We stand and mumble out old hymns to the ostentatious hum of the organ. We repeat creeds and prayers, without any conviction. Why should we? They are written for us. And the sermons, how dull. They are nothing more than the trite moral recriminations delivered only in sanctimonious conviction. But at the same time they completely lack authority.

I guess that is what I want more than anything. Not want, need. I need to walk into a church with authority. Now, more than ever I need it. I need the solace found in knowing that despite the dark madness of the world there is a place, a power that is kind, meaningful and transcending all the petty forces of this place.

Everything I've known or thought I've known stands wrecked and destroyed. The world is a ruin around me. At least in my former oblivion I had confidence in life. Even if it was a confidence based on a lie. Now I am but a leaf tossed on the ocean waves. And as far as I know, this ocean hates me and longs to destroy me.

I need a rock, some sort of dry land beneath my feet.

If the world I thought I knew is deeper and more

wondrous, and also more fearful, than I ever imagined, there must also be out there someone, some man, that walks in the power of good.

Or at least this is the hope that I must cling to.

A raven perched on one of the oaks outside my house today. It hopped down the branch close to the window of the upstairs room I use for a study, and peered inside. Intelligent eyes stared at me, with a touch of amusement.

Surely more than my imagination was at work here. Even now, he stares at me. I know he won't leave. Maybe he wants to drive me mad. Maybe I'll let him.

I found the pistol I keep in the bedroom closet and thought about shooting him. Not yet. I'll wait and see what the bird does. I think about getting a concealed permit. Just because I'm going to die soon doesn't mean I should go down without a fight.

The pale man appeared again. So too, then, did a vision follow. I wonder if he means me no harm but is rather just a herald of some sort. As much as I would like to believe that, I cannot separate the crippling, cold fear that accompanies his presence from the man himself, if he even is a man. He is infinitely worse than the crimson figure and whatever evil he portends. The pale man is impossibly more terrifying. His wide eyes send tremors through my bones. That white, outstretched hand of his stabs me like a bolt of pure fear. My senses leave me completely and I'm consumed with an irresistible urge to flee.

I sat outside the café when I saw him. A sense of being watched came over me and I looked up and saw him across the street. As usual he was garbed in the gray of dark and fiery ash. I even thought I could see wisps of smoky soot blow off his shoulders. His blood red lips mouthed my name and he reached his hand out toward me.

In the midst of my fear I felt resignation. It was the resignation of a lamb being led to slaughter, who knows how futile it is to resist the unmerciful hand that drags him to the killing floor. I knew the pattern and accepted what would happen next.

Still, I wanted to distance myself from that awful, pale figure. I stood and hurried down the street, not running, just stepping quickly.

Where would it be, I wondered. What door would carry me to the awaited vision? Could I choose or was it some specific door?

Something drew my eyes to an alleyway I passed. It looked like any urban alley, filled with trash cans, empty cardboard boxes, perpetual shadow and a feeling of dread. It was normal in every way except for the door that stood in the middle.

A plain wooden door, nothing more. It didn't even have a casing around it. With nothing to support or anchor the door it still stood upright. A tentative push with my hand and it didn't budge.

What point was there in delaying the inevitable? I had survived the other visions, so there was no reason not to think I wouldn't survive this one either. With a deep breath to steady my nerves I took hold of the metal knob, pushed the door open and stepped through.

That now familiar sense of disorientation, followed by the darkness, overtook me. This time, I rode it patiently. When the light faded back into my vision, I looked around to see the book lined walls of a richly adorned study.

Voices slowly filtered in through the thick swell of quiet. Many voices all at once clamored. One raised up in anger, another in laughter.

The scene fully materialized and I could make out seven men gathered in the study. It looked much like the one I had seen in my first vision, but there was much different about it and my memory of that harried experience is broken at best.

Something struck me as unusual about the men and it took me a moment to register what it was I noticed. It was their fashion. Judging from their hair and clothes they looked like men from somewhere in the middle of the previous century. 1950s or 60s as best as I could tell. One older man smoked a pipe, dressed in plain slacks and shirt. Three of the other men smoked cigarettes, one with the slick hair and crisp suit of an old Vegas style gangster. Two of the men wore thick framed glasses. One wore white and donned a white smock, holding in his hand the white hat soda fountain operators used to wear. One man had his back to me, looking up at the shelf of books in front of him.

"Why are we wasting words?" The older man with the pipe said. He spoke with a cultured British accent. "The situation grows every day more out of our control."

"Is it supposed to be in our control?" The well-dressed man smirked. "Isn't that the point?"

The old man sighed with impatient indulgence.

"You know what I mean, Sid," he said.

Sid smoked his cigarette with arrogant amusement. Immediately, I disliked the man.

"Oh I know what you mean," Sid answered in a cloud of smoke. "It's just that if we lose focus there's nothing to separate us from the enemy, is there?"

"Well spoken Sid," the older man said. "I'm certain you will never let that happen. But that doesn't change the fact that things are steadily worsening."

"What are we going to do about it?" One of the men chimed in. "We're not nearly strong enough to challenge them."

"This isn't the kind of fight we're used to," another argued. "It's not like it used to be. They cover their deceit in legitimate business interest."

"At the same time they bribe politicians and flout every single law known to man."

"And yet they go unprosecuted," Sid calmly pointed out. "In fact, they go unnoticed."

"How did this happen?" The man in the smock asked. "Have we become blind? Sir Bradley? Has this always been so?"

The old man with the pipe sighed again and all of a sudden it seemed a great weight had settled upon his shoulders. The skin of his face sagged and his whole countenance seemed to dim.

"This is not the fault of any one generation," he said. I presumed him to be Sir Bradley. "The enemy has been encroaching quietly for a long time now. For how long, who can tell?

"We grew complacent, you see. It seemed we were successful. We've heard nothing but mild disturbances from them here and there, inconveniences easily put down. Why, I remember talk in my youth that we didn't really need the Keepers anymore. We got comfortable. We got weak."

"Not so weak that we couldn't defeat them in Germany," one of the men spoke up.

"Yes, we broke their power in Germany," Bradley shrugged. "Only to find that they were even stronger in Russia. And we start to really confront them in Russia when we discover that, all too late, that these were mere fronts in a worldwide assault. Here in America the enemy was strongest of all. The most hidden and the strongest right here."

"How long do you suspect they've been dominant here?" Someone asked.

"Hard to tell," Bradley shrugged his shoulders. "They've been major players since the Civil War. Perhaps longer."

A somber quiet seemed to settle over the gathering. For a long moment no one spoke. A sense of doom settled cold and palpable.

"There is always something to be done," Bradley answered, forcing a smile to his face. "We are the Keepers of the Flame.

We always find a way. Remember what it says in the book. The light shines out in the darkness, the darkness does not overcome it."

"So what do we do?" Someone asked.

"We bear the flame," Bradley answered. Some of the life had been restored to him. His shoulders pulled back straight and his head held itself a little bit higher.

"We don't control men, as Sid was so kind to remind us. The situation has become what it is because we believed most of these developments, despite how we felt about them, were natural developments. The enemy has been so slow and subtle in this to remain hidden. This is such a departure from his normal strategies. Unprecedented really.

"Still, had we been vigilant it never would've gotten this far. Remember that. As we grew complacent the enemy was massing his troops in secret."

He sighed for the third time and took a deep puff of his pipe. The others waited for him to continue.

"There is nothing to be done about it now. We waste time regretting what could've been. Our job is to show the light. Men will decide what to do then. And if they choose otherwise, then we keep the flame alive and hope in God and tomorrow."

Before anyone could reply a butler came in and stood at the edge of the gathering. He waited with the air of an old world servant. Sober features, white hair, and a gracefully aged face fit well with this crisp butler's suit. He didn't say a word, but waited to be noticed.

"What is it Gerard?" Bradley asked.

"A visitor at the Garden Gate," the butler answered in a deep voice.

"The Garden Gate?" Bradley said with pleasant surprise. "This is unexpected, but perhaps providential. Send him in."

"Her," Gerard clarified. "The visitor is a woman."

This information gave Bradley a moments pause. A

questioning look passed between the gathered men.

"Well, that's unusual indeed," Bradley remarked. "Send her in all the same. It is the Garden Gate after all."

The butler shifted uncomfortably. A hand came up to his mouth and he coughed, apparently to indicate some further complication.

"What is it Gerard?"

"The lady is Elioud," the butler said softly.

A confused pause ensued then the room erupted in a clamor of noise. Voices yelled over each other all at once. Confusion and no small bit of fear had taken over the room.

"Calm down! Calm down!" The man who had to that point been staring at the books, turned and said, holding up his hands for quiet. "This is not any danger. This is how we will win the war."

Silence dropped heavy and immediate. All eyes turned to the speaker. I looked up at him too, noting his somewhat odd features. Thick, black hair waved and curled wildly on his head without any order. His cheeks stood high and fat, pinching eyes that already seemed dark and beady. This contrasted poorly with the man's red, wide mouth. The already strange head perched at an angle upon a round torso from which protruded thin, gangly limbs.

"What do you mean?" Bradley asked an edge of suspicion to his voice.

"Exactly what I said," the odd man stated confidently. "All this talk of keeping the flame, showing men the light, works fine in times of peace. But this is war. And we're losing, badly. To sit around and discuss strategy while the enemy circles outside is pure folly. Talk if you want. I, on the other hand, have taken steps to strike a blow at the enemy. At the very heart of the enemy."

"Rip, what have you done?" Sid asked, pale and ghostly. All traces of his former arrogance vanished.

"What's the matter Sid? Don't like being upstaged by

homely, old Rip? At least I'm fighting while you sit around and smoke like a lazy aristocrat."

"What does this have to do with inviting one of the Elioud to this place?" Bradley hotly demanded. "And to the Garden Gate of all places."

"Because she is our friend, not an enemy," Rip said.

"How can you know?"

"I have made her my friend," Rip insisted. "And she has promised me access to the major players among the enemy. Such an opportunity we would be foolish to turn down."

The room erupted again in protest. Only Sid remained silent. He studied the oddly proportioned Rip with a deep glance.

"Rip, you have exposed us all to danger," Bradley said as soon as he calmed the others down. "How could you be so reckless?"

"Why are you so ready to dismiss this idea?" Rip complained. "This is the opening we need."

"And how do you know she isn't playing you?" Bradley asked. "You know how deceptive they are. Subterfuge is their nature."

"No. She's being honest."

"How do you know?"

"I just do," Rip snapped.

"You've slept with her," Sid spoke up, pointing his cigarette at the bristling man. "Haven't you? She seduced you and now you believe whatever garbage that succubus feeds you."

Splotches of red that ran up Rip's neck to his face belied his guilt. A groan went up from the group. One man dropped his head into his hands and shook it despairingly.

"If you must know, I seduced her," Rip said. "She confesses her love for me quite genuinely."

Sid let out a bitter, mocking laugh. His smile was smug again, full of arrogant certainty. The red across Rip's face darkened in anger.

"Oh, you fool," Sid laughed. "You believe you seduced an Elioud. You're dumber than I thought possible."

"Why not?!" Rip spun on Sid and growled. "Do I have nothing to offer a woman? Because I'm not like you? You pompous ass."

"No, you have much to offer a woman. But I would sooner believe that the sky is green and the grass is blue than believe anything an Elioud says to me. Especially one confessing love."

"You just don't know her," Rip said. "Just talk to her, meet her, and you'll see."

"Completely out of the question," Bradley interjected. "Under no circumstances can she come in this room. In fact, you've compromised us all by bringing her here. Something must be done about her immediately."

"Will you not at least hear her out?" Rip pled. "I know she will convince you."

"Absolutely not!" Bradley asserted with visible restraint on his rage. "Do not entertain that notion a moment longer!"

"We have to kill her," Sid said. The group mumbled agreement.

"No!" Rip yelled. "I won't allow it!"

"What choice do we have?" Bradley asked. "You've put us all in danger. You've put everything in danger."

"How can you say that?" The odd man cried, his voice cracking in desperation. "She would never let harm come to me, to us."

None of the men would meet Rip's gaze. He turned to each of them, pleading.

"Sonny? Marion? Nicolai? Do none of you stand with me? No one believes me?"

"It's not you we don't believe," Sid gently told him. "It's her."

"But you don't know her."

"We don't have to."

Fists clenched at Rip's side and his head dropped despondently. "You'll have to kill me too."

"Don't do this," one of the men implored.

"I swear it, you'll have to kill me first." The conviction in his voice was unmistakable.

A sense of gathered pity filled the room. All the men, I could tell, felt an awkward embarrassment for the odd man. Only Rip stood beyond shame. He defiantly faced the men down.

"Get rid of her," Bradley finally said.

"You can't be serious!" Sid leapt up to protest.

"Tell her if she touches these grounds again it will be her certain death."

"We can't let her out of here!" Sid argued. Other voices joined in agreement.

"We do have some of the Elioud as allies," Bradley pointed out.

"Exactly!" Rip pounced. "So why can't she be one? And she is highly placed."

"But none walk on these grounds," Bradley continued in reprimand. "Even our most trusted allies among the Elioud don't come near this place, much less the house itself. Rip, she may become a valuable ally, as great as you claim her to be. But this is not how we go about securing their help. You have gone too far. Get rid of her now."

Rip seemed to realize his situation. He nodded grimly and turned to leave. As soon as he was out of the room, Sid leaned in toward Bradley.

"You can't be serious," he said. "She cannot be allowed to leave this place."

"Gerard, collect a piece of the Elioud's hair," Bradley said to the butler. "We will set a ward."

"Bradley, don't let this happen," Sid pled.

"I will make it a blood ward," the older man said.

Sid raised his hands in concession, obviously swayed by

whatever it was that Bradley offered. The butler nodded and turned to follow Rip.

On impulse I decided to follow also. I tailed the butler through hallways, a large dining room and into a garden workshop, littered with tools and pots.

Rip also stood there talking to a woman. I looked up at her face and stopped. Her eyes seemed to meet mine, then they quickly fell on Gerard. My heart fluttered in surprise.

It was Sierra.

Although her dress was different - blue, pastel pedal pushers, two–tone shoes, bright red lipstick and hair pulled back by a silk scarf - there was no doubting who it was. The golden, blonde hair, distinctly beautiful features, and the aura of sexuality could overpower any change in fashion. No doubt it was the same woman who had been my brief assistant and had made obvious attempts to seduce me.

Still, it couldn't be possible. I don't know why I say that. It shouldn't be possible that I have these visions, whether the visions be of the past or present. Still, it pushes my credulity that Sierra could have remained unchanged for over fifty years.

But there she was. Rip held her hands in his own, sincere and apologetic. She locked her eyes on his, smiling deep and beautiful.

"It will take time, love," Rip told her. "They're just frightened, that's all. But when they know you like I do, trust me, they're good men. You'll see. They are."

Sierra reached out and touched his face. "I do trust you," she said. "And I'll wait as long as you need me to."

She flashed a flirtatious look and added, "As long as you don't keep me waiting tonight. That, I can't wait for."

"How could I deny such a splendid woman?" Rip gushed then kissed her fiercely.

Gerard coughed inconspicuously and edged up close to the couple. They continued without noticing. Sierra's red nails ran through Rip's already disheveled hair. With a satisfied smack she pulled her face away from his.

"Ah, I can't stand it," she moaned. "Don't keep me waiting too long. I might go mad my sweet Adonis."

"I swear I won't, my beautiful Venus," Rip answered.

"This way, my lady," Gerard gently intoned holding his hand out towards the door.

Pointedly ignoring the butler Sierra turned on her heels. Almost too quick to notice the butler's hand shot out. Even expecting it I almost didn't see. His outstretched hand flicked at the back of her head and a small lock of blonde hair fell away. His right hand caught the hair and disappeared into his pocket. It took less than a second and I couldn't tell you what he cut her hair with. The forlorn Rip noticed nothing.

As soon as Sierra stepped out the door I felt the world around me begin to fade. The walls of the house grew translucent and the stability of the floor beneath my feet began to sag. Just before the darkness closed fully over me, I noticed something out beyond the walls of the fading house. Somewhere in the near distance stood a stone obelisk, looking every bit like the one that stands prominently in the old section of my own city.

I can't help but feel excitement about seeing the obelisk. With that I should be able to find the house where my vision took place, if it still stands. Hopefully, the men inside still operate, or at least others like them. For the first time since all this began I don't feel so alone. There are others like me.

Erin came over for dinner and I tried my best not to talk about her research. It seems she has reached a dead end. We still wait for the Telerus manuscript, and as to the origin of the fairies, or the Dannae or Fae, as they are called, there are no end of theories.

Some say the Fae are fallen Angels. Some say they are

spirits, earth spirits or forest spirits. Other theories propound that they are souls of the dead, especially children.

The Irish tradition proposes one of the most compelling theories on the Dannae. They possess, by far, the richest tradition concerning the "good folk." According to many of their legends the Fae are either the old gods who have lost their power, or children of the old gods. Most of them cannot be easily categorized as good or evil. Like people, some of the Fae are good, some evil. Most are powerful, spurious and unpredictable. There are as many dark tales as well as humorous ones filling the lore of the Fair Folk.

I found it difficult to get Erin off the subject. I found it difficult to get myself off the subject. As much as I want to protect Erin from whatever powers I have provoked, I desperately want to tell her everything.

I can't help but notice the toll this has taken on her. She looks more tired and exhausted every time I see her. Sometimes she stares off into space, her mouth moving silently. Other times she cocks her head as if straining to listen to something only she can hear.

When I ask her about it she only smiles and changes the subject. Happy to see her at least momentarily distracted I never press her on her unusual behavior.

She especially didn't like the ravens outside my house. They have multiplied to four now. Erin shuddered when she saw them staring through the windows. I noticed she never faced the window after that.

I believe she has genuine affection for me, as I do for her. I wish I could bring happiness into her life, but I'm afraid I will bring nothing but misery.

If my estimation is correct, the house of those gathered men is about 200 yards from the obelisk. I'm not sure what I should call them. At one point the man called Bradley referred to them as the Keepers of the Flame. That is who they must be then. The Keepers.

The obelisk I saw from the fading house looks every bit like the Founders Memorial, a like feature in our city center to commemorate the anniversary of our founding. It was erected during the 1920s, a time when all things Egyptian enjoyed popular support.

According to the map there runs only a small stretch of houses within the supposed distance. The older neighborhood south of the obelisk looks most promising. The only other section of houses lies east. All else appears to be taken up by businesses and factories.

I shall go tomorrow to try and find the Seekers house. Of course, this is all assuming there are not many houses to choose from. How I will be able to tell which is the home of the Seekers, I have no idea. I guess I'm trusting that something will clue me in, indicate somehow which is the house I want. If not, I will try something else. I only know that I must find this house.

Plans to find the house were temporarily stalled. It's been three days. Impossibly, it's been three days. The odd passage of time astounds me. Or maybe I slept for most of that. Whatever it is, three days have passed and I have not yet gone to search for the house.

Tonight is also out of the question. I'm still too weak for any major outing. Plus, my mind reels from the experiences of the last three days, or however long it was. Giddiness tickles me when I think of what happened, then fear is not far behind.

My feelings couldn't conflict more. On the one hand, my recent experience has made it apparent that Daniels is friendly to me only as a facade, and that he really means me harm. On the other hand I'm fascinated by him and his family, as he calls them. They live such lives as to defy description.

That's not entirely true. I can describe how they live. It's magical. They live magical lives. There is no doubt they are something more than human.

But it's that same more–than–human quality that makes them dangerous. It not only causes fear for my own well being, I fear for the entire human race. I really have no idea of their intentions. Especially after witnessing the dark ritual with the robed figures, I fear they're not good. The place crawled with evil. It reeked of evil. Evil emanated from the dark and shadowy pit. And whoever was responsible for that perverse ritual is of the same ilk as Lord Daniels and his family. They may even be one and the same.

More and more I begin to think that Lord Daniels is one of the Fae or Dannae from ancient legend. Is that too far-fetched? No more so than what I have already experienced, this latest being just as marvelous as the rest.

Three days ago, not long after the noon hour, a limousine pulled up into my drive. The butler from my previous trip to see Lord Daniels emerged from the car and announced that I had been granted another audience with his master. The request by no means came across forceful. Still, it carried a weight, an undeniable implication that the insult of refusal would not be taken lightly.

Like before, the windows of the car had such dark tint on them that even in the day I could not see out. The drive lasted several hours. When the car finally came to a stop and the door opened, the afternoon had already grown late.

The smell of saltwater hit me immediately. Close behind came the sound of crashing waves and that special lightness of the air that is peculiar to the coast.

The beach was deserted, and for the most part, pristine. Large palm trees grew almost all the way up to the water. Some had fallen and lay half submerged in the rising tide.

The butler instructed me to walk south down the beach until I came to a lighthouse with a stone dwelling at its base. There I was to wait for Lord Daniels.

Cold wind blew in from the water, cutting into me. The desolateness of the place made it seem haunted in the fading light. The incessant churn of the water pressed in on me as much as the cold wind. I began to feel the doubts I should have felt as soon as the limousine appeared. Instead, I was more or less stranded with no idea where I was, and the sunlight beginning to fade.

With no other options I walked south as instructed. After half an hour the coastline turned in, and as I rounded the curve in the beach a huge stone arch stood in my path. It seemed a completely natural rock formation that had been shaped by centuries of erosion. This one was huge though. It stood at least 200 feet high and stretched over the width of the beach. The base of the arch on each side seemed as thick as the redwoods I hear grow in California.

There was no reason to think it wasn't natural. Rock formations sprawled all over the beach. But when I stepped through the arch I felt something wholly supernatural. The atmosphere shifted in some way I can't fully describe. It's like the air became lighter and more electric. The light possessed a sharper quality and it seemed as if I could see further. A burst of energy hit me and the gloom suddenly didn't seem so oppressive. The whole place took on a magical quality, bathed in the orange light of the setting sun, and reflected in the rocky hollows that stretched along the shore.

Not long after I passed through the arch the lighthouse came into view. It almost camouflaged itself, being short and squat and made of stone, the same color as the rock around it. A faint, orange light came from the top window, flickering like firelight.

As I climbed up the rocks toward the house the long structure at its base came into view. A large set of doors stood partway open, allowing the same orange light as the window to creep out into the dusk. In the quickly darkening night the glow from inside beckoned with invitation. I didn't hesitate to push open the doors and step inside.

A roaring fire and a few torches on wall sconces lit the room inside. It looked like something out of Beowulf – a large hall of the old thanes of Europe. A stone floor littered with straw stretched past wooden posts ending at the large fireplace. A long table, placed with iron settings entertained no guests except for one figure who sat at its far end. A cloud of smoke rose up from her face. I could already smell the spices.

Eladora.

This time she wore a cream colored dress. It had only one strap, and a thick braid of hair fell over her bare shoulder. Dark eyes mesmerized me immediately. She sat with her back to the table, one leg crossed over another, exposed by a slit in the dress.

"I see, you still haven't gone into the woods behind your house," she said as I approached.

"I keep meaning to," I told her. "But things keep coming up."

"There are no woods behind your house," she said as smoke drifted lazily from her mouth.

"So I'm told."

We regarded each other for a moment. I waited for her to say something, to introduce my surroundings or explain why I was brought there. She waited for something only she knew. All I can say is that any misgivings I may have felt for my vulnerable position dissipated like Eladora's smoke as I stood before her. You would have to see her to really know what I mean, see her in the flesh. A picture could never do her justice. I felt lucky just to be there.

"So, Danileoth has decided to take you with him tonight," she finally said. Her voice sent a thrill through me.

"Who?" I asked, not recognizing the name.

She laughed that joyful but somehow mournful laughter. "The one that fancies himself as Lord Daniels," she said. "He's always been Danileoth to me. I never gave into his

107

pretensions."

"I imagine you could get away with whatever you wanted," I said with all honesty.

She stood up and walked up to me. Her eyes peered into mine, stripping me naked with her power. And I loved her for it. Never have I felt so smitten. I thought of what Erin had told me about the Fae of Keats's poem. Dame Sans Merci.

I believed.

I believed every murky and supernatural tale. I believed every fantastic legend, every impossible myth. She stood before me. I believed.

"My dweomer," she purred.

"What does that mean?"

"It means your special."

She moved closer to me, so close our lips almost touched. I could smell the spicy aroma coming from her and the sweet floral of her skin. My heart pounded in my chest with excitement. I thought it might burst.

"I want you to do two things for me," she whispered.

As if she really had to ask. She could have commanded me to capture the tide and I would've died trying.

"Anything you want," I whispered back.

"Do not tell Danileoth I was here," she told me.

I nodded.

"Now close your eyes," she said and pulled on her cigarette.

I complied, closing my eyes. Her presence drew nearer. Soft lips touched mine. A thrill ran through my flesh.

Impossible, I thought. I kissed a goddess and yet I lived.

Her mouth opened mine and she breathed into me. The sting of spiced smoke burned my lungs as she exhaled. My body revolted, racking me with coughs. I doubled over, eyes stinging with tears, spewing out the foreign smoke.

When my vision cleared Eladora had left. Male voices came clamoring down the hallway beside the fireplace. Lord Daniels and six other men stepped into the hall. He smelled the air and looked at me disapprovingly.

"Where did you get that?" he asked, gesturing toward my hand.

Bewildered, I looked down and saw Eladora's cigarette burning between my fingers. I scrambled to think of something, wondering if this was her idea of a joke. She must be toying with me, but I didn't care.

"Some woman gave it to me at the Grove the other night," I heard myself say. "Seemed like a good time to try it while I waited."

Lord Daniel searched me with a calculating look. I felt small beneath his withering gaze.

"Do you fancy it?" He asked.

"Doesn't really suit me," I said, throwing the rest of it into the fire. "Think it was stale anyway."

Daniels nodded, and shrugged his shoulders. If he doubted my story then he didn't indicate any distrust.

"I hope rum suits you better," he said. "Because you'll need it."

"Rum is great," I agreed. "What are we doing?"

"Diving," Daniels told me.

"Diving?" I asked incredulously. "It's freezing outside."

The others laughed like they were in on a secret I was ignorant to.

"It will get colder before it gets warmer," Daniels assured me as he took me under his arm. "We must get dressed first though."

He took me and the others back through the hall and out onto a stone dock overlooking the dark ocean. A cold, biting wind drove in from over the water. It pierced through my clothes without effort and sent me to shivers. At the end of the dock a boat waited, one of the old types made of wood and driven by sail.

To my horror the men began to undress. They stripped down to nothing, revealing figures all as godlike as Daniels'.

None seemed to be the slightest bit affected by the cold although their toned bodies showed not a trace of fat upon them. Instead, they stood naked upon the stone landing as if they soaked up the rays of a summer afternoon. Expectant looks fixed upon me.

"You've got to be joking," I said. "I'm already cold."

"Trust me," Daniel said. "I wouldn't lead you astray. Man up now. We have."

Something about that phrase along with seeing other men take up a challenge proved irresistible to my ego. My brazenness rose, determined that if they could do it, I could too. Damned if they were mythical creatures or not. I would not be outdone.

For the second time I stood naked beside Lord Daniels, pudgy and out of shape beside his perfection, beside the perfection of all the other men. They all smiled, enjoying the sight of my pale flesh trembling uncontrollably in the cold. And it was cold.

About this time a servant boy, dressed in his usual white cloth about the waist, came out on the landing with a bundle in his arms. Daniels reached into it and handed me a red flask. I could barely make out nautical figures carved into the metal surface.

"Let's put you out of your misery," Daniel said, instructing me to drink. "Impressive endurance though."

I lifted the flask with shivering hands and took a small sip. The rum was exquisite and sweet. More importantly, a warmth suffused into me, no, a heat, that instantly made the cold bearable. Even wearing no clothes I was immediately comfortable.

The other men began to dress, somewhat. The servant boy handed them red bundles. He gave one to me also and the leathery material felt like a skin of some sort. Imitating the other men I tied it around my waist. A smaller piece of the same material was given me to wrap around my head, along with an empty pouch and a net to hold the flask of rum. Finally, I was handed a knife and told how to tie it around my calf. I stopped to admire the beautiful piece. Out of its sheath the blade glowed blue, like it gave off its own light. The handle was ivory, with carved figures twining up the bone. I couldn't decipher them all. They looked like some sort of sea monsters, mostly foreign to me.

"The ladies of the water are waiting," Daniels cried and led us out to the waiting ship.

As soon as we untied from the dock our ship moved into the teeth of the waves and water. Our sails billowed as if the wind blew from behind us instead of into our faces. I only suffered a moment of confusion, coming to expect such marvelous things.

One of the other men stood at the wheel, Daniels standing beside him from time to time. The ship rocked and slammed into the water. Salt spray soaked my face. I could tell it was cold, that both the wind and the water should be freezing me to the bone. Yet I felt no sensation of cold. After a time the chill became more acute, and I sipped more of the rum which immediately restored my warmth.

We sailed out into this unknown ocean for a few hours. Some of the other men began to sing. Others played dice on the deck. One man carved figures into scrimshaw. I seemed to be the only one with no distraction. Instead, I contented myself with marveling at the rise and swell of the winter ocean.

"The Isle of Beltane!" a voice cried out jubilantly.

I scurried to the rails and looked ahead. Through the dim night I could make out fingers of rock jutting out of the water. The craft deftly maneuvered around these dangers towards the coast. It wasn't until we were almost upon the stone pier that I could see the island in front of us. As soon as we docked the others leapt off, laughing excitedly, offering me no explanation or instruction. I followed, struggling to keep up.

We ran through wind and marsh until we reached the far end of the island. From there the men formed a single line and began to jump from rock to rock out over the ocean. The leader stopped at a single promontory, a rock small enough for one man to straddle. He looked fragile out there, alone on his small island while the dark tide buffeted him.

"Come to me lady of the ocean deep," he yelled out over the water, acting anything but fragile as he confidently faced the ocean. "For a kiss I will give you a treasure to keep."

A splash rose from the water and a figure leapt up to lean against the rock. At first it looked like a long fish. Then, as it burst fully out of the water, the scales shimmered away and a beautiful woman stood in her place. The man placed something in the girl's hand. She pulled it close to her breast, then grabbed the man and kissed him deeply. With a laugh that danced over the cold wind she plunged back into the water, the man diving in right after her.

"Of all the treasures beneath the sea, only gold and silver are lacking," Lord Daniels said, appearing beside me. "Whatever the ocean gets of these comes from men, either from shipwrecks or gifts. Of all the treasures, silver is the most coveted of the merrow."

He pressed something into my hand. I looked down to see a silver coin there.

"Once the Merrow kisses you do not breathe. As soon as you take in air the enchantment is broken. As long as you don't breathe and remain underwater you will be fine."

He pointed to my flask and made a drinking motion. I tipped it up and drank deeply, reveling in the warmth it brought.

One by one all the men stood upon the rock and called out to the Merrow. They all received a kiss after giving them their gift, and dove under the waters.

After the last one had gone under I crept along the slippery rocks as fast as I dared. Upon the promontory a wave slapped into me, almost knocking me into the water. I gripped at the rock with one hand, holding fast to my coin in the other.

"Come to me lady of the ocean deep, for a kiss I will give you a treasure to keep," I yelled out over the waves.

Almost immediately, a huge silvery figure splashed out onto the rock. Its scales glowed and shimmered, like rainbow dancing across its surface. It shook itself and then a beautiful woman sat next to me.

Her skin was pale and lovely, eyes gray, and lips blue. Water dripped from her white hair. Her mouth parted open in wonder, a look of curiosity upon her face, and I could see small, yellow teeth no more than nubs sticking out of her gums.

"You aren't like the others," she said in wonder, with a voice like the churn of water. "You are a son of man."

She reached out a hand and stroked my face. With an expression of intense interest she touched my hair and ears, finally resting her hand over my heart. A deep smile broke out over her face as she felt it beat in my chest. Her eyes closed and she sighed, enjoying for some mysterious reason the mere feeling of blood moving through my body.

"They want to consume you," she opened her eyes and said.

Before I could respond she pressed her lips to mine and kissed me. I felt the rush of salt air enter me. My head swam with the pull of the tides and I felt a deepness that was the depth of the ocean.

I opened my eyes and the merrow regarded me with sadness. She took my hand and pulled me into the water. I felt the silver piece slip from my hand into hers.

I will do my best to describe to you the sensation I felt. Beneath the influence of the merrow's kiss everything appeared and acted differently than I'd ever experienced under the water. For one thing, I could see as clear as if I were in a shallow pool instead of deep, salty ocean. A light suffused all around that gave the ocean a blue cast.

More difficult to describe is the lack of need I felt for air. I didn't breathe under the water. Like normal I held my breath beneath the surface. But I didn't feel the need to breathe. That straining of the lungs, that tightness that tells us we need air, never came. Whatever air I had in my lungs became sufficient. Something in the merrow's kiss had imparted to me the ability to see and live under the water as a natural inhabitant of the ocean.

As soon as I got over my initial amazement I noticed the others had swam deeper towards the ocean floor. I followed as best I could, not catching up until they stopped at an oyster bed stretching as far as the eye could see. They all pulled out their knives and went to work prying open the mussels.

Understanding what was happening, I joined in the work with excitement. I found a mussel and with some effort managed to pry the knife into the crease of its mouth. Once inside the blade forced the shell open. I saw nothing but the pale flesh beneath.

I looked around and saw the others digging into their oysters. Following their lead I reached beneath the slimy tongue and groped through it until I felt something smooth and hard in my hand. I pulled out a small pearl, letting it float in my hands in the blue ocean light. If I could've laughed out loud I would have, like a little child. I carefully put the pearl in my pouch and swam to the next oyster.

Unbelievably, they all contained pearls. At least all that I opened. After the fifth oyster betrayed its treasure to me I knew this could be no normal oyster bed. Perhaps it was part of the enchantment, or it could even be a different ocean altogether. Whatever it was, I soaked it up with excitement.

I had nearly filled my bag with ocean pearls, when I felt a tug on my arm. A blond haired companion of Daniels motioned me to follow him. I noticed the others swimming away, deeper into the ocean.

Despite my treasures I began to feel anxious to get back to the surface. I had not breathed the air in at least an hour, and though I felt not the slightest need, the alien feeling of not taking in air began to make me feel claustrophobic. Some primal need to breathe, even if physically unnecessary, pulled at me. There was only so much I could take of these unnatural wonders.

The others didn't seem to be bothered, and I was, for the time, at their mercy. I followed along and allowed myself to enjoy the splendors of that magical depth that I would surely never see again.

We swam past a bed of multicolored anenomes. Wavering tendrils withdrew back into their bodies as we passed. The water shimmered in color.

The ocean floor fell away into a large rift. Rays of moonlight spilled through, brightening the blue glow of the water. In the canyon I could see a whole new array of sea life. But it was the ship that immediately grabbed my attention.

It was impossible to place the era of the shipwreck. The ship itself appeared to be wooden, fitted with large sails, like the old voyagers of the ocean. Its size though was immense, and the shape completely unusual for oceangoing vessels. Instead of the rounded hull I was used to seeing, this one stretched out long and rectangular, with a flat bottom. I could tell because the ship had landed on its side, exposing the long jagged breach that must have caused her doom.

The group made straight for the shipwreck. I have to admit my own fascination, and my forgotten anxiety as I followed the others through the breach, into the ships hull.

Darkness folded over us as we swam inside. My eyes adjusted to the poor light and I experienced a stillness that could not be replicated on land. To be filled with water as it was made the ship seem frozen in time. A few pieces of timber floated by. All around me the walls seethed with a sense of abandonment. The quiet stillness gave the ship a haunted touch. I knew that living men once roamed these chambers, sang and laughed and celebrated life as they sailed together. And now their absence was palpable, their presence frozen by the dark embrace of the ocean, waiting to be felt by whoever might come to wander where they once walked.

We swam through many different chambers, down a hallway, and into a vast room. At first I couldn't make out his purpose. The colored light that spilled through stained-glass gave the room a strange glow. A chandelier rested awkwardly on its side. I could make out a partitioned area along the floor that looked like the space reserved for an orchestra.

The others beckoned me to the far end where a huge, oval mirror in a gilded frame, still gleamed from its place in the wall. I swam over and looked in. All I could see was the submerged chamber behind me and a wavering, red beam of light that fell across the silver surface.

Daniels touched the gold frame and the surface of the mirror grew hazy and filled with smoke. The fog billowed and churned, then cleared as a new light shone out of the mirror.

I turned to see if anything had changed in the room behind me. We were still in the shipwreck, the water in the room murky and dim. Turning back to the mirror I saw a reflection not of the sunken room, but one full of men and women dancing with joy. Brightly colored dresses twirled as men with dark suits and white gloves led their ladies through the steps of a grand march.

Above the dancers the chandelier glowed warmly. Small globes of light floated down from the chandelier like bubbles. They drifted lazily before being swept up in the wind of the passing dancers, making twirls and turns of their own.

I watched in fascination, wondering if what I saw was the life of this ship in older, happier days. It was like the mirror could watch and remember all that transpired before it, and when beckoned, reflect back those memories.

The dancers passed before the mirror, smiling and full of

youthful joy. More than one young girl would stop and look at herself in the mirror, making small adjustments to her hair or dress. A few of the men might steal quick glances at themselves as they passed by, never looking for long lest they be caught in the act of vanity. It felt like they looked at me when they looked into the mirror, and with every glance I felt more entranced by what I saw.

I started to look deeper into the moving image for details. To the side of the dancers an orchestra played, full of men in powdered wigs. A couple fought in the corner, the man pleading with his date in words I could not hear, though by his gestures I could tell he was earnest.

One couple in particular held my interest. At first I wouldn't have guessed they were together, for they danced with different partners. Once though, he looked up at the mirror, and I took notice of his dark and handsome face. A woman looked up at the same time, she in a blue dress with dark curls falling down in a sort of casual disregard that only highborn ladies can pull off.

A conspiratorial smile flashed across his face. The same smile spread across hers. I realized they looked at each other in the mirror, not themselves. They shared a brief look then twirled away with their partners.

After that I found them looking at each other quite often. They would steal glances across the room, crane their heads this way or that for a quick peek. During one dance they briefly touched hands as one line of dancers moved towards another. They locked stares for a moment, looking deeply into each other's eyes. As the dance pulled them apart they only released their grasps with obvious reluctance.

Several times as I watched I told myself it was time to move on to other things. But I couldn't pull my eyes away. And it had nothing to do with the scene that drew out before me. That was quite pedestrian in and of itself. An impulse kept me fixed on the mirror, an impulse that told me to keep watching, continue to be fascinated.

And I did. Even though I felt the cold slowly creep back into me, I continued to watch. Even when the voice of warning inside me grew louder and more urgent, I continued to watch. I watched helplessly, though still enchanted, as the dancers twirled and dipped and glided tirelessly.

Then someone stopped, a look of confusion on his face, his eyes fixed on something I could not see, something out of the mirror's line of vision. Another couple noticed and stopped mid-dance. Like a ripple over the surface of the water one group of dancers would stop, followed by those just beyond them. Finally, the whole room was milling about, heads craning to see whatever caused the interruption of their festivity.

I could almost hear the mill of confusion turn to panic. It must have been a scream, for the crowd jumped in shock, faces wide in terror. Panic broke out and the people began to run in different directions. Mayhem ruled where moments before reigned the joyous and orderly movement of dance. No one showed the slightest regard for another. Men pushed over women. Some ran one way, then turned and ran another.

The girl in blue appeared in front of the mirror, looming large and taking up the entire glass. Blood spilled down the front of her dress, seeping from a gash across her throat. I hardly noticed the dark curls that fell down her face. I could hardly notice anything but the eyes staring right into mine, pleading and desperate, before something jerked her violently away.

The fright jolted me back to my senses. Fog filled the mirror, blotting out the mass of people running in desperate fear. A bloodied hand pressed against the glass. The red print faded last before the mirror shimmered again, showing only myself floating alone in the room of the sunken ship.

Alone.

A new panic flared in me. I looked around frantically. I was alone. Worse, I could feel the cold quickly seeping back into my body. The bottle of warming rum still hung on my belt, but I feared trying to drink it in the water. I couldn't risk losing a precious drop.

Desperately, I thrashed through the water, searching for the way out. By some miracle I found another hole in the ship which brought me directly outside again. I looked around, but my companions were nowhere in sight.

A thousand awful scenarios ran through my mind as I swam back towards where I thought we had come. I couldn't be sure in the least. I saw myself swimming those waters forever, or freezing to death, or wandering that desolate island in my one strip of leather, living off of oysters and growing a long and ragged beard while my limbs withered away.

I felt like an idiot for going on this insane trip with Daniels. With every desperate stroke I made I cursed my stupidity. Why had I agreed to come here, I asked myself over and over.

As I swam back over the ridge I felt the pit of my stomach drop. Even with clear visibility under the water my companions were nowhere in sight. For all I knew I had been staring at that mirror for hours. Maybe they had long since abandoned me, days ago even.

I swam on though I believed my efforts futile. For whatever reason, it became clear that Daniels had led me here to die. Why he bothered with the elaborate set up I couldn't begin to fathom. The same end could be accomplished much easier for a man as powerful as he.

Just when I believed my situation was hopeless, salvation arrived.

A dolphin swam up beside me and stroked me with her long nose. I pushed it gently away and swam on. The animal nudged me again and lay her body lengthwise against mine. She wriggled against me in a way that made me think she wanted me to ride upon her back.

I reached out and took a tentative hold of her fin. With a

snap of her tail the dolphin shot off. The sudden jerk of speed forced me to tighten my grip to keep from being thrown off.

The dolphin sped me through the water. In mere seconds we passed over the oyster bed. Then we neared the rocks in which we first began our swim. I could see the others just beginning to climb out of the water.

But the dolphin turned and swam past them and around the island, leaving the rocks and the others behind. I hardly had time to realize what was going on much less object. I simply clung to the dolphin's fin, trusting my new savior.

As we turned around the end of the island I could see the stone wharf and our ship floating about 200 yards ahead. I wanted to laugh out loud as I realized what the dolphin was doing. With exhilarating speed we made straight for the wharf.

As we approached the dolphin turned inland. The shore zoomed towards us, water and land converging at a point that sped closer and closer. With a kick of her tail the dolphin broke the surface of the water. I flew up and soared awkwardly through the air, my limbs flailing. I landed upright, knee-deep in water, but on my feet.

Sound and air crashed in on me. The desolate silence of the ocean below fell away with the roar of wave and wind. Air filled my lungs, precious and sweet, and I breathed deep. I coughed first, then laughed, exhilarated just to be standing on land and breathing air.

I turned to look for the creature that had saved me, but saw only a woman standing in the churning surf. It was the same whose kiss had enabled me to swim freely underwater.

We stared at each other for a moment. The wind howled about us, light rain pelted my neck and chest. With a shiver I remembered the cold. I fumbled for the flask and took a deep drink. Warmth faded back into my limbs. Relief and warmth.

The merrow smiled at me. Her tiny, rounded teeth marring an otherwise beautiful face.

"You saved me," I said somewhat clumsily. "Thank you."

She stepped closer and wrapped her hand around the back of my head.

"Will you grant me a favor then?" she asked.

"Of course," I answered without hesitation.

"Then grant me two," she said.

"Okay," I said with a chuckle.

"Pray for me," the merrow said.

"Pray for you?" I asked, surprised by the request.

"Yes. Will you? You granted me two favors, and that is the first that I ask."

"Okay. What is your name?" I asked.

"Mesulina," the sea woman said. "Pray for Mesulina and for her redemption. God hears the prayers of men, and he is merciful to them. Will you do this? Will you plead to the Almighty for mercy on behalf of poor Mesulina?"

"I will," I answered with a sense of solemnity that seemed appropriate.

"What else do you want?"

Mesulina's smile deepened and she drew herself closer to me.

"Kiss me," she said.

"Again?"

"No, I kissed you that time, for breath. I want you to kiss me, for desire. Kiss me like you would kiss a woman you long for, one whose affection your heart craves."

I was struck by the earnestness of her request. Intensity widened her eyes and she gripped the back of my head as she spoke. This meant something to her.

"You just want to kiss me?" I asked in disbelief.

"No. I want you to kiss me," she iterated. "There is a difference man and you should know it."

Her eyes darted to the island and back to me.

"Hurry," she said urgently. "Your companions return. They must not see me with you."

"Just a kiss then," I said.

She nodded eagerly, looking every bit like a young girl at her first dance, then closed her eyes.

I took her head in my two hands and drew her close to me. Her naked skin pressed against mine and I could feel the cold beneath it. I leaned in and touched my lips to hers. Thinking of the look on Mesulina's face, that look of naïve anticipation, a look only the young and hopeful can master.

This kiss felt nothing like the first one with the merrow. I tasted no saltwater, or felt the ocean churn. Instead, I felt something pass from me.

A warmth or fire, one that I had not even known was there, passed from me. I could feel it distinctly. Some heat of mine went out of me and flowed into her. That she felt it too I know because she moaned in delight just when I felt it move.

For a moment I thought I had lost something, that the sea woman had stolen from me with this kiss. Then, as soon as the fire passed from me, another heat rose up more powerful than the one I lost. And this was not from her. It came from somewhere within me. I could feel that by giving Mesulina some of this inner fire I had stoked it even hotter within myself. As if by giving I had opened up some well in me and drawn upon an unquenchable source. More passed to the merrow with my kiss, but I lost none for it.

When she pulled away with a whispering laugh on her lips I felt stronger and more alive. Something of the same blaze shone in her eyes as well, as she had been warmed also.

"The fire of God blazes in men still," she said. "Beware those others. They seek to steal it from you. And do not forget your prayers."

She turned and dove back into the water. One splash of a dolphin's tail and she was gone. Where she had stood only the wind whipped at me and the waves splashed at my knees.

The sound of laughter came from behind me, approaching against the wind. I turned to see my companions—and deserters—running towards the wharf. They didn't see me until their feet slapped the stone dock.

Daniel stopped first. I relished the look of uncertainty that struck his usually smug features. His eyes widened in shock as he froze in disbelief.

"There you are," he said, trying to recover. For a moment he was unable to feign his usual congeniality. "I thought you...you were behind us."

I spread my arms wide, refusing to offer any explanation. "I'm a fast swimmer," was all I said.

"Indeed, you are," he said. His eyes narrowed from surprise to a more sinister cast. "Much more than you appear."

Through the whole ride back to shore I sat alone near the bow of the ship, trying to see into the darkness before me. None of the others spoke a word to me and their avoidance was tense and awkward. I sensed the conversation, or rather an argument, that wanted to break out but had to wait until I was gone. I half expected one of them to throw me overboard.

By the time we docked I had grown irresistibly tired. I remember making it back to the lodge and dressing in my own clothes. A fire still blazed in the hall, its warmth seducing me to sleep.

After I had dressed one of the servants led me outside. A curt and chilly farewell from Daniels, then I was helped into an old, horse-drawn carriage. I hardly had time to appreciate its old world feel, the black finish of his exterior, the equally black, velvet softness inside. I felt the carriage jolt and heard the clop of horses hooves then I could resist no longer, and fell into a deep slumber.

I awoke earlier this afternoon. The stack of newspapers on my front landing told me I had been out for three days. If I slept that long then it was not a peaceful sleep, for I am as tired as I ever remember being. There is an aching in my muscles that screams out that I have pushed them too hard.

As before, it seems like everything I experienced happened

in a dream, if even a vivid one. When I think about it, that's how it seems. I tell myself it couldn't actually have happened. But also as before I have tokens of my adventure, proof, at least to myself, that my adventure was real.

I have a pouch full of pearls, more exquisite than I have ever seen. And I have an ivory handled knife, its blade shimmering blue, and the handle carved with marvelous sea creatures.

The Fifth Vision

Another two days of rest and I'm only now just beginning to feel like myself again. The ache in my joints has subsided, but that was a minor problem. The disorientation is worse. Hardly anything makes sense to me, if even that makes sense. I find concentration impossible. It's like I expect things to be different than they are. Instead of sea legs I have a sea brain. I'm having to get used to being in this world again.

The last two nights I dreamt of Mesulina, or the ocean, or that horrible vision I saw in the mirror of the sunken ship. I can still taste the salt in my mouth. Even though I know Daniels meant evil for me, I can't help but think of my journey with him as a wonderful adventure. So wonderful, in fact, that I find life on this side almost unbearably dull.

But I'm getting used to it again, like getting over a cold, or waiting for a dream to fade from your memory at the break of dawn. Only I don't want to get over this illness. I don't want the dream to fade. Though things will get back to normal for me I have a feeling I won't forget. This will haunt me until death.

Erin came over last night in a strangely exuberant mood. She was bubbly and giggly. She laughed at everything. It thrilled me to see her happy. I could also see that behind the happiness lay something else, something that waited for the joy to pass so it could exert its dominance again.

I mentioned none of this. I wanted to let Erin enjoy herself. She needed it. Even though her happiness had a reckless quality to it, I dared not dampen it in the least.

We drank together. We laughed, she laughed. We walked all over the neighborhood arm in arm. At one point she commented on the ravens that had gathered in a dark mass over the trees in my yard. That was the only moment her happiness faltered that night. She looked at the birds cloaking the old oak trees like a billowing garment, a serious look upon her face. A shudder passed through her and she shook it off.

The smile returned.

Later that night, when the evening had worn old and dim, she kissed me softly. Her lips trembled on mine. Her hands held my head tightly.

I heard a muffled sob, then she wrapped her arms around me and wept. I didn't ask why. There was something in her tears that lay beyond asking.

Eventually we lied down to sleep. Sometimes she would weep again. Other times she held me and stroked my hair affectionately. At one point I fell asleep. Whether she did or not I do not know. When I awoke this morning she was gone.

For some reason the ravens irritate me today. Their mere presence is a mockery, an insult. I don't know why.

I should be scared. But today I am angry. Angry at whatever forces gather around me, around my house, around my property. What right do they have to threaten me? Why should I let them intimidate me? Let them do what they will. They shall not find some docile lamb going meek and trembling to the slaughter.

No, I will be the lion. I know my power is not equal to theirs, but what I have I will exercise to the utmost. I also know I have more than I'm aware of.

I took the gun outside with this thought in mind. My first two shots missed, only causing the dark birds to jump and flutter where they perched. I could hear them laughing at me.

With the third shot came an explosion of feathers and one of the birds fell squawking to the ground. The air shook as the flock of ravens took to the air and flew away.

"I am death to you!" I screamed to the retreating birds. "You hear me?! I am death!"

I know my neighbors must think me mad.

The raven I had shot still lived. He fluttered helplessly on the ground, squawking in pain. One of his wings lay limp while the other flapped in vain. I reveled in his suffering. It made me feel, not powerful, but not quite so impotent.

The bird stilled as I approached. His yellow eyes stared up at me with hate and vengeance. This was no ordinary bird. He was a messenger of the deep. He was a servant of the dark.

I felt in him the brutal wrath of the enemy. One who sought not only my undoing, but the undoing of all I and the world held dear. He served hate and death. He flew at the command of rot and putrescence. He was a harbinger of fear, a hater of happiness and joy.

The bird flapped desperately again as I reached out my hand towards him. He screeched when I took hold of him and tried to scratch me with his pitiful claws.

I held fast, feeling every bit of the righteous indignation that is my due. I may die, but not without a slaughter of my own.

Memories came back to me of the wrapped bundles offered up to the dark pit, the innocence plundered for the cause of evil. I twisted until I heard and felt the satisfying crunch of bone under my hand. The bird fell limp and still.

I too, would have my slaughter.

The ravens came back. I knew they would. They returned with a vengeance in their eyes. Their number had doubled. This is a fight to the death.

But I too will have my slaughter.

This morning I woke up with that irresistible urge to attend church again, this time more powerful than the others. I don't know why I feel this way or can even imagine what good it would do. My recent experiences in church have been nothing but disappointing. When I had been moved by these urges before I explored many different denominations and found them mostly lacking. The old, mainstream churches are dull, full of rote observance, empty repetition and watered-down theology. More contemporary churches fare little better. They have plenty of energy and enthusiasm. Instead they lack depth. They seem to be more concerned with their people having good finances and happy marriages than a deep spirituality.

Maybe I am just expecting too much. After what I've seen, the magic and power that the world is full of, I find it inexplicable that the church does not display some of this same depth and power. Of all places, the church but scratches at the surface of life. It should plumb the depths.

At the same time, though I know I will be disappointed, I feel the need to be in a church again. I feel like I know what it's truly capable of, though I can't say what. I can feel it shuddering on the edge of their repetitive droning and passionless hymns. I can almost see it in the rituals, here it in the creeds, waiting to break free like a wild animal rattling the bars of its cage.

A vast and immeasurable power sparks on their fingertips, yet they do nothing with it. They hold committee meetings, programs and potluck dinners, and yawn while the preacher gives them charming life advice or encourages them to be nicer people. What they have become are dull and impotent people.

I guess what I am drawn to is an urge to feel a touch, a whisper of that power. Even if the oblivious clergymen do not know it, I know it. I want to feel it.

On a whim I chose a Catholic Church. It was one I hadn't tried yet. I found an older one downtown. The building was built in that soaring style that people have forgotten. The gray stone rose up high in towering spires. Carved figures – apostles, gargoyles, whirling designs – covered the exterior walls. Inside, fluted pillars rose up to open a quiet and solemn space. Colored light floated in through stained-glass. Shadows flickered from votive candles. The sound of quiet steps echoed on the marble floor, mixing with the creak of the wooden pews and the whispered rosary from knelt figures. I even picked up the distant scent of incense. The total effect was solemn and quiet awe. My soul felt it, and a peace born of deep strength, not my own, settled over me. I felt infolded in powerful, tender arms that wrapped around me in protection.

I can't say the service impressed me. The mass was said almost mechanically. The effeminate priest tried to sound impressive in his thin and nasally voice. He succeeded in sounding ridiculous.

The presence of the sacred space alone kept the trip from being a complete loss. But it was just as I thought that I would get no more out if it when I noticed a soft whispering beside me.

I looked up to see an old woman praying the rosary beside me. Her brown fingers rubbed each bead, one after another. The cross came up to her lips and she kissed it reverently.

She must have felt me looking at her, for her eyes opened and they turned towards me. Deep wrinkles covered her face. They looked more like wisdom than age.

"Do you have a rosary?" she asked me. A smile touched her voice that made it sound like she knew the secret to peace and contentment.

"Oh, I'm not Catholic," I confessed as a way of answer.

"I didn't ask if you were Catholic," she said. "I asked if you had a rosary."

"I'm afraid I don't then."

She held out hers to me, a beautiful set that looked to be made of olive wood. I tried to refuse, but she insisted, pressing them into my hand.

"The world is full of great evil," she told me, her aged and sagacious eyes looking into mine. "Men need powerful light to protect them."

Her words struck me in a way that only words can when they were meant just for you. Did she know? Was my need written so clearly across my face? Was there something deeper here at work? Perhaps all the deep power has not left the world.

Her warm and maternal fingers took mine and showed me how to pray the rosary. She spoke slowly and carefully, the patience of a teacher in her voice. Just as slowly I repeated what she said, comforted by the sound of her voice and the touch of her hands.

"You seem like a man in need of powerful blessings," she observed.

I nodded.

"Let me teach you another one," she said. "This one is a strong invocation, from men who find themselves in grave danger, or confronting the powers of darkness.

"It's called the Lorica. It is very old, and very powerful."

Her voice chanted the invocation in a low hum. Reverently and softly she chanted it to me. I could feel its power. Something ancient rose on its words, a power deeper than the depth of the sea. I could almost feel the shadows of an old forest, the shade of a chapel filled with incense, a tremor in the bowels of the earth.

I bind unto myself today the strong name of the Trinity
By invocation of the same, the Three in One and One in Three
Through the blood of Christ, His breaking of death's door
His passion and His reign forever more

I bind unto myself today by faith in Almighty God above
His strength to hold me, His eye to look on me in love
His hand to guard in dark of night
His host to save by conquering might

I bind unto myself today
The strength of earth and heaven
Light of sun at height of noon
Radiance of the sacred moon
Blaze of fire burning bright

Brilliant flash of lightning strike
Speed of wind and depth of sea
Rock's immovability

All these I place
By God's Almighty help and grace
Between myself and the powers of darkness

The visit to the church gave me an energy and optimism I had not felt for some time. The old lady's words were a balm to me. They seemed to confirm the power that I knew was possible.

She patiently repeated the chant to me until I had it memorized. It took a surprisingly short amount of time. Something about the words, their cadence and rhythm, the way they floated into one another, fit so well together that made the learning process seamless and simple.

The Lorica, she called it. The power that came from it was palpable, like fire coming from my lips.

Feeling newly empowered I set out to find the Keepers. With the preparations already made I left late in the afternoon.

I started at the obelisk that stood downtown in the middle of an intersection where several roads came together. Endless streams of cars tore around it, their rushing lights blinding in the near dusk.

To the east stood an old church. Behind it, rows of the old market went back nearly half a mile. All I could see to the south was an unending line of strip malls. West of the obelisk was an old neighborhood, so I set out in that direction first.

I walked up and down those streets for nearly two hours without finding anything that looked right. I turned north through a group of derelict warehouses and into a neighborhood of new townhomes. Still nothing looked right.

Staying north I crossed over from the row houses and immediately saw what I was looking for. I can't say how I knew it. The house was large and sat on a sprawling piece of property, built of faded green and white bricks. A carriage house stood beside the main one, along with some other, smaller buildings. Nothing I could see indicated that this was the house I sought. I knew it all the same.

As I approached I could make out a garden wall connected to the main house, distinguished by the ivy crawling up its sides. Something tugged at my memory, the mention of the garden door among the Keepers. Something felt right about it, part of the same rightness I felt about the entire house.

A pair of iron wrought gates guarded the entrance. They pushed open easily, though eliciting a screech along their rusted hinges. The sound cut through the quiet of the night, giving me a sudden bout of self-consciousness. I only noticed then that the house was dark and quiet, looking every bit like a neglected property.

What was it I felt there? I can't say for sure, though the sensation still throbs in me. I can still feel the pulse that ran up my hand as soon as I touched the gates. It's a living thing, I thought. And I think it still. The garden is alive in some sense, though I could not explain how.

A wind blew out of the garden, like a tired exhale, stirring up the dead leaves at my feet. I took a tentative step in. A hedge wall blocked my path. It surrounded me on three sides, forming a kind of foyer. There was no path to access the inner gardens.

I looked the hedge up and down, searching for a way through. I saw nothing but the thick cluster of growth that barred my way. I stepped back into the gateway and looked at the brick path at my feet, wondering if I could find a clue written there as to how to get through. It was then that I noticed the shimmer in the green wall. I looked up and it was gone. I turned my eyes down again, and again I could make out a shimmer in the hedge wall, just in the corner of my eye. When I turned my eyes directly to it, it returned to its substantial form.

Slowly, I turned my head to the side, and as soon as the corner of my vision passed over that place in the hedge, the shimmer returned. This time I kept my head still. The wall of growth continued to pulse and flow. It looked as though at that particular spot the hedge was a mere reflection on the surface of rippling water. But if I were to look directly at it then it looked like any normal bush.

I decided to test it, and approached that spot while only looking at it from the corner of my eye. I'm sure I made quite a spectacle, sliding awkwardly over the brick path with one hand out to my side and my eyes fixed rigidly in front of me.

When I had gotten close enough to touch the space of shimmering hedge, I reached out and felt only air. My whole arm passed through and still met no resistance. I reached in further and once my shoulder was through I felt the confidence to step completely over.

Overall, the maze was small, though frustrating. Every turn was a dead end. I stepped from row to row, finding the doorways by the shimmer I could only see out of the corner of my eye. And every doorway did not lead down the right path. Twice I found myself back at the gateway. And twice I came upon a fountain at the garden center. It had long since been abandoned. Only dark, stagnant water filled the pool. The stone angel atop the fountain with wings outstretched pursed his lips to no avail.

Only after much frustration and retracing of steps did I make it through. One last passage through the surreal break in the hedge and I found myself facing a door recessed into the faded, green brick. A half rotted and molding rope hung in front. I pulled on it and waited.

A tall, gaunt figure opened the door. I recoiled a bit in shock, as he looked exactly like the butler who had served the men in my vision. He appeared as if he had not aged a single minute.

"What is it you seek?" The butler asked.

I was about to answer with, the Keepers of the Flame. Just before the words came out of my mouth I changed them, without considering why.

"I come seeking the Flame," I answered instead.

A small, sad smile crossed the man's face as he stepped aside.

"Welcome, seeker," he said.

I stepped inside, feeling a part of some ritualized activity. The butler guided me in, through the darkened greenhouse and further into the mansion's rooms. Sheets covered most of the furniture in rooms thick with the dust of disuse. Once we entered the library, the same I had seen in my vision, the butler stopped and turned to me.

"Normally, I would introduce you to the company of the men you seek," the butler said with a heavy sigh. "These are dark times. There is but one left, and he is very sick. I'm afraid there is no one left to guide you through your journey."

I nodded, unable to think of anything to say, and unaware of the full significance of his words. The butler turned and led me from the library and up a broad flight of stairs. He knocked softly on the door before stepping into a bedroom where an old man slept in a large bed. A candle burned on the bedside table and the sound of labored, wheezing breath came from the figure underneath piles of down covers.

"Master Bickley," the butler said, touching the old man.

The figure on the bed startled awake. He looked around, confused.

"Gerard? What is it?" he sat up and asked.

"It is a seeker," Gerard answered.

"A seeker?" he squinted his eyes at me. "Corbin? Is that you Corbin?"

"No Master Bickley, a seeker," the butler reiterated.

"Ah, yes, a seeker," he said as the word sunk in. "Very good, a seeker."

The old man's eyes turned back to me and looked me up and down. He gestured to a chair beside the bed.

"Sit down boy, let's have a look at you."

Gerard bowed his head and stepped out of the room. I took a seat by the bed.

A trembling hand reached out to grab a pack of cigarettes on the bedside table. He pulled the candle close to light it. A puff of smoke covered his face and he inhaled deeply.

"They tell me these things will kill me," he said, lifting up the cigarette between his yellowed fingers. "But I'm one hundred and sixty-seven, so I guess not fast enough."

A rattling cough came out instead of a laugh. It receded into a sigh as the old man settle into his pillows.

"Do you believe that?" he asked me. "That I'm over a hundred years old."

I shrugged my shoulders, thinking it would be both rude and pointless to express otherwise.

"It's a curse to outlive everybody," he told me. "I alone am left to drink the bitter draught of failure and loss."

The bloodshot eyes closed and I believed he had fallen asleep. But they opened slowly again and the old man took another drag from the cigarette.

"So, you're a seeker," he said. "Been a long time since we've had a seeker."

"To be honest, I'm not sure what I'm doing here," I confessed. "Some strange things have happened to me, and I guess I'm looking for some answers or some sort of guidance."

"Sounds a lot like a seeker to me," he answered. "Tell me what's happened."

I laid the whole story out to him. Everything I could think of I told him, starting with my old life, the fever, the awakening and all the visions. I told him about the pale man, and up to my last encounter with Daniels. He listened attentively, asking questions for clarification. A smile crossed his face at the mention of Eladora, and a groan eked out of him when I spoke of Daniels. When I first said something about Sierra, he muttered something about a halfbreed whore. And when I told him of my vision of the Keepers meeting I saw a shadow pass over his face. When I was finished he sat for a while in brooding silence.

"So what do you want me to do?" he finally asked in a voice that sounded heavy with weariness.

"I don't even know what I need," I laughed.

"And I don't know that I could do any good," he answered.

As I watched him lean over and light another cigarette, I recognized the arrogant, but well-dressed man they called Sid from my vision. The arrogance was gone, but the handsome, aristocratic features still showed.

"You were at that meeting," I said. "You wanted to kill her. Sierra. Didn't you?"

"If only Bradley would've listened," he spat. "And we could've killed that fool Rip too.

"Ah, but it doesn't matter now. It probably wouldn't have mattered then. By that time everything was already lost. We were just beginning to realize it. Even if Rip hadn't blundered we still would have lost it all. It just went a little faster is all."

Sid seemed to fade into pensiveness. A distant and lost look crossed his face.

"Who are they?" I asked. "Lord Daniels and Eladora?"

"They are the children of the gods," he told me with a sense of finality. "And we are but insects crawling over the floor underneath their feet."

"Gods?" I asked. "Like the old gods?"

"No, not gods, children of the gods," he explained. "Except for that whore Sierra and her ilk. They're Elioud."

"What's an Elioud?"

"Offspring of one of the Fae and a human. Not as powerful as one of the Fae, but it makes little difference to us insects. We are equally helpless."

138

Sid's words battered around my head. Part of me wasn't completely shocked, but I still didn't understand. I still don't understand. Who are these gods? Who are these children of the gods?

"We call them Tuatha De Danaan. The Children of Dannae, or just Dannae" Sid explained, seeing my lack of understanding. "But they have been known by many names throughout the years: fairies, fae, sidhe, the blessed ones, the fallen ones, elves, and it goes on and on."

"What happened to their parents?" I asked. "Are the gods still there? What do they want?"

"Stop it! Stop it!" Sid yelled out, quieting me with a jerk of his hand.

His breath came out faltering and ragged. I heard a wheeze from the depths of his lungs. It took a few long, deliberate breaths from his nose before he settled down.

"Stop it," he said more calmly. "Don't work yourself up over something you can't do anything about. They've broken us already. Danileoth and the rest. They've broken us."

"Danileoth," I said remembering what Eladora had told me. "That's the same as…"

"That little queer who prances around as Lord Daniels," Sid finished for me. "His real name is Danileoth.

"He outsmarted us. Long ago he had us beat. By the time we realized it, it was already over. By the time you saw us having our little crisis with Rip, it was done. That was just the deathblow. Sierra and Rip, that fool, that was just the deathblow."

I wanted to ask more but I was afraid to push Sid. He sat back with his eyes closed, breathing deep and unsteady. It seemed as if he held back some great flood within him only by a great effort of his will.

"What am I to do then?" I asked instead.

"I don't know," Sid shrugged his bony shoulders. "Go dancing until the end comes. Find you a pretty girl, or maybe a few pretty girls, and go someplace far away with a couple of crates of rum. Get drunk and fuck them like there's no tomorrow."

A laugh tried to escape his throat. Instead, he wheezed and coughed. His face turned red with the effort and his whole body shook.

"Why would I do that?" I asked.

"Because there is no tomorrow," Sid croaked between coughs. "Didn't you hear me? We lost. We lost it all. We're just mortal and they're not. Who are we to rage against the gods?"

"It wasn't always like that," I reminded him. I hated to see him so pathetic. Hardly a remnant remained of the passionate and cocky young man I saw in the vision.

"That's right, it wasn't always like that. But we fucked it up good." He thumped his bony chest. "For thousands of years the Keepers have protected men from the Fae. It was up to us to blow it all. Our failure was so colossal that we undid the work of 10,000 years in just over three generations. Thank you for reminding me of that. All the work of the Keepers, undone by us. By me."

"That's not what I meant," I protested.

"Sure, but your effort to inspire me failed all the same," the old man said with an odd sense of triumph.

"Just look around you boy. Can't you see it for yourself? Men today are just puppets. They have no will of their own, no awareness at all. They're pushed this way and that by style and trend. They're not even capable of great evil. Mediocrity. That's what's left of mankind.

"What could you possibly do? There's nothing left but to wait for God to return and wrap this whole nasty thing up, if he even finds us worth the time for that."

"Has God abandoned us then?" I asked despondently. "Are we left all alone?"

"Don't try to blame God for all this," Sid warned me, pointing an admonishing finger. "He lets us make our own mistakes. This, all this mess of the world, this stinking pit of consumerism and pop culture whores, this is the disaster of a dwindling mankind."

"Now go boy," he said with a wave of his hand. "Stress is not good for my condition."

After he closed his eyes and settled back into his pillows I felt alone in the room. Alone again. This abandonment struck harder than the first. I had been lifted by a hope that there might be help for me, only to have that hope broken. The second cut deeper than the first.

Gerard was waiting for me when I stepped out of the dim room. A knowing half smile stretched across his face as he held out his hand to lead me back through the house. I felt sympathy come from him.

"Master Sid is in low spirits," he told me when we had reached the garden door. "Come another time. He may feel better then."

"So what he said isn't true?" I asked him. "We are not abandoned? All is not lost?"

"We are never abandoned," he assured me. "And you are never alone."

Something in the conviction of his words convinced me, if only a little. A small break in the clouds of darkness appeared overhead, and a thin slender of light broke through.

"We've had tough times before, desperate times," Gerard continued. "Faith has seen us through then, and it will see us through now."

Something in the butler's words, or perhaps in the way he said them, filled with a rich and deep wisdom, a wisdom only acquired with many years, made me think that his lifetime stretched back deep into antiquity. "How long have you been with the Keepers?" I asked.

"I have had the privilege of serving the Keepers for a very long time," he said in a way that suggested a staggering number of years.

"How long exactly?"

"Very long."

I nodded and turned to leave. Gerard held out his hand to stop me.

"If you ever find yourself possessing a peculiar thirst, a thirst for exotic things, I suggest you go to the old part of town. You will find there a bar called the Wounded Stag."

"The Wounded Stag?" I echoed.

"Yes, the Wounded Stag," he said. "Ask for a pint of the Hibernian Dark. The bartender will try to discourage you. You must insist. He will ask you why you want it. Tell him you are seeking. He will ask you what you are seeking. You must tell him, the Sacred Flame of Life."

"What happens then?" I asked.

"Who knows?" Gerard shrugged. "You may just enjoy a good beer."

Are we really alone?

It feels so at times. And certainly I am not the first to ask that question. But do we even know how to answer that? Or where to look for answers?

Some look to the stars, for life on other planets. Their idea of not being alone in the universe is having another race, another civilization somewhere out among the darkness of space that shares in the struggles of life.

If we did discover an alien civilization would that mitigate our suffering at all? To discover we are not alone in that way, would that make us feel any less alone? Would any new meaning be injected into our universe if we found civilizations besides our own?

The hope is that any alien race we would discover would be more advanced than ours, possessed of greater wisdom and technology. We imagine them descending from heaven like the gods of old, teaching us their secrets, sharing with us their accumulated knowledge. Maybe they would wipe out disease and old age and war. What then if they did? By simply solving all our mortal problems would that bring us any closer to solving that dilemma of existence that asks why we are even here?

I don't believe any advanced civilization could fulfill such a longing. Perhaps we would be fascinated for a while. Perhaps a new energy would enter our world for a time. But eventually I think we may feel alone again. I think after a time we would become disappointed in what we had received, become disillusioned with our saviors. A hope unfulfilled can provide greater comfort than a hope disappointed. What if that alien race came to our planet seeking to fill their own emptiness? What if they turn to us for answers?

No, I think that if we were to discover any inhabited planets we would not feel any less alone for all the people scattered among the stars. There would just be more lonely people in the universe.

There can only be one sufficient answer to the question of our loneliness. Is there a God? Our loneliness, my loneliness, would be mitigated not by others who live out among the stars, but by a power that has determined their course.

Another civilization is just that, another someone like us. So what if they are smarter, more powerful? They would make paltry gods. Would they not be made of the same stuff as us, subject to the same hungers and weakened by the same vices?

What we need is one greater than us, greater than this whole order of fallen and broken things. The desire stirs in all of us, rarely fully awakened, for a Father, for one who would give us answers that we couldn't understand, though we still hunger for the answers.

Then we wouldn't be the final authority in the universe. That responsibility would rest upon one more capable of bearing such a weighty burden. Maybe then, all might not be lost even if we were to lose it all.

But this God we search for has to be more than greater in

power or greater in knowledge. He must be greater in goodness too.

I look at these gods around us today, not only at those children of the gods, but the idols of our age. They possess a power greater than ours. What they must know would confound our puny little minds. But what are they? Grasping, ambitious creatures. I know little of their motives, only enough not to trust them. I have seen their coldness and brutality. And for all their power and knowledge I can't escape the certainty that their goodness does not exceed that of the average man, or even equals that of a savage and selfish man. What kind of god is that?

The true god is a good god. Only if we can look up to a being that is better than us in all ways can we admire him as God. It must be a moral superiority as well as an intellectual and effectual one.

Maybe that is our true longing when we ask questions about loneliness and our place in the universe. It doesn't matter if there are other beings out there. We need to know if there are better beings out there. Or at the very least, one in all the cosmos who is truly good and right.

The very thought warms my soul. Despite what else may happen, even if our age would consume itself in sloth and avarice and greed, there is still one that is good. There is still a rightness which flows through all things seen and unseen.

Then I would not feel alone.

I find myself caught in this strange place between misery and ecstasy. A gentle snow began to fall tonight, about two o'clock in the morning. The night is still, the street quiet around me. Above, the clouds take on a strange, reddish hue, like the blush of night.

I sit here on my balcony and watch the easy flakes of snow wander out of the sky and light upon the trees of my yard. The ravens have gone, at least for now. I wonder if this snow is holy somehow. I like to think it is. This purity that has wafted down from heaven covers my land with its sanctifying power. The corrupting evil of the ravens cannot stand it. I would like to believe as much. So they have fled.

Or at least that is how I choose to see it. The loneliness inside of me swells so much that it makes me ache. At the same time I am so moved by the beauty around me that I think I might also burst with joy. It is like being torn in two. Heaven and Earth war for my soul, and they threaten to rend me in two.

What a dark and wonderful place this life is.

I am alone, yet I am a part of all things, connected to all things.

I am everyone and I am no one.

I have reached out into the terrible swarm of oblivion.

I have touched the perilous solitude of consciousness.

I wonder how many more of these visions I can endure before they drive me mad. This one felt like it was tearing into that frail curtain I keep between madness and sanity.

Of course, the pale man appeared with this vision also. He is by far the most terrible part of the whole ordeal. In him is a fate worse than death. The vision itself doesn't hurt. It was, in fact, a quite happy occasion that I witnessed.

What do the details matter? What good does it do to either resist or rail against them? In many ways I feel more free than I have ever been, and at the same time I am ground in the gears of an unfeeling and uncaring machine, against my will and with no regard for my good. Is there no escape from this compulsion?

Is not every man in some way slave to the guile of the world? We trample over one another to get the next new machine. We scarf down mindless and popular entertainment without ever thinking to ask for something better. We are as oblivious as driven cattle, and just as careless.

I said it was pointless to complain, yet here I am doing just that. Sometimes I hate myself for being so pathetic.

The vision, though, the vision.

I walked out into the snow covered night. The falling from two nights ago still lay thick on the roads. The streets stood deserted and empty. The city's nightlife had quieted due to the snow as well.

I wandered down the white covered roads alone, enjoying the peace borrowed from emptiness. That special tranquility that comes when noisy places have fallen silent, a singularly unique tranquility, enveloped me in both body and mind.

A deep chill came over me, one that had nothing to do with the cold. The pale man stood blocking my path, his hand stretched out toward me. Fear touched me but not panic. I took a step back. He stretched his arm out further to me.

I looked to my left, at a house that had no lights in the windows. A for sale sign leaned over in the snow-covered yard. It had the empty look, of something long abandoned. The paint peeled off the weathered siding. A piece of rotting soffit hung down. One of the windows displayed a jagged hole in the center.

The door pulled at me. I distantly heard my boots crunch in the snow as I walked towards it. A moan sounded from the pale man, a sound like the sighs of the brokenhearted carried on the wind. The rusted knob turned easily and the door opened by itself. I stepped inside, offering no fight to the disorientation that came bubbling up with the darkness.

Light came slowly back to my vision, and as it did another season opened up before my eyes. The sky burned in orange and deep violet, the display of a magnificent autumn sunset. Just beneath the sky, the turning leaves blended in with the same colors. A few cedars and evergreens rose up, contradicting the fall colors.

A laugh sounded from somewhere nearby. Men gathered in

an open field, surrounded by the shifting colors of the forest. Three wagons came creaking into the clearing, pulled by oxen. Each one was laden down with barrels and bundles.

The men fell happily into the business of unloading the wagons. Each knowing his part, the work went on like a choreographed performance. Before darkness had fallen all the goods had been emptied from the wagons, tables set up, barrels tapped. A huge, roaring fire grew up in spouts of orange flame.

Other people began filing into the clearing: young girls in braids of flower and bright dresses, blushes on their cheeks and eyes wide with wonder, children running in unrestrained jubilation, mothers and fathers walking with irresistible smiles, rich men arrayed in clean clothes, poor men shuffling in their humble best. Finally, the elderly arrived, slower than the others but no less enthused.

It was impossible to tell what year it was. I felt I must be looking at the distant past. The people for the most part wore simple, homespun clothing. All classes gathered there. They all mingled freely and drank freely from leather tankards and clay goblets. Laughter echoed in the descending darkness.

When night had fallen completely a man dressed in what appeared to be branches and leaves stepped up to the fire. The crowd cheered at his appearance as he smiled through a mask of green foliage and waved a willow hand.

He spoke in a language I did not recognize. Though it seemed apparent he was telling a story, gesturing with vivid animation. Sometimes his movements were tender and small, other times wild and violent. The strange language he uttered rose and fell with the cadence of music. I almost believed I could understand what he said. I had the feeling he told an ancient tale of deep romance and high adventure.

The crowd acted as a perfect listener. When the storyteller dressed in green foliage spoke in hushed tones they listened quietly and leaned in close. They laughed as one, cried out in surprise as if on cue, and gestured back to the storyteller at certain gestures from him. And when it was all done, when the green man grandly bowed, they howled their approval.

Music rose up as soon as the story had finished. Pipes and drums and stringed instrument sounded into the night. Young girls danced around the fire while men young and old, watched in fascination and desire.

After a time of dancing an old man walked into the firelight. He exuded the aura of the holy, his long beard flowing down dark robes. In his right hand he carried a wooden staff with a single shoot and leaf peaking from the top.

The crowd looked upon the old man with reverence. They even inched back a step or two when he approached. It was much like the respect they gave the storyteller, mixed with a touch of fear.

As the priest spoke, I couldn't help but feel drawn in by the hypnotic quality of his voice. His dark eyes searched the people, his hand stretched out in blessing. They bowed their heads and echoed back his words.

The rituals lasted for quite some time. A bundle of wood was brought in ceremoniously. The priest threw it on the fire and sparks flew up along with brightly colored smoke. I could smell the rich clouds of incense reeling from the fire.

The people began to step forward, one by one, beginning with the richly dressed people. They each offered platters of goods before the fire. Some meat, some grain, some carved figures or other produce. The priest threw them all on the fire. After each offering, he dipped his fingers in water and sprinkled the foreheads of the supplicants.

With the sacrifices ended, the music took up again. This time, there was a decided ritualistic sound to it. The pipes drew out their sounds long and mournful. The strings accompanied with low and haunting cords. The drums were barely heard, nothing more than a distant rumble.

Young girls stepped forward, each wearing a white dress without sleeves, and began a slow dance around the fire. They moved in unison with large swings of their unclothed arms. Their bare feet traced circular movements in the dust. As they danced their hair swung freely with the rise and dip of their heads. Erotic undertones filled the dance, though subtle. As their bodies twisted, young hands traced their emerging forms. Red lips parted, heads rocked back in splashes of unbound hair and feigned ecstasy.

Somewhere outside the circle of gathered people the priest began a chant, words to the sound of strange music. The crowd stirred and parted, making a broad pathway from the priest to the fire where the girls continued their ritualistic dance.

A murmur rippled through the crowd. Hands pointed to the line of trees on the edge of the clearing. Something stirred in the shadows. Vague movements at first, then shapes, human shapes, stepped out of the trees.

About twenty in all, they moved with the fluid grace I immediately recognized. All clad in animal skins, the women wore short gowns, sleeveless and tied over one shoulder, the skirt rising high up their perfect and golden legs. The men had only this material wrapped around their waists, like kilts.

The crowd parted further as this group neared the fire. A hushed awe fell over the people. Only the young girls appeared not to notice. They danced on, their rhythmic movements circling the fire.

I walked closer to the gathering, fascinated by what was going on. The people who had come out of the forest joined in with the dance of the young girls. They blended in seamlessly, perfectly mirroring the dance.

With the arrival of the forest people, the pace of the dance increased and the energy of the watching crowd grew more palpable. Excited tension coiled about the people as the music grew faster. The drums beat louder, faster, dominating the increased tempo.

I knew exactly who these forest people were. With their fluid grace, and their perfect proportions, who else could they be? Still, I couldn't help but feel some surprise when Lord Daniels rushed by me, spinning in the air. Then Eladora passed with a whirl. There was no mistaking that striking beauty, no possibility that I could fail to recognize her.

Both of them looked different somehow, younger, though they both possessed a timeless youth. Especially with Danileoth, there seemed to be a lightness to his being that I had never seen before. Whatever darkness had cast its shadow over him was gone. I could see laughter in his eyes, what an earlier generation would've called gaiety. His body moved free of tension or burden, full of ecstasy.

The change in Eladora stood out less. She reminded me of a girl, spinning, stretching out her arms. A contagious smile spread across her face and laughter brimmed in her eyes. That glint of mischief that I remember still touched her. It was the look of a child who had just done something devilish and couldn't wait for it to be discovered.

The tempo of the music continued to increase. To keep up, the dance grew wilder and faster. Feet pounded the earth, and drums pounded louder, drowning out the pipes and the lyre. All I could hear were drums. Insistent drums, thundering, rumbling, awakening primitive spirits from the bowels of the earth. The crowd began to sway, half intoxicated by the sound.

A scream pierced the night. I jerked my head towards the source of the sound. A laughing Danileoth had taken a girl upon his shoulders. He burst through the crowd, carrying the girl who gave no other sound of protest.

As if taking a cue, the other men, the other Fae, grabbed a young girl of their own. Each took hold of one until all the dancing girls had been hefted upon a naked shoulder. Except for the single cry of alarm, they made no sounds of protest as they were carried off into the forest. I even thought I saw a smile on one of the young faces peek out through her tousled hair. No one in the crowd made a move to stop the abductions.

By now, the music had stopped and the Fae women stood still. With their backs to the fire they scanned the faces of the crowd. Eladora stood right across from me, her eyes moving lazily over the hushed and tensed people. That wicked smile of hers broke out again as her eyes locked with mine. She stepped into the crowd, impossibly, towards me. My heart pounded in my chest, anticipating what this could mean.

But no, how could it mean anything? She couldn't see me, of that I was fairly certain. And even if she could, would she even know me?

It was a young man she was after, one who stood just in front of me. She ran a finger up the length of his neck and plucked at his chin. The dazed young man followed as she pulled him by the hand, off towards the distant trees and darkness.

My head dropped, as did my heart. A pang of jealousy tore at me, gnawed an empty place where my stomach should have been.

What I wouldn't have done to be that chosen one. I tremble even to think of it. What bliss that young man must have enjoyed. To lie with a goddess, why the very idea is legendary. It is thought that such a thing can only be done in dreams. But there was a time, wasn't there? An age when men could walk with the gods. An age when men could share pleasure with the daughters of heaven. And what can we boast of? Machines? Cheap food and tawdry entertainment? What weak and unremarkable things we have become.

I became so wrapped up in my morose thoughts that I did not notice the change. A cloud of smoke passed over my eyes, then it became the frozen clouds of my own breath. The barren walls of an abandoned house replaced the roaring fire, the open clearing, and the forest beyond the darkness. I turned and looked out the window, into the front yard. The pale man still waited for me on the sidewalk.

We stared at each other for a moment, neither one of us moving. He didn't approach the house so I decided to look for another way out. The back door was bolted shut and had no latch on the inside. With no sense of panic I wandered around the house, waiting for the pale man to leave.

A dull melancholy weighed me down. I walked through the house listlessly, almost not caring if the pale man came in or not. I couldn't muster the strength to care. Our world, even if it wasn't doomed like Sid believed, has little in it worth redeeming. What point is there in fighting for such a joyless existence?

These thoughts echoed off the walls of the house. The vanity of our vain lives was wrapped up in them. I imagined the unremarkable lives that must have lived there. They came and went with hardly a notice from the world.

In one of the rooms upstairs an old Pac-Man sticker slowly aged on a closet door. Once, it had been placed there new and with pride. It struck me as an odd, and somewhat insane ritual. Why do we display the symbols of the things that we love, or the things that are popular? It's not like they make any political or religious statements. We aren't declaring any loyalties or pointing out our view on a certain issue. Brand icons, sports symbols, band emblems; what are we saying when we wear them? Is it an attempt to garner some reflected glory that we bare these symbols?

What was this kid trying to say when he put up the sticker on his closet door? I like Pac-Man. Or was it that since Pac-Man was considered great that by brandishing its symbol the owner of this room would also be considered great?

I can't help but think that there is something akin to worship in this. I will make you, Pac-Man, the god of this room, proudly wear your symbol, extol your virtues, carve out a place in my heart for you, love you, devote time and thought and energy on you. In exchange, you will give me your blessing. And one day, at the day of your eclipse, when you grow into an impotent god I will move on to other divinities appropriate for my age. Metallica, Nike, Red Sox will replace you. If I grow sophisticated, my devotion will grow to Kubrick and Kafka, my symbols esoteric and rare.

At any rate, Pac-Man became a forgotten god. His icon was left to dry rot on the door while the child, devoted to him so many years ago, left him behind without a thought.

Such mediocre gods we raise up. Is it any surprise that we are a mediocre people? Even the ghosts, the old presence of these gods that still haunt the vacant hallways, even they reek of mediocrity.

I turned away from the tattered icon and walked back to the front of the house. I looked out the front window and the sidewalk was empty. The pale man was nowhere to be seen. For the time, I am free again.

I don't know why I bother going into the office anymore. Erin isn't there. She works permanently from home now. As before, I mostly do nothing. Sometimes I go down to the floor where I used to work. Sometimes I pass by my old cubicle, home for how many wasted years I hate to even think about. It is occupied by another desk slave. When I go down there to look at the space I could tell my presence made the new occupant nervous. No doubt the poor guy thinks I am high brass. Technically, that may be true. No way for him to know it is just a façade.

Some strange attachment still has me bound to that desk. Maybe I yearn for the simpler years. There may well be a part of me that still wishes I had never opened that inner door to the deeper world. Even though that life was misery, it was also a life without burden. It allowed me to coast through life oblivious. Empty perhaps, but unaware of the emptiness.

Almost everyone else I see still occupies that oblivion. I can see it in their eyes. A dull glaze masks their features, a dimness in the gaze where light should be bright and blazing. Instead, there is only gray and shadow.

Every once in a while you see a flicker in another person. They may look up from their phone, or from the sidewalk right in front of them, and notice the world around them for a brief moment. Even more rare is the one who walks with that awareness almost all the time. One who sees life around him. That light in the soul, peering out through the windows of the eyes, is unmistakable. I can see it in them, they can see it in me. Few understand what it really is. There is a feeling of kinship, brief, just as our eyes meet. They pass their way, I mine. The moment does not linger. For an instant we don't feel so alone and hopeless. Then we are swallowed by the unfeeling mass again. Despair buzzes around me. Emptiness swallows up fullness.

Oh, but I live for those moments of shared light, brief though they may be.

My children were over to visit when a strange summons arrived. I think they begin to suspect something odd about my life. They look at me sometimes with a mix of confusion and mild fear. I try to ignore it. But when things like this happen, that proverbial elephant comes rumbling into the room.

My son and I were working on the truck, coming closer to completion. My daughter was upstairs, working on her part of a school project. We were all absorbed in our work. My son and I grew visibly excited as the truck looked more and more like what we had both envisioned.

"Dad," my daughter called out, uncertain tone to her voice. "There's a horse coming up your driveway."

Just as confused, I wiped my hands and followed my daughter to the front door. It took a moment to sink in. Just as my daughter had said, a beautiful, and somewhat imposing horse cantered up my driveway.

Not just a horse, a whole carriage came with it, pulled by the large animal. For a moment I thought it had ridden out of a fairytale. Opulence decked out the carriage, with gilded edges bordering the satin white paint. On the top four corners, cherubs silently blew brass trumpets. A liveried footman, complete with powdered wig goaded the horse forward with the driving whip.

As soon as the carriage came to a stop in front of my house, the footman jumped down and opened the side door. A man as lavishly decorated as the carriage – wig, walking stick, red, satin pants and coat, rings on most of his fingers – stepped down and approached me.

He struck an unusual pose with one leg forward, the back leg slightly bent like a half bow. With a flourish he produced a sheet of parchment, folded and secured by a wax seal.

"Lord Daniels graciously extends this invitation to you, Sir," the man announced in a droning English accent.

I took the sheet, painfully aware of the stares my children pummeled at me. The wax seal, impressed with a dancing stag, broke easily. Inside, a coat of arms headed the letter, followed by ornate scripts that read:

Bal Masque
Your presence is respectfully requested by his Lordship, Daniels
'e Dannae, to celebrate Imbolc, beginning at sunset

Dress for Grande Revel
Transport Provided

"What's a Bal Masque?" my daughter asked, reading over my shoulder.

"What's a Grande Revel?" my son chimed in.

"I have no idea."

I shouldn't even consider going. After what happened last

time, surely Daniels will try something similar. Why he doesn't just kill me, I don't know. Perhaps he enjoys the elaborate schemes. At any rate I won't give him the satisfaction of thinking I am afraid. I told the servant I would be there, though I couldn't decipher when exactly this event was supposed to take place or how I should dress for it. Erin is the only one I can think of who would know something like that.

I continue to worry about Erin. After going to see her, I realize that her condition has worsened. I was hoping a bit of rest and sun would help. It hasn't. Even worse, I don't know what is wrong with her. She hasn't gone mad, though at times it appears as if she has. Usually, she possesses a firm grasp on her mental state. Other times, completely unaware, she lapses into an odd stupor. Her eyes take on a distant, glassy look, the muscles in her face slacken and her mouth drops, just slightly.

I went to ask her about the invitation I received from Danileoth, but also to check on her well-being. A ring at her front door received no response. I looked around back, peered in the windows and saw nothing. Her car sat in the drive, so I suspected that she was still home. I tried the back door and it clicked open.

I stepped in cautiously and called out her name. No answer came. I crept through the house, calling out to her, finding nothing but empty rooms. Growing uneasy I made my way up the stairs. Her bedroom was also empty, the bed clothes ruffled and disorderly, very unlike her. The door to the spare room stood slightly ajar, and from there I heard what sounded like whispers.

That sense of unease grew at hearing the sound. It reminded me of a chant though I couldn't make out any words. There was that rhythmic repetition, giving the sound a somewhat magical cadence.

Carefully, I pushed open the door. My eyes widened, taking in the bizarre scene. At first I didn't even notice Erin standing

156

in the middle of the room.

Every bit of furniture had been cleared from the room. The emptiness was filled instead with arcane writings in black ink over every bit of wall and ceiling. Some I recognized as hieroglyphics or runes. A giant ankh occupied the wall that Erin stared at. Most of the other symbols were completely foreign to me, perhaps vaguely resembling some form of language. Arcane though it was, it possessed some sense of coherence.

When I stepped inside the room I noticed the red drawings on the floor. These too were written in symbols unknown to me. In the middle of the floor stretched a circle and pentagram, decorated around and inside with more strange characters. It was here that Erin stood, wearing nothing but a shirt that fell to her knees. Her skin had grown pale, her hair a disheveled mess. She stared at the ankh on the far wall and whispered low.

I called her name. She gave no indication that she heard. I leaned in close and listened. The whispers fell so quick and low as to make it impossible to discern what she said.

Reaching out my hand I called her name again and softly touched her. A small start shook her, and then all at once the glaze fell from her eyes as the light slowly returned to them. Recognition dawned in her eyes and she smiled weakly at me.

"Hello," she said in a hoarse voice. She reached out and touched my arm in a manner of familiar affection.

"Are...you okay?" I asked.

"Of course," she answered in a way that made the question sound ridiculous. "Just doing research."

Sheer horror passed through me at the thought of what research she might be involved in. By the looks of the strange drawings all over the room, including the ceiling, she must be peering into things sinister.

"You're supposed to be taking a break," I reminded her.

"Oh, but we had a breakthrough," she answered with a

weak smile.

Looking at her I had the thought that she hadn't slept in days.

"Come on," she turned and said.

I followed her down the stairs and back towards the kitchen to the basement door. After pulling the light on she took one step down the rickety stairs before furrowing her brow and turning sharply back to me.

"You're not going to steal these, are you?" She asked suspiciously. "The Alfar didn't send you?"

"Who?"

"The Svart Alfar," she said. "The whisperers. They want to steal the secrets for themselves."

"Erin, you were doing this research for me, remember? Why would I steal it?"

The furrow in her brow deepened and her lips pursed in concentration. She looked like one struggling to remember something, or worse, keep her grasp on sanity.

"That's right," she said and nodded to herself. She turned around and continued down the stairs.

A single bulb shed a curtain of light in the dark basement. It swung over a table covered in papers and books. One large volume lay open, it's yellowed pages written in an intricate and unreadable script, and the edge illuminated by meticulous scrollwork. I stared down in awe at the artistry and sheer size the book.

"Beautiful, isn't it?" Erin remarked. She reached out a hand and caressed the edge of the leather cover.

"What is it?" I asked.

"The Secret Book of Taliesin," she told me.

"And who might that be?"

"Taliesin was an old Welsh bard who lived around the sixth century. He was given the title Ben Beidd, Chief of Bards, or poets. Served at least three kings in his life, but is generally acknowledged as one of the greatest, if not the greatest, bard to ever live."

"And I take it this is his book then," I said, peering more intently at the pages. They certainly appeared old but in no way was I capable of dating the work.

"Secret book," Erin corrected, pulling the book towards her.

"There is a very famous Book of Taliesin," she said. "You can get a copy just about anywhere. This is the Secret Book of Taliesin. Most scholars don't even believe it exists."

"And what's so great about this book?" I asked.

"Taliesin was said to have possessed a knowledge so great and deep that he knew the secret heart of things and was gifted with prophecy and the ability to see into the past and future. More importantly, his work contains lots of hidden lore about the Fair Folk."

As she spoke she continued to caress the edges of the book. Her fingers ran lightly over the pages, like the soft touch of a lover.

"It was said that most of his knowledge was written in a secret book that was then hidden in a cave, guarded by enchantments and watched over by a stone hawk that Taliesin fashioned himself. He gave it the power of life by two magic gems, one red and one blue, that he fixed in its eyes."

"Doesn't sound likely to be discovered," I pointed out. "How could you have gotten hold of a copy?"

"Not easily," Erin agreed. "But according to legend a dark witch cut a piece of Taliesin's hair when he was laid out to wake. With the hair she made a glammer over her son, so he could look and sound just like the bard. So disguised the boy was able to get through the enchantments and take the book as the hawk watched on, believing her master had returned.

"But when the witch opened the book, she didn't know that another enchantment had been placed on it. Taliesin, in his insight, had written the book in a secret language, so that any who try to read it without the cipher would go mad. The witch clawed her own eyes out after trying for many days to decipher the secret language. After falling into poverty the son sold the book to a collector. The collector tried to make copies of the book but soon found it to be impossible. Just as the witch, all who tried to work with it went mad. Eventually, he discovered the only way he could make copies was to use an illiterate who could imitate the letters written without making any attempt to understand it. Thus, very few copies were made."

Judging from Erin's appearance and her earlier behavior it looked as if the promised madness had already begun to set in.

"Wouldn't that make this dangerous?" I ventured, gesturing to the book. "Maybe you shouldn't mess with this."

"Am I going mad?" She looked up at me and asked with condescension. "Should I also be careful about saying Bloody Mary in the mirror?"

"Where did you get this?" I asked instead of pushing the issue.

A look of confusion crossed her face. She paused, considering.

"I think I requested it," she said, uncertain.

"And where do you request a copy of a rare and hitherto unknown manuscript?" I pressed.

She shrugged. "I've gotten so many books lately I can't remember where each one comes from."

"Doesn't that sound odd to you?" I asked, hoping to arouse some suspicion in her. "This rare book just comes to you and you don't know from where? It's probably worth thousands of dollars."

"Well they did," she said emphatically. I could hear an edge of irritation creep into her voice. "I don't know what you're worried about anyway. Should I stop reading this because the curse of the bard might get me?"

"Well, I have something else I need you to look into," I said, eager to change the subject.

"And what would that be?" she asked with a total lack of interest. She had already turned her attention back to the book, her eyes tracing the strange script. I could almost feel her slipping back into a trance.

"I received a strange invitation the other day. It came from the same people I had you look into. From our mutual employers."

Her face lit up when she glanced at the invitation.

"A Bal Masque? Is this for real?" she asked with heightened interest.

"As far as I can tell."

"Are you kidding me? A real Ball? You are invited to a real, honest to God, old-fashioned Ball?"

"Well I'm not on the committee or anything," I said. "But in my experience with them so far, when they do things, they go all the way." Memories of my night in the Grove with them came to mind. If that was an impromptu celebration, I could only imagine how one of their planned parties would look.

"This might be one of the coolest things I've ever seen," she said, apparently forgetting the book for a moment.

"What is it?" I asked. "What is a Bal Masque?"

"Oh you know, one of the grand balls where ladies wear these long flowing dresses, and everyone wears a mask of some sort. At midnight there is an unmasking. It's so wonderful and glamorous, like a fairytale. There's nothing like it today. They were the most spectacular things in the world."

Erin had taken on a theatrical air, her eyes wide and wistful. A blush came over her face when she saw me staring at her. She giggled and put a hand to her mouth.

"How do you dress for one of these?" I asked. "It's Grande Revel attire. And it's supposed to take place on Imbolc. Whenever that is."

"February 2," she told me. "That gives us only five days. Actually four, since Imbolc begins at sunset February 1. Not a lot of time to get ready."

161

"No, Erin," I said with my hands out in a gesture pleading for reasonableness. "I know this sounds like fun, but it is actually very dangerous. The people hosting this are not bound by convention, and are in fact, quite powerful and not shy about using it."

"Oh please, you have to take me," she begged.

"Out of the question," I said. "These are the same people I had you look into. You know how powerful they are, and they are not fond of me. I can't expose you to that kind of danger."

"This may be the only time in my life I will be able to do something like this," she pleaded with me. Taking both my hands in hers she looked up at me with wide and almost tearful eyes. I could almost feel her shake with excitement.

"Please, please, please. I'll love you forever. And I'll be good. We'll be careful. I'll help watch out for you. You have to. You just have to. Please, please, please."

I know it was a bad idea to give into her. I know how dark and terrible Danileoth can be. Nightmares of his cat women meting out his punishment still haunt me. And I have already exposed her to greater danger than she deserves.

Another idea motivated me though, or at least I tell myself this. If I took her to this Ball, then she would see that there really are magical dangers out there. She would see and she would have to believe. She would know that this secret book she is looking into is really dangerous. Perhaps that is the only way to convince her. I must show her.

As I looked at that bright, lively face, it became difficult to refuse. This was the Erin I knew and loved. For a moment she was herself again. If I could keep her away from the strange things she was looking into, the things that made her face pale and her eyes dark, then that would have to be good for her too. She may even forget about her research in the process.

"On one condition," I said to her squeals of delight. "You have to put everything aside for a while to make sure we're ready for this. We only have a few days."

"Oh, I will. I will," she readily agreed. "Thank you. Thank you. Thank you. This will be so awesome. We will have so much fun. It will be like a story."

She pulled me tight into a hug and I already began to feel an ominous premonition about my decision. The best I can do now is watch her close and take all the precaution I can.

Sometimes I believe spring will never come. I am not one to mind winter so much. But this one has been so cold and so long.

Perhaps my perception is colored by the doom I know awaits us. Whatever sinister forces have gathered against mankind will soon move against us. Ignorant, we will be numb and powerless.

That is what this winter feels like. It is the gathering of all the enemies of goodness. The cold, dark reach of evil lives on the chill of this winter. It walks on the shadows of our long nights. I can feel it in the ground and in the air around me.

The Raven King comes. The Confounder. The Deceiver. The Lord of Despair. The servant of the Crimson King.

I don't know his face. His voice I hear on the wind. The ravens gather thick on the trees, waiting to devour my flesh. Waiting to devour my soul.

This winter will never end. For me. For all mankind. Whatever the season, cold and darkness have come.

The Raven King comes.

Two nights before the Bal Masque and I am irresistibly restless. Every inch of this house has felt my pacing and restless steps. The snows outside are full of my prints. I even stood at the entrance to the woods behind my house and contemplated going in. I stared into the path that wound beneath the ancient and gnarled trees but did not go in. Something about those shadows kept me away. Or maybe it was what the Fae had said about them. There are no woods behind my house.

Who the hell can decipher anything they say? Why should I care anyway?

Because I am tangled up in their game. Somehow, for some reason still unknown to me, I am not only mixed up in what they are doing, I am apparently some sort of obstacle in their plan. Me against the gods.

What futility it sounds like. What do they want with me? Why do they toy with me? What can I possibly mean to them?

To make matters worse, I am defenseless. Even against these ravens that gather so ominously outside my house. I can kill them. They always return. The only resistance I can offer is my defiance. That, I will hold on to until the very end.

I decided to go to the Wounded Stag, the bar Gerard told me about. Mixed success came from that venture. I learned much there, much I didn't know. What to do with this information I still have no idea. I wanted to find something like the Keepers. That didn't happen.

The bar is located in the old section of town, not far from where I live. I had never heard of it before, and decided to walk to find it better.

The place is hidden in plain sight. Right on a busy street, amid crowded restaurants and bars marked with neon lights. I found a hanging, wooden sign marking the spot, swinging from an iron arm. A faded drawing decorated the wooden sign – white stag rising up on two feet with a bloodstain on his side. Stairs beneath the sign descended under the street to a single wooden door.

Inside, the Wooden Stag looked like an old world pub. Wooden keg handles lined the bar. Men huddled over pint glasses. Smoke filled the room despite the city ban on interior smoking. Places like this defied convention out of custom. None of the patrons would care, or have it any other way.

A few stares followed me to the bar. Most didn't notice me.

I sat down on an empty stool and ordered the Hibernian Dark. The young man dispensing the drinks that night thought for a moment, then told me he would have to get someone else to pour it.

"Who thinks they can take on the Hibernian Dark?" a pleasant Irish brogue called out as a familiar figure stepped behind the bar.

We both took a moment to recognize the other. Then his face fell, disappointment clearly etched on his features. When he sighed I made the connection. It was Gareth, the bartender from my daughter's fundraiser, the one who had given me a taste of that special bourbon.

"Ah, it's you," he said in an attempt at cheerfulness. "Come to try the Hibernian, eh?"

"What can I say?" I answered. "You've whet my appetite for exotic drinks."

He smiled weakly. Reaching beneath the bar he produced a brown, leather tankard. Dust flew up when he blew into it.

"It's an old keg you know," Gareth said. "Probably no good now."

"Wouldn't hurt to try," I answered.

He shrugged and proceeded to wipe the tankard with a white cloth.

"It's got a real weird taste," he told me. "I've never met anyone who actually likes it. In fact, I think it's a failed experiment. The brewer needed to get it off his hands, so he gave it to us cheap."

"It can't be that bad," I countered.

"It's worse," Gareth said. "Like tar with pine nuts in it."

"I love pine nuts."

"Let me get you something else," Gareth offered. "Anything else. On the house. In fact, all of yours will be on the house tonight."

"No thanks. I'll just take the Hibernian."

A dark look crossed Gareth's face. His smile fell away and

he leaned over the bar towards me.

"Don't want to do that friend, trust me," he said with unfeigned earnestness.

"I don't, or you don't?" I countered.

"Why do you want it so bad?" Gareth asked me.

"I come seeking," I answered.

He paused here and searched my face. For what, I don't know.

"What do you seek?" he asked.

"I seek the sacred heart of life."

Another deep sigh and Gareth nodded in resignation. Flipping the tankard over he placed it under a copper tap, aged with a green patina. Dark, frothing liquid poured out.

"Been a long time since a seeker has come here," he said, watching the dark beer spill into the tankard. "I take it Sid hasn't croaked yet. Still rotting away in bitterness I assume."

I didn't answer. Not that he was waiting for one. He scraped off the top layer of brown foam and presented the tankard to me.

"Your Hibernian Dark."

I sipped carefully at the beer, wary of Gareth's warning. Caution proved unnecessary. The drink went down smoothly, full of sweet, malty flavor and a strong hint of molasses. As promised, at the very end, spruce washed over the back of my tongue.

"So what can I do for you?" Gareth asked after I had tasted amply of the beer.

I shrugged, and told him of my meeting with Sid and how Gerard had told me about the Wounded Stag.

"Come on, let's talk," he said, gesturing for me to follow.

He led me to a booth, one that was screened off from the rest of the pub. With him he carried a bottle of unmarked whiskey and two glasses. Sliding into one side of the booth he filled both glasses and handed one to me.

"Chase it with the Hibernian," he instructed. "It'll taste like vanilla.

"So what do you need with me?"

"I have no idea what I need," I confessed. "Things just started to happen. I don't even know what. I can't make sense of anything. Someone is trying to kill me, at least I think so. Crazy shit is happening that I can't explain. Or maybe I'm just going crazy. I don't know. Maybe what I need is the loony bin. I don't know. I don't know what I need."

A sudden swell of emotion took over me. For the second time I laid my story out as tears pooled in my eyes. He listened carefully and drank as he listened, nodding and asking questions at the appropriate places.

"Well, there's a lot of questions going on there kiddo," Gareth said apologetically. "What do you want to know first?"

"I want to know what's going on?" I said. "What's going on with me? What do they want with me?"

Gareth looked out thoughtfully over his shot glass. He tipped it back and quickly refilled.

"All right, how do I explain this?" he asked himself.

"Sid already told you a lot about Danileoth it seems," he said.

"Not really," I told him. "Children of the Gods? Whatever that means."

"It means what it says," Gareth explained. "The first thing you're going to have to do in order to understand what's going on is to forget what you think you know about the world. Got it? The world you know is a very predictable and regular place. It's ruled by laws you are familiar with and it carries on with all those forces and scientific principles modern man is so proud of. Yeah? What you see is what you get.

"Bollocks is what it is, all of it. Man has spent the last several hundred years trying to forget the true depth and nature of the world. Granted, he has done a damn good job. For the most part you've got this down; well-regulated cities and pretty decent explanations for the weird stuff. You've narrowed your world enough so that you rarely encounter anything extraordinary. And as long as you do that, you're blissfully ignorant. Problem is, it's all a lie.

"You see, as you are beginning to discover, there's a lot more to the world than meets the mortal eye. There are forces, there are powers, deep and dangerous. Some mean you harm, others are a bit more kind."

"But what do they want? These Fae?" I asked.

"Well, that's the real question," Gareth shrugged. "At one point they just wanted to stay alive. They wanted to flourish. Some did so by being nice, others by scaring the shit out of everyone. But that's all changed now, changed for a while now. Something is different. Their goals have changed."

"Changed? How?"

"They've become uncharacteristically focused. They don't seem content with the usual mischief. They seem to want something, want to do something. They're working together too, and that's unusual for them. Usually, they go a bit rogue. Here and there they might work together, but for the most part they fight with each other more than they get along. Lately, and I say this on their timescale not yours, they've all been getting along like one big happy family. And that frightens me. Really frightens me. What it is they're up to, I couldn't begin to guess. It's like the rules have changed and they're acting like different creatures. They want something. They want it really bad. And I feel sorry for any poor bastard who gets in their way."

"How long has this been going on?" I asked. "I mean the change in behavior. You said it wasn't always like this."

"About 400 years or so," Gareth answered. "Or that's the best guess. The Keepers didn't really take notice until about 200 years ago."

"How did the Keepers find out?"

"At first they just noticed a lack of activity. Then some of them started noticing that the Fae were getting involved in human affairs. Business, politics, religion, higher learning, you name it, all of a sudden you started seeing the Fae become an intimate and influential factor in every facet of human life. The Keepers began to see their hand on everything."

For once, things began to make sense to me. Memories of my conversation with Danileoth in the tower, the vision of his board meeting with the world's business leaders, all focused into something that resembled a coherent picture. Hadn't Erin mentioned something about shadow corporations, organizations behind the scenes that reached out all over the world. Now Gareth said it had been going on for at least 400 years. What they could accomplish in that span of time I couldn't begin to fathom.

"All right, the Keepers then," I moved on. "Who are they? What exactly do Sid and his people do?"

"What they did –" Gareth stressed the past tense. "The Keepers are, or were, the protectors of mankind."

"Should I even ask who they're protecting us from?"

"All things dark and terrible," Gareth answered with a toast and another shot. "Usually that includes the Fae and their offspring, or whatever monsters they unleash upon the world. There are also a variety of spirits, demons and otherwise unpleasant creatures that hunt the night and give men the willies. Stuff to scare children, that kind of thing. And the Keepers were always there to balance things out. They would win some, lose some. But for the most part they kept man safe enough to pursue his own life freely."

"How come we don't see these things?" I asked. "Especially with the Keepers all but gone? We can't be that good at ignoring the dark."

"You're better than you think," Gareth pointed out. "But you make a good point. Run-ins with evil and magical creatures has been happening a lot less. For a long time the Keepers thought they were just getting better at stomping out evil, that they were tipping the balance. What really happened is that the Fae had turned the heat down on purpose. The decline of the fantastic breaking into the normal world seems to have been part of the plan. Why? Who can guess? But it seems to have worked. The Keepers are broken. Danileoth pretty much rules the world. So even if all these nasty creatures return there isn't anyone left to keep them from having their way with mankind."

These words sunk into me with cold realization. I felt like the insect Sid told me I was. Or maybe this is what the gazelle feels like, knowing the lion prowls somewhere out there in the deep grass. We are prey. What can we do? We put up a paltry little fight, but we are at the mercy of our predators.

"Fine, they have their plan, or whatever it is. What does that have to do with me?"

Gareth gave me a searching look, rolling the empty glass between his fingers.

"That's what they're trying to figure out," he said. "You've become a player all of a sudden. They want to know why."

"I'm not a player," I protested. "What have I done? Up until a few months ago I was divorced, stuck in middle management, eating bad take-out every night. The only high point in my week was late-night soft porn on Cinemax. What do I have to do with all this? I get a fever and wake up to find myself in a 400-year-old war. I wonder sometimes if this is all a fever dream. Or maybe I lost my mind, like my temperature went too high or something. Now I can't tell the difference between reality and fantasy."

"Bit of a mind fuck, isn't it?" Gareth wryly observed.

"Is that what dweomer means?" I asked with a chuckle. "Is it the Celtic word for mind fuck?"

"Should be, but no. The important thing is not the dweomer you started, but the dweomer you've become," Gareth clarified.

"So I'm a dweomer now?" I asked, still not clear on the subject.

"Yes, but we don't call them that. That's what they call them. We call them gregori."

"And what exactly is a gregori?"

"It means the awakened ones, or the watchers."

"So that's what I am?" I asked. "I'm a watcher?"

"That's right," Gareth nodded. "When you started what they call a dweomer you became something new. You opened a door deep in your mind and woke up. You're different now and you know it."

The fever dream came vividly back to me. I could see again the tunnel under the mountain, the old man, the door opening, and then...whatever happened then, the dweomer, it doesn't matter. I woke up different. There was awareness in me, an awareness to me that I felt instantly. Then the strange things began to happen: Eladora, the visions, the pale man.

"Okay, so I'm different," I conceded. "So what? What now? How does that make me a threat to them or give me any part in what's going on?"

"That's the problem with you humans," Gareth said, pointing at me with his now full shot glass. "You don't realize how powerful you really are."

"You say that like you're not one of us," I pointed out.

He shrugged. "I'm not. At least not completely."

Recognition struck me when he said that. His charm and good looks, his knowledge of the Keepers and the Fae, his understanding of the dweomer and all these other strange things, it made sense now.

"You're one of the half breeds?"

"Elioud," he corrected. "We prefer to be called Elioud. But yes, we are only half human. The rest of our lineage, in my case my father, is of the Fae."

"But I thought your type was against us, on the side of the Children?" I asked. "Why would you help me?"

"Not all of us are bad," Gareth explained. "Just like everything else. Some want to help men, some wish them

171

harm, Elioud as well as Fae. I've been an ally to the Keepers for a long time now."

"So you can help me," I said, growing excited. The possibility of his kind of help made the odds seem a little more balanced, especially if he knew others like him. "Are there others like you?"

"Slow down there, cowboy," Gareth said with a hand up. "There are some of us who help here and there, but we don't get involved like the Keepers do. I'm available for special jobs upon request, advice, that sort of thing. We have to lay low, we helpers. If Danileoth were to get hold of us...well, you've seen his brand of punishment."

Visions of the cat women came back to me. I shuddered, hearing again the crack of bone in their feline mouths and the sound of the wet flesh they devoured.

"There's no one to help me then," I said, thinking I would have to face those cat women someday.

"Did you not hear me?" Gareth asked insistently. "You've got more power than you think."

"What power do I have?" I complained. "I can't do anything special. I don't have any magic."

"Who said anything at all about magic? I'm talking about power. There's a lot you have that I or Danileoth don't have."

"Like what?"

"Two things," Gareth said, indicating with his fingers. "Freedom and passion."

"Freedom?" I asked scornfully. "You seem to be able to do whatever you want."

"You're misunderstanding me. Freedom isn't about doing what you want. We all make our own decisions. But one thing we can't do is act outside of our nature."

"What does that mean?"

"I mean true free will," Gareth answered, growing animated. "You don't really know what it's like because you've never experienced anything different. You don't have a defined nature, nothing written in your being that tells you how you have to be. I mean on a deep, spiritual level."

"You mean like being good or evil?" I asked.

"Yes and no. Being good is an exercise of freedom. But what I mean is the ability to make choices not dictated by your nature, or determined by your nurture. It doesn't really matter what your genes say, or what your environment was like growing up. At least it doesn't matter like scientists and psychologists think it does. They treat the universe like it's a machine when it's really a living thing. Man more so than anything else. And you men really have a will that is free. Doesn't matter how you were born or how you were raised. At any time in your life, at every moment, you can make your own choices independent of any and all influence on your life."

"Then why don't we?" I asked the obvious question. "It seems to me that most people just mill around following the herd, or their base impulses."

"That's because most people haven't woken up and discovered what they're capable of," he said. "Or at least very few of you have. And while you still slumber you allow yourself to be slaves. Willing slaves, but still slaves. Whether by deception or fear or force, all slavery is willing. If you want to be free, you will."

"I don't really see how this helps me."

"Ha! He doesn't see how it helps," Gareth said incredulously. His hand came down and slapped the table. "Lord help me! It only means your made in the image of God. But yeah, that's nothing. Couldn't possibly help.

"Don't you get it? Creativity, innovation, acting in wild and unpredictable ways, mastering the forces of nature; all these you can do and more. There is a magic in you because of that freedom, a magic and a power that makes the gods tremble. The Fae may be strong, but they have nothing on man, at least a man that is awakened as you are. They fear you, my friend.

Someone like you can be a game changer. You can do something unpredictable, mess up everything they've worked for over the last 400 years."

I had a hard time believing what Gareth told me. Whatever power lay inside of me lay dormant. It was inconceivable that I could even be a mild irritant to Danileoth, much less a force he had to fear.

"What about passion?" I asked. "Where does that come in?"

"Ah, human passion," Gareth said with a smile. "That is the fire and fuel of life itself. There is no limit to its power. Its glory shines like the sun. We may have a touch of the gods in us, but that is true divinity."

"Don't you have it too?" I asked. "You're half human. Seems like you would have the best of both worlds."

Gareth shrugged and looked away from me. He played with the cup in his hands and refilled it. I could tell he was avoiding my eyes. Instead, he focused on the brown liquor in the small glass.

"Let's just say I have enough of both to know what I don't have," he said slowly and with obvious regret.

I felt it best not to say anything else. A sore spot had been touched, and it put Gareth in a pensive place. I could tell he nursed a deep and secret pain there. For once I didn't envy the Fae or Elioud. They may be powerful in ways I couldn't comprehend, but they were not free from the pains and miseries that inflict all living things.

"Is there anyone you know that can help me?" I asked, eager to move on. "Someone who can tell me what I ought to do?"

"There is one who's been trying to, but you've been avoiding him so far." Gareth said. "This pale man."

"You've got to be joking," I said. A trickle of fear crept into me at the mere thought of the dark clad stranger. "If anyone is dangerous, it's him."

"Oh, he's dangerous all right," Gareth agreed. "But not to you. He's your guide. He is sent to help you with these visions."

"That can't be," I said. "I feel nothing but fear when I see him."

"That's because he's powerful. A thunderstorm doesn't mean you any harm, yet you shrink from it all the same. That's because it's powerful. It can hurt you without trying. This pale man is the same way. Being that close to that amount of power is always frightening."

"Look, you don't understand," I argued vehemently. "You haven't been near him."

"And you won't find me near him. I play in thunderstorms and I won't go anywhere near that guy. Still, he's the only one that can really help you. He's the only one that can tell you about these visions. You've been given them for a reason."

"That just can't be," I said, sounding like a child trying to talk his way out of a shot. "Anything but him."

"Sorry lad," Gareth replied. "I feel for you, I truly do. I wish I could put a different spin on it for you." He shrugged to communicate his helplessness. "The fact is that he's appeared for all these visions. He's a harbinger of them. There's no doubt he's the guide. It's happened before, you know."

"Oh yeah? To who?"

"Every single one of the Keepers," Gareth said with solemnity, emphasizing his point by jabbing his cup at me.

"They had to go through this? They had to confront the pale man?" I asked, feeling intense sympathy for them.

"Every single one," he said. "All part of the game."

It was my turn to withdraw into pensiveness. I felt a profound respect for the Keepers, for anyone who could face anything so powerful. At the same time I felt an anticipatory pity for myself. I knew, one day soon I knew, I would have to face whatever terror he possessed. The price of my awakening.

175

"I see I've hit you with a lot at once," Gareth said. "Take some time to let it sink in. But remember this."

Gareth leaned across the table and grabbed my arm. He looked into my eyes, intense and serious. Something of the same power Eladora possessed emanated from him. Nothing overt, just an emphasis on his words that made them feel extremely important. It was like he could bold or underline them by the tone he used.

"You must confront this pale man," he spoke to my mind and soul. "Your awakening is not complete without it."

I am a fool. To think even for a moment I could play with the gods! What an idiot I am! How did I not see this coming? I put myself into their hands as if the rules of the world I know matter to them at all. And not only my life, but Erin's as well.

I am a fool.

A full five days ago Erin and I attended the Bal Masque. Five days! And only today did I realize the great passage of time. To me, it was only a night. What happened to those other days I can't begin to guess. Each time I venture out with the Fae my lost days increase. Time is a funny thing with the Fair Ones. It becomes slippery, moving in jumps and starts, or not at all.

As promised, Erin had figured out not only how to outfit us for a Grande Revel, but had acquired all the necessary trappings. I felt ridiculous in the get up she dressed me in. I looked like a dandy from the seventeenth century.

"That's the point," she said when I protested.

Embarrassment flushed over me when I looked at myself in the mirror. The only solace was the mask that went over my eyes. I doubt it detracted much from my light blue, silken coat and matching breeches, the ruffled shirt with massive cuffs flowing out of the jacket, and the stockings tucked into black, leather boots. Erin even strapped a rapier to my side. She only laughed at my discomfort, assuring me everyone else would be dressed same.

"I think you look dashing," she said, admiring me in the mirror.

It was easy for her to be comfortable in this situation because she looked absolutely stunning. Her curled hair framed a face that I noticed had regained considerable color. Like me she also wore soft blue. The dress clung tightly to her waist and breasts, then flowed out in voluminous pleats. She lifted the hem to show me her satin, embroidered shoes.

"Just like a fairytale," she observed, placing her mask on. It was much like mine except for the peacock feathers that flared out the top. I didn't bother mentioning to her how much like a fairytale this actually was.

Misgivings still plagued me about taking Erin along. I had to keep pushing away the thought that I was exposing her to great danger. But just look at her, I told myself in consolation. I had never seen her so happy, like a teenager about to go to her first formal dance. Whatever distress she had been under these past weeks seemed to be erased completely. She appeared light and joyful, like one embracing life. I was happy for that.

What I didn't want to admit to myself is how relieved I was to just have her company. It had nothing to do with safety. There was nothing she, or anyone else, could do to protect any of us. I was glad simply because she was there. She made me feel not so alone.

"Don't worry, I told you you look fine," Erin said, misreading the signs of consternation on my face.

"I hope I'm not making a mistake," I said, turning to face her. I really meant it.

"Everything will be fine," she assured me. "You will see. This will be a legendary night. We will remember it forever."

She was certainly right about that. She was so right it was prophetic. I will remember that night forever, whether for triumph or tragedy, is much too early to tell.

As if on cue, the sound of distant horse hooves fell on our ears. Erin gasped and gripped my arm in a spasm of excitement.

"No way, horses," she exclaimed, and darted away.

The same white, gilded carriage that delivered the invitation drew up in front of the house. Erin beamed. I had to smile, forgetting for a moment the danger I knew certainly waited.

I had to admit, the whole affair did have a distinct, fairytale feel to it. The driver of the carriage, capped in a white wig, stepped down with the bow. He opened the carriage door and held out his hand to Erin. She entered with all the grace of a queen, though I gather it would be hard not to look regal outfitted as she was.

I slid in behind her on to the plush, leather seat. The carriage door closed and it fell dark inside except for a lantern that burned beside me. The first signs of disconcertment passed over Erin's face as she noticed there were no windows to the carriage.

"This is how they travel," I remarked.

She shrugged and fell to admiring the carriage interior. I reached over to look at the bottle of champagne waiting in a bucket of ice, and poured us two glasses. The carriage rattled and pulled forward.

The ride itself began ordinary enough. We swayed to the movement of the carriage, chatted and sipped champagne to the sounds of hooves on asphalt and the flow of passing automobiles.

"I would kill to see their expressions," Erin laughed, indicating the people outside on the roads.

I felt an odd certainty the cars and people outside the carriage had no idea we traveled among them. I kept this to myself.

Eventually, the sharp ring of hooves on pavement gave way to softer sounds. The carriage rattled a bit more, indicating a change to dirt roads. Then without warning, the car shuddered and jerked, like it had fallen into a hole, then stood still.

"Are we there already?" Erin asked.

"I don't think so," I answered, hoping we had not gotten stuck in a pit somewhere. The image of us walking back to town, dressed as ridiculous as we were, had me cursing myself for agreeing to such a preposterous outing.

I reached a hand to the carriage door, when we jerked forward. Erin cried out and fell into me.

"What's happening?" she asked with a quiver to her voice. "Is that supposed to happen?"

"It's fine," I assured her, though not believing it myself.

She continued to hold on to me as the carriage picked up speed. Without reference to the outside world it was impossible to say exactly how fast we were going. But I could tell it was fast, and feeling faster by the moment.

Tentatively, Erin let go of me. I released her with reluctance, relishing the heat of her presence, the smell of perfume that surrounded her.

The carriage lurched again and I felt the unmistakable sensation of being lifted into the air. Erin steadied herself and gave me that pleading look for reassurance. This time, I could only shrug my shoulders.

"You did say it was going to be a legendary night," I reminded her.

She sneered at me, then laughed despite herself.

"Just please tell me we're not in the air," she pleaded.

"We're not in the air," I complied dryly.

She slapped her hands over her eyes. "How is this possible?" she asked. "We're on a horse drawn carriage."

What could I say? Any explanation I could offer would sound ridiculous. Better, I figured, that she discover for herself.

We soared for several minutes before it felt like a descent began. With some preternatural sense, or perhaps an affinity with man's native place on earth, I felt the ground approach. I could see relief visible on Erin's face as well.

A small rumble, then the sound of hooves on the ground returned. An eerie sort of reality sunk into me. Until then, I hadn't realized the sound of the horses hooves had ever stopped.

Not long after we touched down again, the carriage came to a stop. Erin and I waited in silence for a few moments, expecting the driver to open the door for us. When it became clear this was not happening we crept out on our own.

Our feet crunched in the powder of newly fallen snow as we stepped out of the coach. A pink tint lay over the ground, reflecting the light of the fading sun. All around us stood the tall trees of ancient and undisturbed forest growth.

"What now?" Erin asked, looking around. She appeared every bit like a story book princess; her flowing gown, twisting curls set against the innocent beauty of her face as she turned in wonder amidst the backdrop of the snowy wood with the sunset spilling over the scene like paint on a canvas.

"Not sure," I shrugged.

We walked over to the other side of the carriage and found a path carved out in the snow. Smooth paving stones formed a small road recessed into the white powder. It led straight to a soaring, though decrepit, structure.

It would be impossible to identify the architectural school of the building in front of me. For it was only a single wall, nothing else remained of the building. At first glance it reminded me of a cathedral. The long windows tapered off to a pointed arch. Fluting decorated the corners and edges. Here the cathedral similarity ended. It appeared too light and thin. Spikes and angles stuck out in a very non–cathedral manner. And it possessed a decided asymmetry, that while splendid and carefully artistic, defied definitions.

"My lady," I said, stretching a hand out to Erin.

She smiled and delivered a small curtsy before placing her hand in mine. The cleared path in the snow was wide enough to accommodate us both and I ushered her along it like I thought a noble lord should.

We passed under the arched doorway of the crumbling wall together. In the fading light it looked as if it shimmered when we walked through. It could very well have been a trick of the eye or a glimmer of the fading light. But the shiver that passed through me at the same time was unmistakable. And by the tremble in Erin's hand I knew she felt it too.

Once through the arch we walked over a stone floor in equal disrepair as the wall. A single figure waited at the far end. A herald by the looks of him, he was dressed much like our driver and held a decorative staff. He stood rigidly at attention at the top of a white, marble staircase.

A gasp escaped Erin's lips as we approached the stairs. Below was stretched a vast, snowy landscape, as far as the eye could see. In the last light of the sun a garden maze could be made out in the distance to our right. To our left lay a forest, sheathed in the cold of winter. But it was what lay directly below us that stole Erin's breath.

At the foot of the marble stair a host of dancers, arrayed in all sorts of splendor, twirled about in a grace of motion that I doubt has ever been witnessed by human eyes. The sight was unbelievable. I can hardly fathom any human body moving in a way I saw them move.

The timing, first of all, was impeccable. Machines could not move with such perfect synchronicity. Even the smaller movements, the dip of the head, the flick of a hand, was carried out in flawless unison.

As incredible as the timing was, it didn't compare with the sheer feats of dexterity I witnessed below me. The dancers executed moves that should have been impossible with the human body. Women spun while tipping at forty-five degree angles. Men somersaulted and pivoted on one hand. Ladies pirouetted on one toe in the palm of their partner's hands who held them either over their heads or straight out in front of them. I can't tell you what an odd site it is to see a man with a hand casually outstretched with a full grown woman spinning on his palm. And all this in time to the orchestra that played beside them.

"This has got to be a dream," Erin gasped. I was only hoping at that point that I wasn't expected to dance.

Before I could say a word the herald thundered his staff on the top of the stairs. The sound rumbled through the air. The music fell silent and the dancers stopped their impossible motion all at once. Every head turned and looked up. The feel of 100 alien eyes, all peering out of masks, bore into us. Erin gripped my hand and I could feel a cold sweat break out over her palm.

"Lord and Lady Avalon!" the herald boomed, then stretched out a hand to indicate we were to pass down the stairs.

Thankfully, the music started back up and the dancers turned away from us and rejoined their revel. I took Erin down the stairs, painfully aware of how out of place we were.

"Who is Lord and Lady Avalon?" she whispered to me.

"Apparently us," I answered. We both laughed and some of the tension relaxed.

At the bottom of the stairs a new marvel presented itself. The floor the dancers raced across shimmered as if made of pulsing tiles of color. We walked along its edge, admiring first the dancers, then the strange floor that glowed in strange twists of color.

Then the floor underwent a more dramatic shift, turning completely blue. As I stared at it small figures began to swim underneath. I realized it was a picture of the moving ocean beneath my feet, appearing as if I stood on a glass pier.

The dancers continued on, not seeming to notice the strange transformations of the floor. Even when it shifted again, this time to reveal the earth from a thousand feet up, they missed not a single step of their intricate and impossible movements.

I recoiled and stepped back. The illusion, if it was an illusion, appeared so real I thought we really might be suspended high in the air. I saw through the floor, beneath the blur of quickly moving feet, a mountain village far below. It wasn't until both my feet felt the snowy earth beneath them that the queasiness in my stomach completely subsided.

Mixed in with the dancers walked those servants particular to the Fae. Both male and female servants worked the floor, carrying trays. As usual, they were very young, very beautiful, and wore only tunics that left their chests bare.

One of the serving girls bowed to us and stretched forth the silver tray she carried. Erin looked with alarm at the girl adorned in beautiful, red curls, and seemingly unashamed at her partial nakedness. She didn't make any move to take hold of the wineglasses offered. I reached past her, took hold of two golden stems and handed one to Erin. The girl bowed and hurried away.

"What...what...that poor girl," Erin stammered as she watched the servant retreat. "She can't be more than sixteen."

"If that," I remarked.

"What is this?" she demanded. "These kids don't even have shirts on. Shouldn't we...should we do something? This isn't right. It isn't."

"I don't think these people operate by the same rules we do," I told her.

"These are kids," she insisted. "You don't get to pick which rules you follow. My God, they could be slaves. How could this happen? People just can't do this kind of stuff. I don't care who you are."

"Look around you, Erin," I said, taking her by the arm.

The army of dancers continued to whirl by us. Most were dressed as we were, imitation of the seventeenth century nobility. But we also saw more exotic dress from different eras. All the dancers wore masks as we did, and when they passed they turned their heads to fix their eyes unmistakably upon us.

The floor beneath us shifted again. This time, the shine of stars and galaxies, and the dark of space appeared beneath the dancers. They all twirled like tops, spinning around the floor as if moved by unseen gears.

"Think about how we got here. Ask yourself why no one looks cold."

"What place is this?" she whispered in a voice that carried a touch of fear.

A familiar scent drifted on the wind as I opened my mouth to speak. Before I turned I knew who would be approaching me. Even knowing, I couldn't be fully prepared to lay eyes again on that divine form.

I turned, and Erin followed my gaze. Eladora walked towards us, masked as the others, but unmistakable in her identity. She was dressed as a Celtic princess, or in what I always imagined a Celtic princess looked. Even with the mask, though, a princess of any race never looked so stunning.

A cream colored gown adorned her flawless figure, the sleeves long enough to almost cover her hands. The dress accentuated her beauty perfectly. It hugged her hips close and swooped down in the front to give a tantalizing view of the smooth, olive toned skin over her neck and chest. A gold belt hung loosely around her waist matched with a circlet on her arm. Two braids fell down the side of her head. A blue cloak, with swirls stitched into it finished the look. As usual, I was stunned by her immortal beauty.

"You two aren't going to dance?" Eladora asked with a smile as she approached.

"It looks a little dull for us," I answered, feeling playful with her around. "We were both hoping for a more complex routine."

"Well met," she said in a puff of smoke.

Eladora drew near to me, her eyes fixed on mine. Unable

to resist I returned the stare. I became vaguely aware of Erin pulling up closer beside me.

"I was hoping you would be here," Eladora said. She stepped even closer. I could smell the exotic spices that emanated from her. A fierce heat began to pulse through me, even to the tips of my fingers.

"I've been thinking about you," she continued. Her eyes darted briefly to Erin then back to me.

"Save a dance for me," she said. One of her soft fingers reached out and touched my cheek.

Both Erin and I watched her retreat through the crowd of dancers. Without any apparent effort she passed through them untouched, nor did she disturb the dance in the slightest.

"Who was that?" Erin asked with more than a touch of defensiveness in her voice. I hope she had not noticed my helpless staring. But it was just that – helpless.

"That," I said. "Was Eladora."

Erin whipped a questioning look at me. Her mouth opened to ask the inevitable question but no sound came out. I shrugged and sipped at the cup that had gone untouched in my hand. The warm taste of spice and fruit flowed over my tongue.

A boom sounded that shook the air. All the dancers stopped and turned to face the herald at the top of the stairs. Beside him a couple waited in regal stillness, both dressed in the fashion of Egyptian royalty – white, cotton tunics, headdresses, sandals laced up the calf in leather thongs.

"The divine Osiris!" announced the herald in a voice that carried out over the winter air. "And his consort, Isis!"

This time the dancers did not resume. They waited in respectful silence as Osiris descended. Once he had reached the dance floor the people separated, opening up a path wherever he walked. That path happened to be right to Erin and me. The crowd parted in front of us and the godly couple approached.

"The reborn god greets you," the Osiris dressed man said to me with a nod of his head. I knew immediately by his voice and bearing that it was Lord Daniels – Danileoth, that stood before me.

The woman I didn't recognize. She stared out blankly, seeming to register nothing. Her hand rested in Danileoth's almost absently. The smile on her face reminded me of one subdued and dully thrilled by medication.

"Lord and Lady Avalon, at your service," I said with a bow.

"Lady Avalon," Danileoth repeated, looking Erin up and down with obvious interest. He reached a hand out towards her.

Erin gingerly offered her hand as he pulled it towards his mouth and kissed her fingers. He looked up at her face with hungry eyes, the gaze accentuated by the mask he wore.

"A lady indeed."

"Would you care to entertain me with a dance?" he asked.

Erin blushed and looked to me for help.

"I...I don't know..." she stammered. "This looks...I don't know this..."

"Nonsense," Daniel said with a wave. "Simply follow my lead. We'll start with something simple."

Without waiting for a reply he handed me Isis and took Erin. She laughed nervously but allowed herself to be led away.

Danileoth stopped and jerked his head back towards me.

"You haven't gone into those woods behind your house, have you?" he asked sternly.

I shook my head.

"There are no woods behind your house," he said and led Erin into the crowd of waiting people.

Once Danileoth was in place the orchestra began a slow waltz. As promised, the dance was simple. From what I could see Erin kept up adequately. Through the brief glimpses between swirls of costumes I saw her smile turn from one of rattled nerves to pure enjoyment.

The pang of jealousy at watching the two dance surprised me. It was ridiculous I know, especially considering how moments before I had helplessly stared at Eladora. Perhaps it was because I knew I could never compete with the attentions of a god. If Danileoth wanted to take her from me, he probably could without effort.

The girl beside me seemed not to care or notice. She stood passive, her eyes glazed with a drowsy smile. Like everyone else there, she was quite pretty. Though unlike everyone else, she lacked that liveliness of feature you expect from a normal human being.

"Pretty amazing, isn't it?" I said, trying to engage her.

"It's magical," she answered with a lost sound in her voice. "Tonight will be magical."

"Yes it is," I agreed. "Do you live around here? Wherever here is."

She didn't answer at first. Her fixed and listless stare remained on whatever invisible visions kept her so rapt.

"Magical," she whispered. "Tonight will be magical."

"She is a freshman at the University," Eladora said from behind me.

I turned as she walked around me and the girl dressed as Isis. Eladora didn't pay her the slightest glance.

"Last night she sat alone on the quad, dreaming of home," Eladora continued. "She misses the wide open spaces of her hometown, the river a few miles outside of town, the old farms, her grandmother's Victorian house. While she dreamt of these things Danileoth came and promised to give her all the lost magic she longs for. She won't remember most of this, only that she experienced something amazing beyond words to describe. It will be a dream that haunts her the rest of her life, a longing that gives her pain and pleasure all at once. In nine months she will give birth to a child whose eyes will remind her of that lost magic. He will be the only consolation

187

in a life that will never equal the longing that hides in the deepest recesses of her heart."

A surge of pity welled up in me for the unlucky girl. Her only sin had been dreaming of home at the wrong time. She had fallen into the hands of these cruel gods that stalked the world like bandits in a lawless country. A cursed life waited. And to Danileoth she was only a decoration for a night, a moments pleasure, a brief distraction.

I can see it already written on the girl's vacant features. I turned to voice my frustrated rage to Eladora, but found that she was no longer beside me. A few yards ahead I saw her walking off into the snow.

Who could say why I followed her? It was not unusual for Eladora to disappear. That was her nature. But something about her retreating figure enticed me, called out to me. It had to be something she did on purpose. For whatever reason, I felt an irresistible urge to follow her and I trudged out after her.

As if she felt my presence, Eladora walked faster as soon as I began to follow.

"Eladora!" I called out to her. She turned to me then began running through the snow. Spurs of desire dug into my soul and I too broke into a run. Surely, I thought, I could catch up to a woman running in a dress.

What a fool thought that was. Eladora, perhaps looked like a woman in a dress, but she was of the Fae. She is of that race of creatures that makes sport of men.

She always stayed in front of me no matter how fast I moved my legs. Almost without effort she moved further away the faster I ran. My lungs burned with the cold air rushing in. I ran in futility, even thinking myself a fool for running after her. And then I ran harder.

She stopped at the entrance of the hedge maze I had seen from the top of the stairs, and turned to look at me again. The lure in her eyes called out across the snowy distance. I felt the tug on my soul, the deep stirring in every fiber of my body. She waited until I came close enough to see her bewitching gaze, then plunged into the shadows of the hedge.

Winded, I reached the maze entrance. With hands on my knees I stopped to catch my breath. Clouds of air billowed out of me in great puffs, gleaming blue in the moonlight. The air was still except for my breath. A heavy silence fell over the night.

Softly, the sound of feet crunching in the snow rose up. A figure appeared within the hedge, shadowed in the night, then ducked down one of the many pathways. Ripples of laughter bounded off hedge and snowfall.

What happened next, happened as if in a dream. I felt myself moving towards the turn in the maze, following the figure that appeared and laughed. I heard the sound of my own laughter, distant though, like the laughter of another. A fog settled over my mind, a sense of it all being surreal. At the same time my mind lit up with a deep awareness, every sense suddenly acute and feeling every atom of my body.

I chased Eladora through the maze. Echoes of laughter led me on, like Theseus' yarn, guiding me through twists and turns I hardly noticed.

Glimpses of flowing hair disappeared behind another turn, then another. Laughter beckoned me again. I followed the invisible skein, towards damnation or salvation I could not tell. Nor did I care. Hell and Heaven were all the same to me. They all rested in the countenance and gaze of Eladora.

The swell in my heart rose as I pursued her. A hook set in my flesh, it's barbs pulling at my veins. Pulling. Pulling. Feet ran without thought. Heat swelled in cold air.

I could have followed her by smell alone. Rich spices mixed on crisp winter air. Long ribbons of exotic scent trailed behind her. Intoxicating, opioid and dense, forbidden highs in long forgotten oriental dens.

And laughter, always the laughter. Mocking music and the

promise of ecstasy. Tantalizing. Rich with the sound of summer. A summer long ago. I, a young man. Fresh in love. Watching the girl with strawberry blonde hair and a dust of freckles across her nose. She wore a thin, white shirt over a pink bikini top and cut off denim shorts pulled over half sunburned legs. A painted toe played in the sand. Salt air drifted over the waves. She laughed too, and kicked water at me while we strolled the beach at sunset. At night we watched the stars blaze unashamed overhead. We lie side by side on the dark sand. I reached out and touched her fingers. They wrapped gently around mine. Bliss for me then. Such simple bliss. Wisps of hair tickled my face as she nestled into my shoulder. Stay moment, you are so beautiful. Stay, and never pass from this fixture of time and space.

But summers pass. Forever and forever they fade. And only the listless scent of longing remains. We dream as old Odysseus dreamt, in the bed of aging Penelope. Only the longing remains. Only the dream. The agony of age that has not spent its youth. Empty hunger and dark wanderings of half sleep.

All of this I heard embedded in Eladora's laugh. It was magic that pierced my heart. And I chased on. I can't say how long. Days? Hours? Surely not that long, but an eternity and more.

A turn in the hedge and I found myself in a vast garden covered in snow topped trees. A rocky outcropping rose in the center, the dark rock standing in stark contrast to the snow all around me. Smoke drifted from the top like a dormant volcano.

I closed my eyes and shook away the remaining haze. Passion still burned in me. At least I had my senses, or so I thought.

Eladora's shadow peeked out from a tree, then disappeared behind it. I ran to the tree and found it deserted. She didn't even leave tracks in the snow.

Laughter sounded again. I turned to see her shadow ducked behind another tree. I ran to that one also and found she was not there.

Laughter again.

This time I didn't turn.

"Why do you do this?" I asked, exasperated even as I still raged with desire.

"Do what?" she asked in return. Laughter in her voice. Could she do nothing but mock?

"Why do you torture men? Do you hate us that much? Do you despise us so that you toy with us and use us as your playthings? You hate us for our weakness?"

Crunching snow sounded close by. Eladora's scent filled the air. I could feel her behind me. I could even sense a hand stretching out to me, but I didn't turn around.

"We don't hate you," she said, stepping closer so to that I could feel her heat and the wind from her breath on my neck.

"We don't hate you at all. No, we love you for your passion. There is nothing in all creation that feels or loves as fiercely as man. The fire that burns in your hearts would consume you. But do you shy away from the flame? Do you turn from this fire?

"No, you embrace the flames and you feed your all-consuming passion. You reach out towards that which would consume you. You even seek it out, sing about it, praise it. It's a power so overwhelming it clouds the mind, it numbs your reason, it even pollutes your judgment. But do you run from it? You run towards it. How many of you men have risked their reputation on a single night of love? How many risk their lives for a moment of desire? You would even die for love of country or freedom or the triumph of your faith. What a magnificent thing this human passion is. And we gods can only look and marvel and lust after it.

"Why do you think the gods would shun the affection of their own kind and take a mortal lover? Your fire may be brief, but it blazes hot and bright. Ours is always the colder love. Believe me when I say that there is nothing so powerful and deliciously intoxicating as the fire of human passion. We Dannae crave and hunger for it because it is something we cannot have of our own. And we all crave it. Some more than others. I more than any."

Her presence drew even closer as she spoke. I felt her tender and full lips brush my ear as she whispered to me. Her hands reached out and took hold of my arms and pulled me close. Her body was so near to mine I could not help but tremble.

"I am addicted to man's love," she confessed softly. I can't express to you how those words thrilled me.

"I crave it more than air. I thirst after it even more than the ambrosia we used to eat when we sat at our father's table and he fed us with his own hand. It is a thrill like none other. So I cannot hate you. I can envy you. I can covet you. I can hunger for you. But no, I could never hate you."

"Why me?" I asked without any thought to my words.

"Passion has all but left men today," she said. "What once was a blazing fire sputters weakly in the modern soul. I have starved for many years while men waste so much of that vital energy. What little they have is tossed away on idle pursuits.

"But you, you burn like the men of old. You blaze like men did when they made themselves into legend. Your fire is the fire of life – the real flame that Prometheus stole from Olympus. That was always the lure of the dweomer. And that was always the danger."

Could it be the gods envy us? Hadn't Gareth said the very same thing? Perhaps, though it was hard to think I had anything to envy when I stood shivering in the snow, in complete thrall to Eladora and her magic. I felt like a child, an adolescent boy about to ask a girl out for the first time. To think this was what the gods envied – how the world is different than what we reckon it to be.

"What do you want from me?" I managed to ask a weak voice.

She walked around so that her eyes looked up into mine. I saw the universe reflected in her eyes. "Kiss me," she said. Electricity shot through every cell in my body.

"Kiss me like a man kisses a woman whom he loves with all his heart. Kiss me like you would trade the world for the touch of my lips. Kiss me like you want to devour me, consume me. Make your rapture mine. Give me the fire of your touch and the passion of your heart."

It was the same request that Mesulina had made. I could feel, though I don't know how, that she used none of her strange powers on me. Something about what she wanted required that it be a free gift. If there was any compulsion on her part, it would all be empty. Still, I couldn't refuse her.

No words can describe that kiss. The whole world melted away, the cold and the snow and all the danger and fear I felt, all ceased to matter. At the same time, they mattered even more. Is that nonsense? Yes, it is. But such are the magical things of life.

I took her head gently in my hands. She didn't lean forward to meet me. Our lips touched and the heat I felt roiling in me passed to her. Again, it was just like the encounter with the merrow woman.

At that moment, I realized the truth. I could feel Eladora feeding off of me, consuming my fire. She moaned and pulled me close, her warmth stoking the flames of my heart. The more she drew from me, the hotter I burned. I felt the well of energy inside me empty, then fill up again, over and over, as if it drew from an inexhaustible source.

She pulled away from me abruptly. A satisfied smile crept over her face as she readjusted her mask that had fallen askew. I still raged inside, my desire pulsing as wildly as ever.

"Don't think me cruel," she said, reaching out a hand to touch my cheek. "If I don't satisfy you completely it's because

I adore you. It's not what you think. I'm not like the others who would take all your fire. See? We both can benefit, can't we?"

I had no idea what she was talking about. All I knew is that she pulled away from me, turning away and walking through the snow towards the rocky promontory in the center the maze.

It took a moment for my mind to register what my eyes saw. I moved to follow her on weak legs that almost buckled with the first step. A sense of normalcy began to slowly fade back in and assert itself amid the rage of my still inflamed desire.

I pursued Eladora up the narrow path that was cut into the dark rock. About half way up the mound the path turned into a dark grotto. Still led by passion I plunged into the dark cavern without fear.

It took a moment for my eyes to adjust to the darkness. Some light glowed in the distance, illuminating the turn in the tunnel ahead. Sounds echoed off the rock: a grunt, a low, gurgling laugh, excited talk, the ring of metal on metal.

Was this another of Eladora's games, I wondered. I stepped through the rough tunnel, desire mingling with anger, and turned the corner into a small cavern.

Orange torchlight sputtered in a wall sconce, throwing up black smoke. It mingled with the water that dripped down the cave walls. My mind, reeling as it was, could barely take the details in. I had eyes that only wanted to see Eladora. Only when I realized that she wasn't in the cavern did I notice the hunchback. He leaned forward, working on some black structure that dominated the cramped space.

"Ah, there she goes," the hunchback muttered, adjusting a metal rod in the structure.

I stared in curiosity, first at the deformed man, dirt and grime smeared his swollen face and his thick fingers moved with surprising dexterity. Then my attention drifted to the black, metallic thing in the middle of the cavern.

It was impossible to tell exactly what I looked at. Dozens of black, metal spikes of different heights rose up in a pattern I could not quite discern. They reminded me of teeth of different sizes, each one terminating in a slanted knife edge. All the spikes were connected at odd places by girders running in geometric patterns through the whole structure. In the middle of these jagged teeth rose a central tower, dominating the structure. Reeded with thick bulges this middle tower stretched higher than all the others, also tapering to a slanted point.

"She's a beauty, ain't she?" the hunchback said as he adjusted a rod in the maze of dark metal.

"What is it?" I asked, taken in by the grotesque structure.

"Ha, what is it? What is it? He asks what it is," is all the answer I got.

"It's not as beautiful as the one we built at Shinar," he continued. "But styles change and that one was torn down. Oh, torn so cruelly down. She was beautiful. Yes, very beautiful. Shinar shined across the whole plain. But they tore it down and styles change. They change and we build new things, though not as beautiful."

"Yes...it's quite interesting," I said, thinking of no better complement.

"Interesting, he says. Ha!" The hunchback muttered. He pulled a file out of his dirty apron and began working on one of the prominent spikes. A flurry of sparks flared up as he ground the metal impossibly fast.

He worked without any notice of me. Every once in a while he would muttered to himself or laugh. Only every third word was intelligible. He seemed to love the terrifying thing that he built as most of the muttering was affectionate talk directed at the odd array of dark spikes.

I watched him for a moment then remembered the elusive Eladora. A pile of tallow candles lay on the cave floor

195

underneath the sconce. I picked one up and lit it off the torch. I found the tunnel again on the other side of the cavern and plunged in with my little candle.

It wasn't until the sounds of the hunchback faded that I began to think how foolish my venture might be. The cold of the rock tunnel closed about me. Water seeped out of the walls. My little candle fluttered in the damp breezes. Stories of men lost in caverns warned me, too late, of my folly. Fortunately, after a short walk, the candle lit on stairs that led back up to the surface.

I stepped out of the dark to a stone archway, and back into the winter night. A forest of old and looming hardwoods surrounded me. Dim pockets of blue moonlight filtered through the gaps in the trees and lit the snow-covered forest floor.

Somewhere in the distance the sound of the ball, still in full swing, came floating into my ears. I followed the sound, picking up a woman's laughter amid the swell of music, the clap of hands and a man yelling something out. Damp from the snow began to seep into my boots and I began to feel the cold in earnest.

Just before I reached the edge of the forest, a clearing opened up in the trees. I stopped at its border staring in amazement at a circle of glass paneled coffins. Moving among them was the hunchback I had just seen in the grotto. This time, he was wiping the glass of the coffins with a cloth.

"You," I called out, more amazed at the reappearance of the hunchback than the circle of glass coffins in the forest. "How did you get up here?"

"Eh?" the hunchback grunted and swung his head towards me. He squinted as I approached, looking me up and down.

"Get where? What you talking about?" he asked gruffly.

"Ah yes, the grotto," he then said in understanding. He turned back to polish the coffin that lay in front of him. "You must've met my brother, the architect."

I looked closer, past the obvious resemblance. For one, this man was much cleaner than the one in the grotto. And for all his rough manner he still came across more amiable than his counterpart.

"So what is it you do?" I asked.

"I am the caretaker," he said, not looking up from his work.

I stepped closer to one of the glass-paned coffins and wiped away the thin veneer of frost. A pale face, cold and still, appeared in the frame. Red lips stood out against the milk white skin of a young girl. Snow White came to mind. But there were dozens of such coffins.

A tickle of warning teased the back of my neck. I walked to the next one and looked inside. A boy this time, blonde and as still as marble, slept peacefully inside. I cleared the frost off a third and found another young girl within.

"Don't smear the glass," the hunchback complained. "Here, if you want to look inside use the cloth."

"Are they dead?" I asked.

The hunchback paused in his work. A stubby finger tapped on the pane.

"Not really," he said. "Not really sleeping either."

"Then...then what are they doing?"

"They keep winter company," the hunchback told me. "It's the only way to get spring here early. We need a lovely couple to keep winter from getting lonely. And it's been so long since we've had new ones. The winter is not given up easily. He needs company you see. Maybe this Imbolc will be different. They told me it would."

Something about what he said made that touch of fear grow until the hairs stood up on my neck and my blood ran cold.

"What did they tell you?" I heard myself ask.

"They told me to get the beds ready. It's been so long since I've been out here, you see. Not that it's my fault. The

Children don't care for Imbolc like they used to. Or any of the other old rites for that matter. They don't watch the fire so carefully anymore, or dance for the spring, or frighten the children at Samhain. Sure, they went too far sometimes, but that's the way things go. No reason to just ignore it altogether.

"Not my fault the place was so dirty. They don't care anymore, so why should I? What good is a caretaker for those who don't care?"

The ramblings of the hunchback faded into a hazy background. Panic throbbed in the forefront of my mind, and clawed at me with cold insistence. I turned to see two other coffins sitting apart from the others, their glass lids open and waiting. Somehow I knew. I knew with certainty these waited for me and Erin.

"When?" I asked the hunchback. "When is this going to happen? When are you going to fill those two coffins over there?"

"They're not coffins," the hunchback said. "They're beds."

"Beds...whatever," I said as urgency filled my voice. "When will they be filled? What time is this supposed to happen?"

"Why at midnight," he said as if it were the most obvious fact in the world. "At the unmasking. That's when the Children show themselves for what they really are."

"What else could it be?" he continued, seeming to talk more to himself than to me. He bent to his work again, wiping down the glass panes. "They can't really use their power as long as they are masked. Well some, but not all. No, they have to be unmasked. Yes, unmasked. You look at them that way and who can resist them? Why no one, of course. Because they have no masks. Not as beautiful perhaps, but indeed..."

The hunchback's voice faded into the night as I bolted out of the trees. A long expanse of open field stood between me and the Bal Masque. I could see it in the distance, what seemed like miles across snowy field. The costumed figures didn't dance anymore. They mingled with one another, laughing and talking. A fire burned at the head of the dance floor, blazing high on a tripod.

"Prepare to unmask!" a voice cried out. Cheers rose up in response.

"Midnight comes! Midnight comes!" another voice called.

Snow hindered every step I ran. The dance, and Erin, seemed impossibly far away. I churned through the snow, praying to close the distance.

"Ready!" someone announced. The crowd began a countdown in unison. I tried to make my legs move faster. Cold air burned my lungs like acid.

The countdown had reached five when my feet slapped against the dance floor. I burst through the thick crowd, shoving people out of my way. They only laughed at me, their hands at their masks, ready to pull them away. Some stepped in front of me as I shouldered through. Rough hands shoved me in the back and I sprawled on to the shifting tiles. A volcano roiled in spouts of lava beneath the floor.

I jumped to my feet, ignoring everything but the faces before me, desperately searching for Erin. The countdown reached one when I saw her. She stood, laughing with a group of masked revelers, oblivious to the danger that smiled back at her.

"Unmask! Unmask!" boomed the command over the crowd.

Without thinking I ripped a cloak from a woman's back and dove at Erin. She cried out as we crashed to the floor. I held her tight to me, one hand holding the cloak over us.

"What are you doing?" she yelled as she struggled against me. "You're hurting me! Let go!"

"Don't look, don't look," I warned her. "Trust me Erin. You have to trust me. Whatever you do don't look up at them."

There must've been something of mad desperation in the sound of my voice. Erin looked up at me and nodded. Traces of fear appeared across her face and in her eyes that widened so the whites stared back at me.

Awful sounds rose up outside the cover of the cloak. Popping of bone, flesh being forcefully ripped, the sound of tearing and rending assaulted my ears.

The floor had turned a slate gray color. Shadows morphed across it. Human shapes rose up into things tall and grotesque. Erin trembled in my arms as a low growl rose up, her eyes held tightly shut.

One of the shadows approached where we lay desperately covered. It lingered over us. Bony protrusions stuck out of monstrous and twisted shoulders. Two glowing, red eyes flared up. I felt their hungry stare on me. It was Danileoth, I'm sure of it. There was nothing but malice in that look.

He left us alone, though. Somehow we had escaped his plans, inexplicable as that may sound. Why didn't he throw off the cloak and subject us to whatever evil he desired? He certainly possessed the power. What could I have done to resist?

He didn't though. Acting under whatever strange laws govern him, he left us alone. His red and hateful eyes stared at me, then left amid the scatter of clawed and leathery feet.

Erin and I remained huddled under the cloak. Long after the last sounds had faded we still clung together beneath our meager shelter. Cold air began to seep in as the temperature plummeted.

After long minutes of silence had passed I threw off the cloak. All the revelers had gone, replaced by a thick mist that hugged the ground. Moonlight dissipated through the fog lighting the night like a gray predawn. A shiver passed through me, as I couldn't help but notice how haunted the place looked. All the stone, even the stone floor beneath our feet, looked old and weathered. It resembled nothing like the bright and happy place it had been just moments before. The quiet was unsettling.

"Is it safe?" Erin asked, holding tightly to my arm.

I nodded and pulled her towards the stairs. We passed through the ruined wall, and back to where the carriage dropped us off. We found no sign of the carriage, neither did we see anything to take us home again.

"What do we do?" Erin asked.

I had to chuckle at that. We had by our best knowledge flown there. There was nothing at our disposal that could get us back home. Home for us could be as far away as the moon.

"I guess we walk." I shrugged. I reached out my hand and Erin took it in hers and we started off down the road.

"It was a fun ball," Erin said tugging on my hand. "And who's to say I'll ever go to another one again?"

"Well, that's something to brag about if we ever make it home," I said.

"We'll make it," she said, sounding more calm than she should. Perhaps she was just relieved to be away from whatever horror we narrowly avoided. Sometimes when we narrowly avoid great danger, a small danger seems extremely manageable.

The path took us into a forest. Great oaks arched over our heads, shading out what meager light the night offered. We held close to each other, talking little. In fact, hardly a word passed between us until we saw a little stone building with light spilling from its windows.

"You think it's..." Erin asked, trailing off a question.

"Safe?" I finished for her.

"I was going to say, normal," she corrected.

"No way to tell. But I think we're still pretty far from normal."

We stood for a moment staring at the building that tempted us with its warmth. The stone walls held up a red, tiled roof. Brown timbers made up the windows and trim.

We stepped closer and peered in. The windows were bubbled and contoured, so that although we could make out movement from inside, and hear the noise that you would expect to come from a village pub, we could not make out anything for certain.

"I don't think we'll find anything better," I said, trying to allay my own trepidation. "This might be all there is for miles."

Erin gave me a nod and I pushed open the door and stepped in. Warm air and noise spilled out with rich, yellow light. All at once the noise fell silent. A quick glance around the tavern told me that the stares directed at us had nothing to do with the costumes we still wore. I don't think a more eclectic group of people existed anywhere in creation.

The inside of the pub looked normal enough. Round, wooden tables filled the space along with benches lined up along the walls. Patrons sat among them talking and drinking out of mugs. A fire burned on the far wall and a long bar took up most of the back. Barrels and bottles piled behind the bar above rows of copper taps. The normalcy ended there.

Every person that stared at Erin and me looked to be from a different age or nation. One man wore silk, Chinese robes. Another was outfitted in the armor of a medieval knight. What looked like an Aztec warrior sat at one table next to an Australian aborigine. I picked out a sixteenth century explorer, two men in togas, one in animal skins and a few dressed in materials and styles I had never seen before. One man even looked as if he had stepped from the set of a science fiction movie. He wore a shiny, black flight suit, and a dark helmet rested on the table by a frothing mug.

"Don't mind the stares," a friendly voice called out from behind the bar. "We just never know what's going to walk in next."

I nodded, noting at once that none of the stares directed at us carried any trace of hostility. The faces wore open and curious expressions, even kind ones. More than one nodded a welcome as Erin and I made our way to the bar.

"What will it be?" the bartender asked, smiling at us. He

struck me at once as a handsome man. His eyes were a sharp and rich blue, and blazing with intensity. For some reason I found myself thinking of fire.

"Well, I was hoping you could help us," I ventured. "You see, were kind of lost. Not sure how to get home."

"Ha! Sounds familiar," a man said beside me. He wore a leather flight jacket.

"Welcome to the Inn of Lost Souls," the bartender said grandly holding his arms wide.

"And where exactly is this place?" I asked.

"Hmmm, that's a little difficult to answer," the bartender said. "This establishment is not any where in the literal sense of the word."

"How can that be?"

"Let's just say it rests in the junction of many places. So it is really nowhere and many wheres all at once. Understand?"

I shook my head.

"Figured," the bartender shrugged. "Doesn't matter really. Wouldn't help you if you did."

Exhaustion welled up in me deep and powerful. A combination of the long, harrowing day, and the strange nature of this other world drained me completely. I wearily rubbed my eyes.

"Look, we're tired and lost and have no idea how we got here or how we get home," I said, almost pleading. "If you could help us at all or give us any information, whatever I can do to pay you, I will. I promise."

"Peace friend," the bartender answered, and I believed he meant it. "Just sit down. Relax. Have a drink. You'll feel better, I promise."

With a resigned shrug I fell into a bar stool. The bartender started to pour out a beer, stopped, shook his head, and reached for a bottle. He presented to me a silver goblet filled with clear liquid.

"I think this might be what you need," he told me.

"Water?"

"Hardly," the bartender said. "Lonicera. A very rare drink. It's full of spring."

I lifted the glass closer to my mouth. A sweet, floral aroma wafted up. I took a tentative sip, tasting flowers and a sharp sweetness like nectar. My head filled with images of field upon field of wild lilies and roses. It tasted like the bud of new life. An irresistible smile broke over my face.

"Good? Yeah?" The bartender asked.

"Outstanding," I marveled. Never have I tasted anything so unique in my life.

"Lonicera," I whispered, letting the word linger on my lips, as sweet as the drink itself.

The bartender pulled out a cloth and began wiping down the already shining bar. He hummed a tune to himself I found at once familiar and foreign.

"So..." I began. "Everyone here is as lost as I am."

"Not in the same way," the bartender shrugged. "But yes, in one way or another they are all lost. Just not like you are."

I nodded, uncomprehending. Strange enough though, a part of me did understand. Or at least it felt that way.

"You see, this place, this one we're in right now isn't at the same here as the place from where you stepped in from. You stepped in from one here to another here. Where you were and where you are are not in the same place. Or in the same when for that matter."

"So where was I?" I asked, trying to get a bearing on the situation.

"That was an odd place too," the bartender laughed. "Very few mortals walk those realms, especially where you're from. You were in what many call the Eternal Realm or Other World."

"Eternal Realm?"

"Land of the Fae," he explained. "Fairyland. Dreamscape. Spirit realm. Tir Na Nog. Call it what you will. It's all the same."

"And what is it exactly?" I asked. "And how do I get back?"

The bartender stopped his cleaning and thought for a moment.

"Imagine all creation as a tree," he explained, spreading out his arms like the branches of a tree. "Now imagine that on the tip of every branch is a world, a different world. Where you were, the Eternal Realm, is a step closer to the trunk of the tree. A level up."

"The Eternal Realm," I said for clarification.

"Yes. Imagine there are levels of existence, all existing on top of each other and touching one another. They interact and affect each other, but creatures of one realm rarely pass through to the others without special powers or under special circumstances."

"So how did I get here?" I asked. A feeling of doom began to settle over me. I was more lost than I knew.

"I'm sure I don't know," the bartender said, going back to polishing the wood surface. "Someone of great power would've had to get you through. Or maybe you passed through a gateway. You remember passing through a gateway?"

Several options for a gateway passed through my mind. I shrugged, thinking of the trip over in the carriage without windows.

"I guess I'm pretty damn stuck then," I said out loud. "How the hell am I supposed to find a gateway?"

The bartender shrugged and took up humming again.

"You shouldn't worry about getting back," he told me. "That is done easy enough."

"You know how to get me back?"

"Like I said, the place we are now is not the place you were before. Once you passed through that door over there you stepped into this place, which is at the junction of many places. Just because you stepped through from one place doesn't mean you'll step out into the same one."

An odd sort of understanding began to shine dimly in me.

"So this enchanted realm I was in," I said. "I stepped out of it when I stepped over your threshold, into whatever nexus this place is."

The bartender nodded in agreement.

"But when I step out I could be somewhere else entirely different."

"Precisely."

"Any chance you can make that my living room?" I asked.

The bartender only smiled and kept to his work. One of the toga–clad men stepped up to the bar and ordered another round of drinks. They were efficiently produced before the bartender spoke to me again.

"No need to hurry off," he said to me. "Stay, rest a bit. You need it. I can tell."

"Honestly, I could rest better knowing I got us back in one piece."

"There is no place you can rest better than here," the bartender said with earnestness that came from deep in his blue eyes. "You're safe here. Nothing can harm you as long as you are behind these four walls. Relax. Release all that tension you have bottled up inside."

A strange power carried on the sound of his words. That, and the expression in his eyes had a powerful effect on me. All at once, the tension that had been building up in me over the past few months burst out from wherever I had been storing it up. The fear, the uncertainty, that awful sense of powerlessness and doom; all these tempestuous and morbid feelings came crashing out of me like a flood.

I wept. No one said anything or pretended to notice or even made any move to comfort me. They let me weep as the tears rolled unrestrained down my face and I moaned like a broken hearted old man.

"I don't know what to do," I bawled as soon as my crying

slowed down enough for me to talk. The words still came out choked and sobbing.

"I'm scared. I'm confused. There's all this weird stuff going on and I have no idea what to make of it. Something terrible is about to happen, or has happened. Or maybe the world has turned into a terrible place without us knowing it. And I don't know what to do."

"And above all, I'm alone," I confessed this most painful of my hurts. Tears came pouring out anew.

"I'm all alone and there's no one to help me. There's no one I can turn to. No one wants to get involved or if they ever were involved, they've given up already. And I just wish I wasn't all alone."

Another glass of the Lonicera was pushed to me. The pilot beside me patted me once on the back. I drank the clear liquid that tasted like spring and the tears slowly receded.

"You're never alone," the bartender said when I had fully composed myself. "I know it may seem that way at times, but you aren't alone. It may be little consolation to hear it now, but one day you will discover how un-alone you are and always were. You must believe that.

"As to all the mysteries and uncertainties you are facing, all I can tell you is that there are answers to the questions you seek, though I do not have the answers. Those you must find on your own. Those you must discover for yourself. That is your burden. But the answers are out there. They await for you to uncover them."

I nodded, still indolent, though comforted by his words. I felt a great weight had been lifted off of me. The tears had cleansed me somehow. There was a lightness in me that made me smile.

"Don't suppose you could give me a hint?" I only half joked.

"What would be the fun in that," the bartender answered. "The whole adventure in life is figuring these things out for ourselves."

"Oh what a blast it is."

"Does that sound like fun to you?" I asked, turning to Erin.

Erin didn't answer. The lids of her eyes had fallen down so she stared out of narrow slits. The muscles of her face had relaxed, her mouth slightly open. She looked to be under the effect of a mild sedative.

"Erin?" I called to her, alarmed at the startling change in her appearance.

"She'll be fine," the bartender said. He regarded her somewhat coldly. "She doesn't belong here, that's all."

"What you mean?"

"She was with you so she was permitted to enter," he explained. "She doesn't belong here. She will remember nothing of this place or anything that was said here."

"She's no danger to you," I said emphatically.

"That is yet to be determined," the bartender said, continuing to stare at Erin with a somewhat hostile look. "Her course is not completely set. But she has the potential to be more dangerous than she seems."

"No matter," he said, brightening. "We will afford her whatever safety we give to you. She will be fine."

With reluctance I allowed her to be as she was. She sat perfectly still, features glazed over but otherwise unharmed. There seemed no arguing with the bartender anyway. He was resolved in the matter.

I allowed the restful and easy atmosphere of the Inn to overtake me. More of the Lonicera was served and more was readily consumed. I talked first to the young pilot beside me then moved among the tables to engage the various and strangely dressed men who shared the mysterious public house with me.

Never in my life have I mixed with such a crowd. Neither have I heard such wonderful tales of exotic places. One man even claimed to have come from a place where magic is common, and men called magi are regularly employed to exercise it like we employ a doctor or carpenter. He even said... ah, but what is the point of going on and on? It was just one of several long stories I heard that night, a night that could have lasted several months.

But this night grows late. My hand cramps with writing. I've been sitting here all day in order to get the events down while the details are still fresh in my memory.

I don't know why I work so hard to do this. Will anyone ever read them? Will they even care? Will I be as alone in posterity as I am in life? Will the ripples I make on the water of time ever be noticed, or ever matter?

Regardless, I feel it does matter. It may be I will never see the full impact of what I do, but I feel it is important all the same.

Anyway, I spent the night talking and drinking with the men there who looked so different from me but were very much like me. After the hours grew long the bartender led me to a room by candlelight. I collapsed into a bed and turned over to see him regard me with the sad expression.

"What is it?" I mumbled sleepily.

"I do not envy you the road that lies ahead," he told me. "It will be difficult. And you will be seriously tested. You must be strong and believe, for much hangs in the balance, for your world as well as many others. But believe and all will be well. Persevere and all will be as it should be."

"I wish I could be certain of that," I said, feeling sleep quickly overtake me.

"There is no certainty," I heard the bartender say as he turned away and the nighttime shadows fell over me.

"There is only faith."

I awoke sometime later with my back resting against a small pine tree. Jumping up I looked around in alarm, but the pub was nowhere in sight. A light fog lay over the morning, casting a gray, dawn light. Though I found myself still in the forest, there was something familiar about it. It took a moment to notice, then my eyes fell on the trash scattered about the scrub trees. Somewhere nearby the unmistakable hum of a car engine faded in and out of the still morning.

Excitement overtook me and I ran, crashing out of the small wood. The relief that washed over me when I saw the streets of my own city is beyond description. A sigh sounded from deep within my soul. I was home. Or at least home enough.

It took a while to get to my actual house, walking through silent and empty factory yards and into the streets that surrounded my neighborhood. Few cars were out at that early hour. The ones that did pass slowed down to look at the ridiculous figure I cut, traipsing about in my powder blue, 17th-century formalwear. A car full of young men nearly stopped so one could hang out of the window and yell at me.

"Time for high tea Lord Queer Bottom!" he yelled in a fake British accent, mimicking the tipping of a teacup with his pinky sticking out.

Laughter sounded out of the car as it sped off. I smiled despite myself.

Home came into view as the fog dissipated and the morning began in earnest. Five newspapers scattered about the front of my house. Five? I stood for a moment and stared at them. Five days.

How could I have been gone five days? The travels with the Fae are strange in many ways, and it seems I lose more time with them at every new venture.

Not that I would ever join their company again. Our hostility was in the open now. Why? I still can't say. But it seems clear they see me as an enemy. For whatever reason, I've been marked as a threat to their plans. Maybe I should be more deliberate in that.

Too much to think about now. The night is late. I've been

writing all day and exhaustion seeps into my bones. But it's down now. This part of the story is written. Tomorrow brings...what?

No, I won't think about that now. Let tomorrow worry about tomorrow. For now, I rest.

The Sixth Vision

It's funny how things can change so quickly. That's life. Your momentum can move so inexorably in one direction, every event in your life ruled by one grim inevitability, and just when you believe that nothing will ever change, something happens to reverse the course completely.

Maybe I exaggerate too much. But much has changed for me. In the course of a single day, a single event, I no longer feel my life hurdles on a crash course with tragedy. I still think I am to die soon, perhaps before the winter is over. What I feel about that death has changed. I no longer think of my death as a tragic affair, the swallowing up of one man in the gears of an indifferent machine, while the world moves unchanged by the man or his death.

No, my death will mean something. How or what I don't know. I'm still not entirely sure what's going on around me or what part I am to play in all these strange events. But I am learning. Or at least I'm learning enough to know that my situation is not as desperate as I thought. Though the forces that have arrayed themselves against mankind are powerful and vast, they are not invulnerable. There are powers beyond these powers, those which move me, powers that have chosen me.

I may die. I will die. But my death will not be tragic. My death will not be meaningless.

My death will be heroic. Perhaps it will mean more than my life.

That is not for today. Perhaps it may never come to pass. I doubt it. I can't say why. May it be enough that the hour is not yet upon me.

After getting home from my strange adventures at the Bal Masque and the Inn of Lost Souls, I slept for the better part of a day and another. When I awoke the following morning, my thoughts first turned to Erin. I leapt out of bed, dressed hurriedly and drove over to her house. No answer came from the bell. I knocked on her door, windows, called out her name,

215

all to no avail. I peeked inside and saw no signs of her being there.

My anxiety for her grew deeper. I couldn't be sure that she had even returned safely from the other night. And if she hadn't, what could I possibly do to get her back?

Sick with worry I drove back home. Had I not been so lost in thought I certainly would have seen him earlier. Distracted as I was, I had already half pulled into my drive when I slammed on the brakes. All thoughts and worries of Erin scattered from my mind.

The pale man stood in front of me.

My house! My land! He had finally invaded my property. Where can I go from him now?

I backed out of my drive, frightened of him all over again. Gareth's advice to face him sounded like the stupidest thing anyone's ever said. How could I face those horrible, blue eyes? That pale and terrifying countenance? I would die and more. He would destroy me, I thought.

I was not sure where I could drive. If he came to my house he could take hold of me anywhere. Eventually, yes, eventually.

I drove around the block, to the property that bordered mine on the back. It was an old mechanic's shop, so I could see all the way through into my own property. I slowed down and peered through the old cars growing grass around their rusting bulks. Nothing stirred in my yard, nor did I see any figures moving in the windows. I almost drove on when the realization hit me full and I slammed on the brakes again.

I could see into my backyard.

But there were woods in my backyard. Thick trees, tall and ancient, spread wide and deep through the back of the property. The woods in my backyard was one of the things that drew me to the house in the first place.

Now, I was looking through the yard of the mechanic's shop and clearly into my own backyard. There were no trees to obscure my view. There were no trees at all.

There were no woods behind my house.

The admonition of Danileoth echoed clearly in my mind.

There are no woods behind your house.

I had always dismissed the comment as a part of their cryptic gaming. But they were right. There were no woods behind my house.

And if Danileoth wanted me to avoid them, then surely that is where I should be.

Still trembling with shock, but resolved, I drove back to my house. The pale man no longer waited in the driveway. I knew exactly where he would be. All these events had been set into motion long before I knew of them. They were already in place before I bought the house, before I had achieved my new awareness. These were forces more vast and wise than I could even comprehend.

Without hesitation I got out of my car and walked directly to the backyard.

The pale man waited at the entrance of the forest. He fixed his gaze firmly upon me, then turned and disappeared into the trees.

The trees. They were there again. Giant and sprawling with thick trunks and knotted roots twisting above the ground, the trees waited. So dense grew the trees of this forest that I could not see through to the mechanic's shop I knew sat idly on the other side. How had I never noticed before?

A small trail wound deep into the shade of the woods. The pale man had disappeared into its depths. I breathed deep and followed, for the first time stepping into the borders of the wood.

The air shimmered as I moved from the backyard into the forest. I felt the pull on me and a twinge of disorientation. The distinction between where I had been and where I was now felt clear and unmistakable.

A gateway perhaps? The idea sounded right to me. This

must be one of those gateways to the Eternal Realm the bartender had mentioned. Have I been living next to one this whole time? Was that the cause of my awakening? Or was it my latent stirring to consciousness that drew me to this place? Or more alarming yet, did this place draw me to itself? Did it call out to me?

However it may have happened, I am certain now it was providence. I was meant to walk, as I now walked, through the path of that wood to wherever it led me.

Strange sounds rose up from the shadows of the forest. Bird calls high and keening, whispers, laughter, something resembling breath drawn quickly in; even music, or something like it, bounded through the trees. I walked as they sounded around me, marveling all the while at the beautiful forest, so full and ancient, hiding the secrets of uncounted ages.

The path ended abruptly at a rocky cliff side descending to a river and gorge hundreds of feet below. A natural bridge arched over the chasm to the other side where the path continued.

I crept out hesitantly, the stone bridge hardly wider than my foot. Dizziness threatened me more than once. Something flew over me. Out of the corner of my eye it looked like a human with wings instead of arms, though I couldn't be sure. At one point I fell to my hands and knees when a stiff wind rose up and threatened to knock me off. I crawled the rest of the way, making it safely to the other side, though thoroughly shaken.

On the other side of the bridge the path led me only a short way before opening up to a clearing. A small fire burned in the center. A domed hut, made of twigs and thatch sat off to the side. All these I barely noticed as my eyes fixed on the figure of the pale man who stood with his eyes – blue eyes that reminded me more of fire than ice – fixed on me.

"You have been running from me," he said in a voice unexpectedly warm.

"You frighten me," I admitted.

The pale man didn't seem offended by this. He stretched out a long hand to indicate that I should sit by the fire. I obeyed, and he sat across from me.

What came next I can only describe as an initiation of sorts. I will not reveal the details of what transpired, for that knowledge is only for the initiated. It would be profanity to reveal it. Suffice it to know that I spent several hours with the pale man. He told me the name he is known by, as he also told me my name, my true name. Many other things he said for my ears alone, and many things said to all those who have proceeded by the same path.

At the end of it, my awakening was complete. What started as an increased awareness flowered fully into a state I can only call total wakefulness. Though it is not a state that is anywhere near total awareness, it is as much as I am capable of becoming at this present time.

Not to say that I am perfect now. Far from it. There is more potential to be reached, even more awareness to be achieved. Only at this moment I have awakened fully to who I am and the place I occupy in the universe. With time my potential will increase, and God willing, I will grow with it.

I realize how foolish I was to avoid the pale man as long as I did. For certain, he was more than death to me. He did more than kill me. He destroyed me. But in destroying me he liberated me. At the end I thanked him for that destruction and mourned that my cowardice did not allow me to be destroyed earlier.

The visions I had experienced were not supposed to be viewed alone. The pale man is my guide. He was meant to walk me through them, explain them as they happened. Much hid in those visions that I needed to see and hear. I needed to be shown more than what I saw. No matter, he said, to my grief. There are more visions. And what is left must be sufficient for the task at hand.

The task at hand. Yes, he told me that too. There is a work, laid out before me. He wouldn't say I was destined for this work. Nor would he deny the force of providence.

"You are free and fated all at once," he offered by way of explanation. "You are called and destined to these times and places, yet your freedom is what allows you to fulfill your destiny."

"There are seven visions in all," he also told me. "Three of what is, three of what was, and one of what yet may be."

I knew immediately which of those I had already experienced. The first three – the dying Keeper, the board meeting with Danileoth, and the robed figures offering sacrifice in the pit – all showed me things of the present. The other two – the gathering of the Keepers and the celebration in the woods – clearly showed me visions of the past. That meant I had one vision left of the past and one of the future. Then perhaps all might be made clear.

The pale man told me as much. After the rites in the woods had been completed he gestured toward the hut. The doorway of my next vision waited.

He placed his hand on my shoulder as we stepped through. Warmth flowed out of his hands into me. I felt strength in that warmth as well as peace. I felt capable and sure of confronting anything that might lie ahead.

The transition into this sixth vision felt different than all the others. The darkness fell over me but I did not feel as profound a disorientation. As light returned I felt more outside the scene than a part of it. It was like I stood behind a window watching a scene unfold before me. At the same time, I could move about the scene, change my perspective or move closer or further from the action.

The world that transitioned into view glowed with deep and primordial power. Great swathes of green forest stretched as far as I could see toward the eastern horizon. Long fields of open grassland rolled to the west. Blue mountains stood in the distance, giants whose rocky peaks touched the vault of heaven.

The scene moved beneath my gaze. It felt like I soared through the sky above. I had no body that I could perceive, only sight and hearing and a will that moved.

The whole land glistened with either dew or a freshly fallen rain. As I drew closer it seemed more soaked than wet. Everything was saturated. The land appeared to have just suffered under a great and torrential storm.

The vision passed to one man, dressed in tattered robes, walking through the empty world. A light brown beard hung from his face. Deep green eyes peered out solemnly, searching for something. He looked down at his hands, at the sapling he held. Fresh, wet earth clung to its tender roots.

I felt the same deep power in him as I felt emanate from the whole land. Something about him, and the world around him, felt more real than anything I had ever experienced. They seemed more alive. I would swear to this day that the world I looked at then was a world more vibrant than ours.

"This is the world after its cleansing," the pale man said from somewhere nearby. The man who held the sapling appeared not to hear.

"Cleansing from what?" I asked, my voice echoing as if I stood in a cavern instead of under the clear sky.

"Evil that had festered ever since the Fall," he answered me.

Of evil I could see none. The world appeared pure before my eyes, cleansed by more than water.

"When all creation was fashioned by the hand of the Father, it was made good," the pale man explained. "All living things obeyed their nature as they were made to do. The living creatures of the earth as well as the spiritual creatures of heaven, each obeyed the Song as it echoed in their hearts. The creatures of earth to tend the things of earth, those of heaven appointed as watchers and overseers.

"Then man was made, most terrible of all the beasts. Not only did he have in him the substance of earth, but also the spirit of heaven. Even more amazing, the spirit that coursed through him was the very Spirit of the living God. A thing too staggering to behold, all creation trembled.

"For within the confines of an earthly creature dwelt the essence of the Divine Father. Who could fathom the mind of God? For in this beast was granted the freedom to act, not according to his nature, but as free as God. And he had placed within him God's passion, God's creativity, wild and unleashed upon the good world.

"Then the man fell, as we all knew he would. This animal with divine breath chose something not of his nature. When he made that choice, a corruption and darkness entered into the world. And as man fell, all creation fell with him."

The man with the sapling slowed down as he neared the edge of a pit. Dark smoke billowed out of the hole, flashing with the red light of magma and earthen fire.

"With the Fall, evil came into the world. Something other than the Song of God rang through the young earth. What was impossible became possible. Things defied their created selves and pursued the illusion man crafted from his disobedience. Corruption tainted all things. The tree no longer had to bear fruit, now it might wither in famine. The swine could turn and savage its young. Even the smallest things, so small they swam in droplets of water, resisted their nature and became disease and plague.

"So too fell the Sons of Heaven, first made to watch over the work of creation. Man lifted up his eyes to them and worshiped them as gods. Fat with the praise of man, the Watchers took themselves to be divine, and what was made to serve became a master."

The pit came into view as the man approached. He shielded his face as angry, red light glowed hot against him. I felt a note of hesitancy in his approach, and something like

222

fear, the kind brought about with a touch of reverence and awe. Except that he seemed more terrified than anything else.

"While some regarded themselves as gods, others fell into even greater darkness. All the Sons of Heaven hungered after man's divine essence, but thirteen of them would gorge their endless appetites. These dark lords warred with the gods, and between them creation was rent asunder. Man was reduced to fear and ashes. What was made in the image of God and gifted with his essence squirmed in the dust and groveled before his gods and demons.

"The gods saw that the daughters of men were beautiful, and desirous to feed upon, and they took some for wives. The nephilim sprang from their unholy union, most deadly of all corrupted things. Being demigods they held the power of heaven and earth, full of divine essence and human freedom. Terror followed in the wake of the nephilim that neither god nor demon could stand against. Great rose up the cry of man."

I began to recognize the story. The world, still wet from his cleansing, the one man before me, all echoed of an old tale, told from the rim of time.

"God grieved that he ever made man, that he had breathed life into him as he looked upon his good world torn apart and dying. Only one man did God find righteous as he opened the vaults of the sky and flooded the world. Noah and his family were spared, and when the waters receded they alone were left to rebuild the world.

"The gods were cast into Tartarus, imprisoned until the Day of Wrath. The nephilim were locked away among the celestial heights. For the Dark Lords, another prison was fashioned for them."

The man whom I thought must be Noah, held the sapling over the seething pit. With trembling hands he lowered it, closer to the hole in the earth. Dirt fell from the roots, and howls of agony, ungodly in its noise, rose from the smoke and fire, as if the soil felt like acid to whatever lay beneath.

Roots webbed out from the sapling, taking hold of the earth. The man fell to his knees as he gingerly, reverently planted the tree. Screams full of wrath and hate echoed out of the closing pit.

I somehow willed myself to move so that I could peer into the flaming hole. As it closed, the roots of the tree snaking out and pulling it shut, I caught one glimpse into its depths.

A swirl of raven feathers coalesced into the form of a man. Black eyes stared up, seething and angry. Hands outstretched in futile wrath, ashen gray skin pulled tight over a thin frame. Another scream and the figure exploded in a flurry of dark feathers.

"Branches from the Tree of Life were cultivated to seal the prison of the Dark Lords. All that was corrupted and foul among heaven was locked away so man might freely pursue the purpose that God had made him for."

The scene began to move in quick, jerky motions, like film that is fast forwarded. I watched as the tree sprouted up, forming into a large, green ash. Day and night flashed on and off. Snow and heat, autumn and new spring all came and went as I watched. Native Americans erected tents by the tree, then disappeared in a flicker of dark. Time passed more quickly and the white man appeared. A city grew up around the tree. At first only log huts and dusty streets surrounded it. Then the houses rose up higher with glass windows and bricks and painted siding. The streets grew wider, filled in with cobblestones and ridden over by horse and carriage, then paved and traversed by automobile.

The tree stood untouched as the world grew up around it. It didn't pass the seasons as the other trees did. Its leaves remained green, even in the snows of winter.

The city grew taller, casting shadows over the lot where the tree stood. Then the progression of time seemed to slow, and for the first time I noticed a blush on the leaves of the green ash tree. Night and day flew by. The leaves redden to full autumn. Slowly, they fell away, as if being stripped of its skin.

The progress of time stopped and I knew that the vision had arrived at the present day. The perspective spun around, affording me a view all around the tree. A light snow fell on the now bare branches. Somewhere in that vast lot, stripped of its leaves, the tree kept its lonely vigil. It felt lesser somehow than on that day it sealed the ground shut.

"The tree is linked to the spirit of life in men," the pale man told me as I watched the bare and winter assaulted tree. "As the spirit of man fails, so fails the tree. As the life of man grows dim and corrupt, the Dark Lord gnaws on the roots of his prison. If the Confounder were to emerge again he would cast confusion and ignorance over the world. His shadow would blot out all truth and beauty. The weakening of man would hasten and his spirit dwindle as the light is obscured from his heart. Those who seek the liberty of the Dark Lord must not succeed. At any cost, they must not succeed."

The vision began to fade even as the pale man's words echoed in my head. I struggled to hold on but the night grew dark and I felt myself slipping away.

"Why?" I screamed out. "Why do they want to free him!? What am I supposed to do!?"

No answer came from the gathering darkness. The vision faded completely and I awoke again in the clearing. Night had fallen. A strangely large moon shone bright above me.

And I was alone. I looked around, but found no sign of the pale man except the ashes of the dead fire and the empty hut beside me.

Finally, everything with Erin is okay. She is safe. Or as safe as can be made in this strange and dangerous world. Indeed, this world, being filled with greater danger than I ever thought possible, is not the world I had believed it to be. Where did we get the idea that life is predictable and safe? Nothing could be further from the truth. Danger fills every crevice of life. We walk by it unaware, step-by-step. Invisible, it surrounds us. We breathe it, speak it. It fills our dreams and enfolds us in sleep. We consume it in our daily bread. To be alive is dangerous. From the moment of birth until that grateful day when we rest from trouble, it is all danger and peril and toil.

Erin, at least, presents me no more worry. I didn't realize what a burden weighed on my heart until it pulled on me no more. I had made myself responsible for her safety, believing I had placed her in this danger.

I was at least partly wrong. Erin had been in danger for longer than the brief time she has known me. And most of it not of my doing. Long before we met, Erin was marked.

Still, I felt, I feel responsible for her. And now she is as safe as I can make her. My heart rests easier with that knowledge.

Not that things began that way. When I returned from the meeting with the pale man I realized it was still early in the morning and I was exhausted. I slept through the remainder of the day and didn't wake again until sunset.

As soon as I awoke I went to Erin's. I found the doors still locked and no one answered my knock or my calls. I could see light coming from the upstairs window, and knowing she might be in there gave me more, rather than less, anxiety.

Certain I had to do something, I smashed in a back window and forced my way into the house. Dead and eerie silence greeted me. I called out her name. No one answered.

I remembered too well how I found her last time, and wasted no time getting upstairs to the room with arcane figures drawn over it. My heart thumped as I pushed open the door, knowing she would be there. A sliver of light flowed out of the room and into the dark hallway.

There she stood, in the middle of the room stripped naked with her arms held wide. A glaze covered her eyes, and they stared out blankly. Her face had gone slack. Only her lips moved.

Shock and horror hit me all at once when I looked at her.

The strange symbols written all over the walls now covered her naked body as well. Some had been drawn in black ink. Others still were carved into her flesh. Those markings had already scabbed over and the streaks of blood dried on her cold and trembling skin. A kitchen knife lay at her feet, its tip died red.

"Erin," I called to her hoarsely.

She didn't answer or acknowledge. Some barely audible whisper came from her, rhythmic and chant like.

"Erin," I said taking hold of her shoulders, feeling a touch of panic.

Her only answer was that same dim whisper. She stared at nothing, lips moving fast and inarticulate.

"Erin!" I yelled, shaking her.

Her eyes shot wide open and her body went rigid in my hands. Fingernails dug into my shoulder as she gripped my arm. She yelled out, and I finally heard what she said.

"ENIM VERO DI NOS QUASI PILAS HOMINES HABENT!"

I didn't know what to do. I had no one to turn to. Doctors couldn't help this. Doctors wouldn't believe this. A hospital would only shelve her away as insane, left to mutter out her days in a drugged stupor.

I wrapped Erin in a blanket and carried her out to my car. Gareth was the only one who could possibly help.

He was furious when I brought him out to the car. Erin still muttered that one phrase, oblivious or uncaring to her environment.

"What the fuck?!" he yelled out when he looked in at her. "Why the hell did you bring her here?"

"What am I supposed to do?" I yelled back at him.

"Bloody hell, man. I can't get involved like this."

"What's wrong with her?" I asked. "Why is she doing this?"

"She's got a glammer on her, man, and a big one," he answered, rubbing his hands through his hair.

"How?"

"Looking behind doors she isn't supposed to," Gareth told me. "There was a mind fuck waiting behind one of them and she sprung it wide open."

The book came to mind immediately. It had some curse on it. I told Gareth about it.

"Could be," he said, calming visibly. "Maybe that was it. But if someone wants her like this then they'll come looking if she gets better."

"Then you can help?" I asked.

"Hell no, this is way beyond me. I can't have my mark on this anyway. You understand? I'm all alone out here. Once Danileoth decides not to tolerate me anymore I am through."

"So this was Danileoth?"

Gareth threw up his hands and shrugged. He sighed deep and paced up and down the sidewalk. He seemed to be fighting with himself.

"Look, I can give you a name," he said, coming to a resolution. "Maybe he can help, maybe he can't. Tell him I sent you. You can tell him it's for old time's sake."

"Fine, whatever you want," I readily agreed.

"He's a doctor," Gareth said.

"A doctor?" I echoed, confused.

"No ordinary man of medicine," Gareth assured me. "His name is Canta, Eric Canta. He works over at Main General in the ER. Go see him. No one else but him. Understand?"

It took a dose of firm insistence and a lot of waiting, but we eventually were given a room in the ER. The nurse that first looked over Erin kept shooting incriminating glances at me. She left and we waited, what seemed like for hours.

"They tell me I've got some big fans in here," a voice spoke up as the room curtain was pushed aside and a white coated figure stepped in.

The doctor looked up at us and froze. I locked eyes with him and a sensation of dread passed through me.

On the surface, Dr. Canta struck a handsome figure and seemed harmless enough. His blonde hair and rugged features, the swagger of his undoubtedly muscular physique, made him extraordinary in his own right. That he reminded me of Danileoth and the Fae made me freeze with immediate fear. Whatever heightened awareness I had achieved told me, without a doubt, that he was one of the children of the gods.

"What do you want with me?" he asked with repressed aggression. "I've done nothing to warrant your attention."

"I need your help," I explained, motioning to the inert and mumbling Erin. "Gareth sent me to you. He told me you could help. For old time's sake."

"He said that?" Canta asked. "For old times sake?"

"That's what he said."

"Ole Gareth," the doctor sighed with a shake of his head. "Getting involved all over again I see."

"Not really," I said. "There's nothing to get involved with. There's...there's nothing. It's only me. There's nothing going on."

"Just as well," he shrugged. "So you're the dweomer all that chatter has been about."

"And you're Fae," I shot back, eager to show my hand wasn't helpless.

One of Canta's perfect eyebrows arched up. "Indeed," he murmured. "You've come a long way. I can see why they chatter."

"I can't," I confessed.

"So what happened to her?" the doctor asked, nodding at Erin.

"I just found her like this."

He pulled up a rolling stool and sat in front of Erin. His fingers reached up and traced small circles on her forehead.

He pulled the lids of her eyes open wider and looked inside.

"So what's this chatter about?" I asked as he examined her. "Why do the Fae care about me?"

"You really don't know?" he asked without looking at me. I shook my head.

The doctor continued to study Erin's face. I looked down at my feet and pondered the white, tile floor. I heard him get up and pull the curtain aside and ask the ER staff for something, then he sat back down and rolled the stool in front of me.

"You see, men like you, awakened ones, are the only real threat to the Fae. Men like you are the only ones that can keep them from what they desire."

"And what do they desire?" I asked. "What is it your kind is after?"

"We just want to survive," the doctor said. "Well, maybe thrive would be more accurate. That's not so bad, is it?"

"What does that have to do with us?" I asked. "Why would I get in the way of your thriving?"

The doctor smiled and considered for a moment, then held out his hand. He blew gently on the open palm, and a flame appeared, floating just above the surface of his skin.

"All living things have a fire burning inside," the doctor explained. "A spirit. Most living things have an animal or a vegetable spirit, very basic, and not very bright."

The flame hovering over his palm dimmed until it flickered like the single tongue produced by a candle.

"But man, man has a human spirit, one fired by the breath of God himself." The flame grew larger, not so much in size, but in brightness and intensity. It glowed like a small star in the doctor's hand, blazing with glory.

"Man's freedom, his awareness, his passion, burns like no other thing, be it of the animal or spiritual world. His spirit is like God's. No other being in the created order can boast of that. Nothing, not the Fae, not even the old gods.

"We may be eternal because we were made of the eternal order, but we lack the God-fire. Man has it in abundance, though it is housed in the body of an animal and even mingles with animal spirit. We may be eternal, but man is truly alive."

"So we have our existence, and you have yours," I said. "No reason to put us at odds with one another."

"Yes, we exist," Canta said with a smile. "But long ago, our fathers first drank of that divine essence."

The doctor pursed his lips and sucked in air. A tendril of light flowed out of the fire and into his mouth. As he drank of the fire, the flame dimmed. A glow suffused into Canta's features, making him seem larger, more substantial.

"For the first time our eyes were opened, and we became like man. We became alive like man and we shared in his glory."

A sick realization washed over me. "You feed off of us," I said, horrified. "Is that what you do? Like parasites?"

"It doesn't have to be that way," the doctor said. The fire flared to life again, as bright as before.

"Man can cultivate this fire," he explained. "It has endless potential for growth. It can be fed, stimulated, increased. There's no reason we can't take a bit here and there that won't be noticed. Besides, the old avenues of our power have been shut off. We're helpless without a bit of man's fire now and again. Without it we wouldn't even be able to manifest in this realm at all."

"Is that supposed to make it better?" I shot back. "Because you need it we're supposed to lay down and be your feast?"

"It's not as bad as it sounds," the doctor said in defense.

"Then why would the Keepers try to stop you? Why would men like me be such a danger to you?"

"There have been some that have gotten greedy," the doctor confessed. "There have been some that have taken more than a bit here and there. They've used...unsavory tactics to satisfy their lust for human fire. And the more they take the hungrier they get. They will draw and draw and draw until there's nothing left to feed on."

The light in his hand dimmed until it barely glowed at all. The flame looked cold and pale, flickering over his palm.

"When these others feed too much, when they feed the wrong way, man is one day left but a shell of himself. He is spent and drained, floundering the rest of his days, listless and empty, wondering where all the passion and power of his life has gone."

Canta closed his hand and the fire vanished. The light disappeared with a finality that struck my own heart. How many times has just such a scenario played out? How often does it happen still today? Had I not felt the same happen in my life?

A nurse came in and gave Canta a leather bag. It looked like the old physician cases that doctors used to carry.

"How does it work?" I asked. "How do you take man's fire?"

"It happens quite naturally," the doctor explained. He opened the medicine bag and pulled out items never associated with the scientific treatment of disease. Black chalk, a crimson candle, a vial of water, and a clear piece of quartz he laid out on the rolling table beside Erin.

"You see, man is an idol maker. And when he gives something his love, his devotion, his faith, he gives with it a part of his fire. Normally, when he is devoted and loving towards the right things, his fire increases. But when he gives that devotion to an idol, he just gives of his fire and doesn't receive a corresponding increase? Does that make sense?"

"I think so," I said. "When we worship something we give it our fire. Worship the right things and we get some back. Worship the wrong things and we just lose."

"Exactly."

"That doesn't really explain our situation," I said. "How are the Fae feeding today? There's hardly any religion left in our culture, much less idols. There's no idol to Danileoth. There's no idols at all."

"No idols?" the doctor asked incredulously. "You've got nothing but idols. You're drowning in idols. In fact, your culture is surrounded with more idols than any other in the history of mankind."

He walked over to the curtain and beckoned me over to him. We peeked out into the large, busy emergency room.

"You see that purse over there?" he pointed out the designer pocketbook that sat at the foot of a woman's bed. "Do you think that woman would love the purse the same without that symbol on it? It designates it as something special and she feels a sense of glory when she carries it. In return, she gives it love and devotion. She gives it her worship."

As the doctor spoke I could see, even as the woman lay prone and sick, a connection she felt to the designer bag.

"That doctor over there with the orange tie," Canta pointed out a fellow physician wearing a tie decorated with a Tiger paw. "He loves that symbol. He feels a sort of grandness when he wears it, a reflected glory of sorts. He will tell you he loves the team, but that love is inextricably connected to the symbol.

"The nurse over there drinking coffee. She may like the drink, but that mermaid on the cup makes her feel like she is drinking something more. All these things go by different names, even have the veneer of sophistication upon them, but they are idols. People look to them to make them complete. They look to these idols to give themselves a place in the world. And in return, they offer up their devotion, their love, their worship. They give of their sacred fire, and then give some more. The most they get back in return is a tasty latte. It doesn't begin to compare with what was lost."

It was hard to believe corporate logos could be so menacing, though it began to make a strange sort of sense. They are all over the place. On our computers, our cars, our clothing, everything we own or pursue or occupy ourselves with carries a symbol. We wear these symbols proudly and sport them before others. We think more of ourselves for having the branded item, and even impart a sense of quality to a thing just for having the right symbol upon it. We brandish the logo of a sports team, and think somehow that whatever glory they accomplish is reckoned on to us.

It is true. We give these things our loyalty, our esteem, our love. We trust them to make our lives better, more fulfilled, grander somehow. Even as they never fulfill us, we pursue them with undiminished vigor. When we find one unworthy of our worship, we quickly seek out another.

"Those are corporate logos," I pointed out. "What does that have to do with the Fae? How do they benefit from it?"

"Behind every major logo in the world, corporate or otherwise, you will find the Children of the Gods," Canta said. "The big ones at least. From sports on down to shoes. The Fae are attached, just like the old gods used to latch on to idols. You worship the idol, and you give your strength to spirit behind it."

He walked back over to the table and lit the crimson candle. Returning his attention back to Erin he held the candle up to her eyes, muttering softly. He drew faint traces on her forehead in black chalk.

"What about you?" I asked. "How do you feed? Is there a logo you're attached to?"

The doctor sighed heavily. "It used to not be this way. There are other ways of getting a little fire than posing as a deity. We used to do little favors for men, help their crops grow, facilitate an easy childbirth, that sort of thing. Some would abuse it. They might take too much, or use fear to harvest the fire. Others might use more...direct methods of feeding.

"This is where the Keepers came in. They protected man from the evil attacks of the Fae. Most of us were left alone. As long as we gave a little we could take a little."

I thought about the kiss I shared with Mesulina and Eladora. When our lips touched, I felt something leave me. But in the moment after, I also felt something grow. I could see where Canta was able to take what he needed.

"So this is what you do? You offer healing, and in the process take a little fire from your patients."

"I don't take anything," Canta said. "People give me what I need. I do it like we did in the old days. I heal them, and in return they give me gratitude."

"So you can feed off of gratitude?" I asked.

"Sure," the doctor shrugged. "It's not as potent as religious zeal, but it's more than adequate. When a patient shakes my hand and thanks me for saving their life or the life of their child, that gratitude transfers a healthy dose of fire to me. But it doesn't hurt, because the happiness a person feels at being healthy again, or having their loved one restored, that recharges them with much more than they gave."

As I digested everything he told me, the doctor continued to work on Erin. He washed off all the symbols she had drawn on her body. The water from the vial closed up the ones carved into her flesh as he sprinkled it over the scabs. Once clean, he laid her down on the bed and picked up the quartz crystal.

"What are they doing?" I asked. "What's Danileoth up to? Something big is about to happen. I can feel it. But I don't know what."

"I haven't had anything to do with them for a long time," Canta said. "I leave them alone, they leave me alone."

"What do you know about the Raven King?"

The doctor stiffened at the sound of the name. "He shouldn't be spoken of."

"I think he's a part of this," I said.

"Impossible," Canta insisted. "They would never bring the Confounder into whatever it is they're doing. We fear the Dark Lords as much as anything."

Canta placed the quartz on Erin's forehead. Arcane power wove in the air as he uttered strange words. Erin's lips fell still, the muttering finally silenced. She closed her eyes all the way, and her body relaxed as she fell into a deep sleep. A surge of relief coursed through me.

"She'll be fine with some rest," Canta said.

I walked over to look at Erin, as if to confirm she was really well. She appeared more peaceful than she had in months. The tension of whatever had consumed her was gone.

"Thank you," I gushed, taking Canta's hand. "I can't tell you what this means to me."

"See what I mean?" the doctor beamed, taking in a deep breath. "Gratitude. It didn't cost you a thing, did it?"

It was true. I felt no weaker for the exchange. As promised, my relief and joy at seeing Erin recovered filled me with real and discernible strength.

"It would be better if she came with me," Canta said. "Her kind recovers differently."

"What do you mean..." I began, then stopped when I realized what he meant.

"She's Elioud?" I asked, though it all of a sudden made perfect sense. Her uncanny ability to research, her inability to put it down, being chosen to watch over me, that undefinable differentness she possessed; it was all there to see, that there was something more to her.

"I take it you didn't know," the doctor observed, seeing my surprise.

"I don't think she knows," I said, still reeling from shock.

"Not uncommon. Most halflings don't discover their lineage until later in life. Some never at all. They live out their days feeling different and out of place, like they don't belong anywhere. They will display some particular talent on an uncanny level, and this keeps them even more at a distance with others.

"But if they discover who they really are, they can live as an Elioud. It is not as free as a human life, though it is blessed in its own way. They live much, much longer, and will not grow old as humans do, provided they learn how to thrive."

"You mean feed?" I asked, still appalled at the thought. "You will teach her how to feed."

"There are many ways to thrive?" Canta assured me. "We will teach her to be a help to humanity. If she has a good heart then she will choose a good way."

"She has a very good heart," I told him.

"Then you have nothing to worry about," he said, clapping my shoulder. "We will keep her safe, safer than you ever could. I will make sure she stays out of all this."

"I can see her, I hope."

"You're awakened," Canta said. "I couldn't keep her from you if I wanted to."

I nodded my silent consent. Reaching out I took her hand in mine. Her hand squeezed back. At that moment she looked more beautiful than she ever had. Perhaps it was the color that had been restored to her features. Maybe it was because I knew of her extraordinary origins. Or perhaps I missed her already, knowing she would likely begin a life apart from me in ways greater than distance. Whatever the reason, I ached for her then. She was with me when I was all alone. Now I felt lonely again, even more than I had before.

The doctor put a hand on me in sympathy and turned to leave.

"Doctor," I called out to stop him. "What was that she was muttering? She was saying something over and over. It was Latin or something."

"Yes," Canta answered with reluctance I could hear. "It was Latin. Enim vero di nos quasi pilas homine habent."

"Do you know what it means?"

"I do."

"Will you tell me?"

Another pause from the doctor. Then he told me. "Man is the plaything of the gods."

How have I never noticed before, what a beautiful place the world is? We have tried to cover it up, man in his race to be master of the earth. Concrete and ugly buildings, smokestacks and parking lots, all to obscure the natural wonder around us. Are we afraid of it? I think we may be.

But there is magic yet in the world. I feel it emanate from the earth, crackle on the air of the cold wind. Power screams out in the stars, flashes in the sun and caresses us in the light of the moon. If only we would see it.

I stood out in the snow tonight. Giant flakes of white powder fell all around me, like angels flitting softly from heaven to earth. There was magic here too.

It is nothing you can see with the eyes or touch with the hands. The words spoken on the wind are inaudible to the ears. There is that deeper sense here, more than mere feeling. Often it manifests as feeling. But this perception, this deeper awareness is not a feeling. It is the vision, the sight of the mind and soul. I would call it imagination except people would mistake it for make-believe.

This couldn't be further from the truth. Imagination is not merely what exists in the mind. Imagination is the faculty whereby we perceive what lies beyond the fabric of this material world. And what lies beyond is more real than the surface we tread upon. It is energy and essence. It is ideal and eternity. Creativity and life well from here. It is the realm of God and all things divine.

Magic waits for us. It bubbles up on the surface of what is tangible and floats into the light and air. It waits patiently without urgency or haste. It wants to be uncovered, and rejoices when I behold it. Like a bride who uncovers herself for the first time to the eyes of her husband. She trembles in anticipation, and awaits the moment in ecstasy. And so does this magic. It wants to be seen, and felt, but like a new bride, only to those who love her.

This magic could still be ours. This greatness could still be ours. If only we would open our eyes. If only we would desire for something different, and see.

Resolution came over me that I must not be passive anymore. I can't wait for the enemy to act. My passivity plays right into their hands. As long as I am still, their plots move forward unhindered. I must act. That much is certain.

What exactly I should do is the only question that eludes me. The visions were meant to be a guide, but as most of them appeared without any help I cannot gauge them accurately. All of this is my fault and the fault of my cowardice.

I keep hoping to discover more, uncover that one piece of information or undergo a massive epiphany that will tell me exactly what I need to do. I even keep walking into the woods behind my house hoping the otherworldliness of that place will inspire me. It is a place full of wonder, and I have seen many strange things there. As of yet, it offers no stroke of inspiration.

It frustrates me to no end, knowing I must do something but having no clue as to what. I pace about my house like a prisoner on the eve of parole.

What do I do? What is there to do?

Nothing. I can think of nothing.

Waiting is all I can think to do. But I cannot wait any longer.

I have decided what to do, though I doubt it will be effective at all. It's nothing more than a stab in the dark really. Futile, like everything else.

More information is what I need. So I have resolved to find it. I can't wait for it to drop in my lap. Perhaps if I know more then my road will become clear. I hope this is so.

So far, what I know is that Danileoth has amassed incredible power around him and those loyal to him. He has been gathering this power for centuries. There's little I could do in my brief lifetime to thwart him there. I don't even know if he is the highest power on his side. Does he make all the decisions? Or does he answer to someone higher up?

However, I can frustrate him. Whatever he is planning it has something to do with that pit I saw in one of my visions. It was the one with the crimson figure floating out of its depths, and the bodies – oh merciful Lord – the bodies of children thrown in as sacrifice to something dark and merciless. Whatever is going on in that place must be key to the whole plot. Why procure such a costly sacrifice if the need was not dear?

I will go there tonight and perhaps find something to lead me further on. The pistol will go with me just in case, though how effective it will be against the Fae and their minions I cannot tell.

It seems strange how excited I am. Nothing may come from this expedition. But I am doing something. God willing I will find something too.

I almost died last night. Rather, I was almost killed. Strange how exhilarating it feels, how exhilarating it still feels. Now that the terror has worn off I can revel in what I've done. I have begun on a course of action, and that action gives me joy and peace.

Of course, in the moment, the fear itself almost killed me. I cursed my foolishness when I felt most helpless and doomed. And yet in that moment I did not regret having acted. After so long feeling helpless and inactive it feels good to move, even if misery greets your first steps.

Back when I first had the vision of the pit, as I fled that awful scene before me, I had recognized the surroundings of my own city. Last night, I retraced my steps and searched for the place where the vision had occurred.

The city stood mostly deserted and quiet. Being dominated by the towers of corporate industry, it held very little activity in the late hours after work. A light rain began to fall as I walked around the Telecon building and onto the main boulevard running north to south. It took a moment to get my bearings before I saw the construction fencing across the street surrounding a giant lot.

Doubt pulled at me for a moment. The Halycon Construction sign on the gate, the smell of oiled engines and the dirty, blue plastic over the fence made it look so ordinary, so appropriate, that it couldn't possibly hold anything sinister. I had to look though.

A locked gate was the only entrance. Surprisingly, no guard stood watch. I fumbled over the fence, ripping my pants on barbed wire, and splashed into the mud on the other side. Yellow excavators loomed over me, towered over by a large crane. The yard lay littered with the scattered tools common on construction sites. It all looked normal. All except for the black tarp stretched out over the middle of the site.

The tarp wasn't plastic, but a heavy, oiled cloth. Strange symbols had been drawn on the surface, almost too faint to make out, too faint unless you looked for them. Cords staked into the ground held the tarp in place.

Even as I pulled one of the stakes free and threw back the cloth I knew what I would find. A black and gaping pit opened beneath my feet, a puncture in the earth.

I shined a flashlight into the darkness below me. It was just as I had seen in my vision. The pit fell away to impenetrable depths. A ledge wound around the perimeter of the hole, like a walkway carved into the walls. Deeper down I could see the outcropping where the black robed figures had conducted their grim ceremony.

A sense of someone else being there with me tickled at the

back of my head. I whipped around and saw nothing but the empty worksite and the rain pelting freshly turned earth.

I had to make myself turn back to the pit. That eerie sense of being watched wouldn't leave. I tried to shrug it off as paranoia and turned my light back towards the hole.

Rocks crunched under my feet as I stepped in and made my way around the perimeter ledge. The hole was massive, spanning nearly 150 feet by my guess. Though impossible to tell, I had the impression that all the digging had been done by hand. There was something about the way the Fae acted, something about the rules of their strange world, that demanded something like this be carved out by human sweat and labor.

About 40 feet down I reached the outcropping of rock. It looked to be a single stone that stretched out over the center of the pit, dangling over the blackness beneath.

Memory of the vision came back to me as I knelt on the stone. The sinister men in black robes, the crimson figure floating over the darkness, the small bundles consigned to the void, raven feathers; all came crashing into my mind with stark lucidity. I could see them around me again.

The sound of cloth snapping yanked me out of my memory. I peered up to see a corner of the tarp flapping in the wind. Rain tumbled in and splashed on my upturned face.

I turned uneasily back to my search, the sense of being watched magnifying by the second. The light picked out an odd shape on the floor of the stone outcropping, something that didn't belong. Memory flashed again.

I knelt down and touched the pool of red wax that had dried on the rock. I could see again the ghostly candlelight illuminating the ritual. And here it was. It felt real. I traced the smooth lumps and saw again the little figures draped in cloth and held out over the maw of the hungry chasm.

The snap of the tarp sounded again. A sense of some presence nearby returned. I could feel eyes burning into me.

I looked up. A familiar shadow loomed over the pit.

"I told you to stay out of the woods behind your house," Danileoth said from above.

"You told me there were no woods behind my house," I shot back.

"I thought we were friends," he said, waving my comment away. "Do you want to oppose me now?"

"I thought our friendship ended when you tried to leave me at the bottom of the ocean," I said, perhaps feeling more confident than I should.

I felt him regard me coldly though I couldn't make out his features. He appeared as a silhouette against the dim sky.

"These are things that don't concern you," Danileoth said. "It would be best if you left them alone."

"Best for you, or best for us?" I responded.

"You reach too high for yourself, mortal," he spat.

"What do you expect me to do?" I asked. "Am I supposed to stand by while you hurl children into this pit?"

If his regard for me was cool before, now it was black hatred. He held a hand out over the pit, as if passing judgment.

"So you will be my enemy," Danileoth said with finality. "Then you will meet the fate of my enemies."

Two more figures walked up to join him at the edge. My courage faltered at the site of them and threatened to fail me altogether. Both silhouettes stood tall and slender, their lithe, feline features undeniable.

"Beautiful specimens, are they not?" Danileoth mused, no doubt reading the fear on my face. "Egyptian bred. Two of only a few Bastet left in existence. Sylvie here has an insatiable appetite. Felia, on the other hand, likes to savor her meals."

In my mind I could hear the crunch of bone and the tearing of flesh by feline teeth as the cat women leapt off the lip of the chasm and bounded toward me. They darted with superhuman agility from one ledge to another, making their way down.

I fumbled the pistol out of my belt. With trembling hands I fired wildly. A puff of dirt flew up with my errant shot. Three more missed as the Bastet leapt easily away.

I forced myself to calm and timed my fifth shot with the leap of the next creature. Aiming for where she would land next I squeezed the trigger as the dark figure touched earth.

An ungodly shriek rose up, stabbing into my ears. The other Bastet stopped and leapt over to her sister. She turned to me and hissed, yellow eyes shining in the dark.

"Felia!" Danileoth yelled and jumped into the pit.

He landed on the stone ledge in front of me. The rock rumbled and I feared it might shatter.

"Enough of your games!" he screamed at me, his voice reverberating through the dark chasm. The air shook with his wrath.

The pistol came up as he strode towards me. Two shots buried in his chest.

He seemed not to notice the wounds as he slapped the gun out of my hands and grabbed me around the neck. The stone left my feet as he lifted me up like a child and brought me close to his face. Malice gleamed in his eyes.

"You will learn not to defy the will of the gods!" he spat at me.

"You're not gods," I managed to choke out. I tried to peel his fingers from my neck. They were as unyielding as stone.

"We are to you, insect," he said and stabbed a finger into my forehead.

Electricity exploded in my brain and the world went dark.

When my senses returned, I was no longer in the pit. A musty, underground smell and the sound of water dripping on rock came to me before my sight cleared. Slowly, vision returned with a stabbing ache in my head, and I found myself in some sort of cave.

I struggled to rise but was pulled back down onto the hard, rock floor. Something bound my hands. They were buried, half way up to my forearms, each one in a pillar of rock.

I tried to rise up again, this time more slowly. I made it to my feet but was unable to stand to full height. The muscles in my arms felt knotted and sore. Orange light flickered from a tunnel ahead of me.

Just when I assumed myself to be all alone a shadow moved in the dim light. Danileoth stepped into the mouth of the tunnel. I pulled at my bonds in panic, but they would not budge, firmly imprisoned in the rock.

"You children of men," Danileoth spat. I could hear contempt thick in his voice. "How easily you are subdued. You think you're so great, riding those awful machines. But you're nothing without them. Nothing. You're stupid, ugly, disgusting animals. Look at you, fat and pale, confused, sweaty, hairy, ignorant. Barely more than a beast."

"And yet you must feed off of us," I shot back. "If you're so great then why must you take from us?"

"That's the way of things," Danileoth shrugged, undisturbed by my provocation. "It's normal for the superior creature to prey upon a lower one. Just as you feed off of any beast of the field. But you don't consider yourself inferior to your livestock, do you? That's what you are to us. Nothing but stupid cows milling about, eating and mating, fattening up so you can feed your betters."

Such a different story than what Canta had presented. Yet beneath the bluster I thought I could see...anger, hatred, envy. Yes, and fear was there too.

"Whatever is yours, whatever portion of light you have, will soon be mine," Danileoth said, taking a step closer.

"I'll never give it to you," I answered, tugging again at my unyielding bonds. The muscles in my arms almost seized up.

Danileoth's laugh echoed through the cavern. "Do you think I need your consent? It may come purer that way, but that's not the only way. No, I will steal the fire from you in pure terror and mortal agony. I will draw it out over decades until you don't even recognize who you are. And I will delight in your screams, and in every drop of life drawn out in the throes of your pain and nightmares. In the end, you will beg to give me your devotion, will weep to be my slave. And after a lifetime of feeding off your terror, I will hand you the blade so you can open your own veins in my name and spill your own blood to my glory and honor, so even that last drop, that last flicker of light in your fading soul will be mine, sacrificed by your own hand. Then, you will simply cease to be, snuffed out like the pitiful candle you are. The world will continue unconcerned, no different for you having been born and died. A pitiful life and a pitiful death. And the greatest thing you will have accomplished will be feeding me."

I tried to put on a mask of brave indifference. Inside, I roiled in terror. Did he speak truly? I believed he could take my fire, Canta had said as much. But could he steal my soul as well? Or more directly, could he drive me to the point where I would give it to him willingly?

Not wanting to find out I struggled anew against the bonds that had me cemented into the rock. Danileoth laughed again while watching me struggle.

"That's it," he said, to goad my flailing. "We're already off to a good start."

I forced myself to stop struggling, to still the panic that threatened to overtake me completely. The rock was immovable. Instead, I closed my eyes and breathed deep, trying to calm the storm that raged inside of me.

"Resist all you want," Danileoth said. "I haven't even begun to break you."

As I calmed, I realized the extent of my helplessness. I had nothing at my disposal with which to fight Danileoth. He mocked me and stirred my fear as I stood bound and helpless. His words cut into me. And I only had words to resist.

Words. That is the only power I had at my disposal. Words.

Something flared in my memory. The old woman in the church. She had given me words. She said they were powerful words. The Lorica. That's what she had called it.

I closed my eyes more tightly and tried to remember.

"I bind unto myself today the strong name of the Trinity..."

A barking laugh broke my concentration.

"You think you have words powerful enough to overtake me?" Danileoth scoffed.

"I bind unto myself today the strong name of the Trinity," I began again. "By invocation of the same, The Three in One, One in Three."

A trickle of power entered into me as I spoke. Strength filled my limbs, clarity filled my mind. The weight of oppression that had filled the cavern began to lift. The darkness lightened, ever so slightly.

"Enough of this," Danileoth said, his voice louder. Currents of fear hid in his voice.

"I bind unto myself today the strong name of the Trinity. By invocation of the same, the Three in One, One in Three. Through the blood of Christ Jesus, his breaking..."

"Shut up!" Danileoth screamed in rage. The flow of power fell away at his outburst. Oppression crashed over me again, darker and heavier than before.

"Shut up! Shut up! Shut up!"

I opened my eyes to see him doubled over, hands over his ears. He looked up, eyes bloodshot with rage. My insides roiled at the sight of such potent wrath. But there, I saw it, unmistakable. Fear.

Ignoring the screams of Danileoth's rage I closed my eyes and began the Lorica again. I opened myself to its power, the power that flowed in the words, rendering the angry cries impotent.

"I bind unto myself today the strong name of the Trinity.
By invocation of the same, the Three in One and One in Three.
Through the blood of Christ Jesus, his breaking of death's door.
His passion and his reign forever more.

I bind unto myself today by faith in God above,
His strength to hold me, His eye to look on me in love.
His hand to guide me in dark of night.
His host to save by conquering might.

I bind unto myself today
The power of earth and heaven:
Light of sun at height of noon,
Radiance of the sacred moon,
Blaze of fire burning bright,
Brilliant flash of lightning strike,
Speed of wind and depth of sea,
Rock's immovability;

All these, I place
By God's Almighty help and grace
Between myself and the powers of darkness!"

The last words tore like screams from my throat. A shattering broke the darkness, like glass cast upon stone. Silence descended. Echoes of my cries lingered in the caves, then faded away.

I opened my eyes slowly. Danileoth was gone. I fell back to my knees, exhausted. My breath came in ragged gasps.

"Those are powerful words you speak," a familiar and inviting voice said.

I didn't have to turn my head to know Eladora approached. If not the sound of her voice, then the smell of her spiced cigarettes told me she was near.

With hands still bound in rock I attempted a shrug.

"I don't know how," I said. "But, hey, it worked."

"You spoke the name of the Holy One," Eladora answered. "Danileoth...he has changed. And not for the better. That name hurts him now. The evil in him cannot abide the name of righteousness."

She ran a finger along my aching arms, over the muscles that had knotted up in tension. With her touch, a shiver went up their length and I felt them relax.

"You know you can just let go," she told me. "There is nothing that binds you to that rock except your own grip."

When she told me that I noticed my fists were clinched. That's why my forearms ached so much. There was something in the rock pillar I gripped with all my might. How had I not noticed it before?

Even knowing, it took effort to let go. Pain shot through my arms as I forced my muscles to relax and release their death grip. My hands throbbed and my knotted forearms screamed with released tension. I pulled my hands free of the pillar, cradling them close to my body as they shook uncontrollably.

Eladora stubbed out her cigarette and took my hands in her own. She massaged the knotted muscles with her soft touch, magic and tenderness flowing from her fingers. All the tension and pain melted out of me.

"How come it didn't affect you?" I asked, noticing that she remained untouched by my words.

"They weren't directed at me," she answered, still working on my hands and arms. They felt better instantly, but her touch granted ecstasy, and I never wanted her to stop.

"Besides," she shrugged. "I'm not quite as far gone as Danileoth. I hate to think of what he's done, how he has corrupted himself. His true form now..."

She shuddered instead of finishing the thought. I couldn't

help but remember the twisted silhouette and the red eyes that loomed over me and Erin at the Bal Masque.

"And yet his change is nothing compared to yours," Eladora said. She stopped massaging my arms. Her soft hand moved to my cheek. Our eyes met quietly.

"You went into the woods behind your house," she said. I noted sadness in her voice.

"The pale man was there."

"I told you he would have his way with you," she reminded me. "It is the way with men like you."

"Like who?" I asked.

"Men who are marked," she answered. "You have been set aside, marked for purpose."

"Is that a bad thing?" I asked. Her sadness had become my sadness.

"It is the greatest thing a man can become," she answered, voice still rich in sorrow. "But the price of the hero is always the same."

Something unspoken passed between us then, a thing I cannot fully comprehend or explain. Respect shone in her eyes, along with admiration. Behind this ran a sorrow, deeper than I have ever felt. One that she had felt before. What might have been, perhaps. Hundreds of times over, what might have been. Played out again and again over the centuries. And even though she knew it would come again, she embraced it. Eladora, queen of an endless tragedy. It was her burden, her punishment, and her joy – to love a hero doomed to give his life. It was the sadness and the glory of the universe, its crown and scourge of grief.

"Why are you doing this?" I asked, taking her hand from my cheek and holding it in my own. "Why all these plots against mankind? What can you possibly want? Is it just power? What?"

"We used to be the children of the earth," Eladora said. She pulled her hand away and turned from me. "We only want to be so again."

"And this is the only way?" I asked.

"I don't expect you to understand. You weren't alive then. You can't possibly know the joy that we danced with at the dawn of the world, when creation was still young. Under our father's care the earth flourished and was beautiful. Is it so bad to want to make it so again?"

"Is this how you do it?" I shot back. "You make this ugly thing of machines and cities? Is this your beautiful world reborn? Strip malls and concrete parking lots?"

"We only give man what he wants," she turned back to me and said. "All we've done is indulge you. This world is man's folly, not ours."

"You've indulged what's worst in us. You've encouraged it."

"Perhaps," she shrugged.

"You know I can't let it happen," I said. Even then I was unable to come close to hating her.

She smiled weakly and leaned forward to kiss me.

"Of course," she said. "Come now. Danileoth will return eventually. Neither of us should be here when he comes back."

Taking my hand Eladora led me through the twists and turns in the cavern. The tunnels led us to an opening into the forest. Darkness still held, but I could make out a path that wound into the trees. Eladora stopped here and faced me.

"Follow this path," she instructed. "Stay on it until you recognize something."

A sense of finality seasoned the moment. Eladora wore a pensive expression, her eyes deep and rich with old anguish. She appeared more beautiful than I had ever seen her. The way she looked at that moment, framed in soft moonlight, will remain forever in my memory. I do not believe death could even wipe out such a vision. If there is any eternity to the soul, any essence that lasts beyond the corruption of this mortal life, then Eladora will always live in me. That moment, perfect and sublime, may it remain in me an immovable monument to the day when I touched the face of divine beauty.

I reached out and kissed her fiercely. I breathed out my fire into her, giving willingly of myself, all that I could. She moaned beneath my lips, and the heat raged all the hotter in my soul.

A glow suffused her features as I pulled my lips away from hers. She smiled. I turned and ran through the forest path.

As I ran I looked back behind me. The cave mouth was hidden in trees, and with it, Eladora. Beyond them, I saw the palace of the Fae, dark and grim. A single tower rose up higher than the rest. Within, a shadow looked out, silhouetted in orange firelight. I could feel Danileoth's eyes on me, malicious and full of hatred.

For a moment I enjoyed a swell of victory. Then, another shadow rose up in the night. A large figure, soaring in front of the moon, spreading out large, leathery wings. A screech pierced the darkness, and the figure dove.

I knew it hurtled toward me. Fear gave me wings of my own. I fled through the forest, hearing the screech first behind me, then beside me.

I ran until I found something familiar, as Eladora instructed. It was the clearing, the one where I had met with the pale man. By then my pursuers were dangerously close.

Normally, I would have been overtaken easily. But here, the power that emanated out of this enchanted place filled me. I was partly a citizen there now. Here I could run faster, longer, with long, loping strides impossible to me in my native world.

I ran over the natural bridge spanning the chasm. Through the forest again, then I burst out into my own backyard. The screech of my winged pursuers still rang through the trees, out of their world into ours, but I knew they would not pursue me here.

I fell into my house, breathless and giddy. Once again, I have brushed with death and survived. Even more, I have struck back at the enemy. It may have been a feeble strike, but I have confronted them, been captured, and escaped with my life intact. I can almost rest easy tonight...almost.

The ravens still gather thick in the trees. The branches are almost completely black, pulsing in wicked feathers. I see them out the window, their hateful eyes fixed on me, waiting. They wait for the return of their lord. They wait to devour.

For today, I am still alive.

The Seventh Vision

Death comes. How soon I cannot tell. Tonight perhaps? Tomorrow? Can I get all these things written in time? Can I do what needs to be done? All will happen in its appointed time. My death is certain, it approaches close. No need to rush towards that hour.

There is much that needs to be recorded before I can complete what has been set out before me. I have been negligent in my writing. So much has happened since my capture and escape. So much has been learned.

I believe know now what Danileoth and these children of the gods are planning. There is much I am still ignorant of, but I know enough. More importantly, I know what I must do, and that it requires my blood to do it.

Before that happens I must make this record complete and tell the last chapter of all the things that happened to me and how the schemes of the Fae were revealed. And then...then my destiny waits.

It begins with the vision, the seventh and last of all these strange things revealed to me. And in this beginning, it ends.

I felt a presence one night as I studied late in the hours. I can hardly remember what I was researching. There have been so many arcane and obscure texts passing beneath my eyes that they begin to run together now.

Before I stood up, I knew it was the pale man. He waited outside my house. No words came from his mouth. He only beckoned with his hands and I followed.

A door stood, alone in that small grove of trees in my front yard. It was the same place where I found the first door, that first disorienting, bizarre vision. It waited as it did that first night, mysterious and alone.

Unlike that first vision I didn't approach the door alone. The pale man walked beside me, the same presence that once terrified now gave comfort. As I pushed open the door I felt his hand upon my shoulder. His presence stepped with me through the dark threshold.

The darkness covered me, but this time it didn't fade completely from my sight. I saw the city come into view, covered in a thick night. Some dense, black fog hung over it, choking the streets and obscuring the few weak lights that sputtered above the sidewalks. It looked like some dark cloud had passed over the city and settled down in the alleys and avenues.

I saw these things through the perspective of one who floated over the city, like a disembodied spirit. I had no sense of body. I hovered in the thick, choked air, festering with a noxious miasma. I moved by will alone, feeling, hearing and seeing all that happened around me without the aid of a body, and unrestricted by its limitations.

Although I still felt the presence of the pale man near me he said nothing nor gave me any instruction. I took the liberty to examine the city on my own. It looked mostly like the one I lived in and had known for so many years. A few differences stood out. Most notably, the heavy darkness and black fog obscured what I recognized. But the light seemed different too, weaker somehow, as if all the streetlights and office lights that spilled out of the tall buildings glowed from bulbs only half their normal brightness.

And a despair hung over the city. Something more than the fog caused it. I could see it in the people hurrying on the sidewalks, their shoulders slumped and backs stooped in that characteristic look of weighty oppression.

I moved myself closer, noticing the downtrodden look on their faces. Their eyes stayed fixed on the ground. Feet shuffled mechanically, without any intent or purpose.

It took a moment to notice, but it became quickly apparent that all the people dressed the same. Black pants, white shirt and black overcoats donned every figure on the sidewalk, male and female. They all moved in the same direction in that same mournful gait. A grim and featureless monotony gripped the city, draining her people of all character and depth.

As I followed the people shuffling on, the crowd grew. One street met another and all the slow steps began to converge. The throng grew thick until I became certain that most of the city must be marching together in one direction.

They turned a corner, one homogenous flow of featureless conformity, and I turned with them. Whatever power I moved under recoiled when I saw what lay before me.

A tower, tall and dark stood at the nexus of the city streets. The people flowed as one towards it, mingled as one sorrowful mass.

It wasn't just any tower I saw ahead of me. It was built in exact detail as the one I found under the grotto, the one the hunchback was building.

This one rose hundreds of feet in the air in massive scale. One jut of black steel flared up in the center, it's point angled like a blade. Buttresses stuck out like spider's legs, connecting it to other, smaller towers, stabbing ominously at the dark sky.

The presence of the pale man touched me, sensing my reluctance. At his prompt I moved forward again, forcing myself to ignore the fear that told me to get as far away from the tower as possible.

Features came into sharper focus as I moved closer. The massive tower stood upon a black, obsidian base, sleek as glass. Steps cut into the volcanic rock led from the ground to the complex of dark steel stabbing at the heavens. The crowds of people slowed as they approached the steps, sensing the dangerous presence.

The crack of a whip sounded, followed by a woman's scream. I pressed myself forward to see figures clad in dark, purple robes lashing at the crowd with whips.

"Forward, you unworthy filth!" one of the purple clad men cried out, thrashing the leather goad randomly at the cowering people. "Forward!"

"Show some gratitude, filth!" another shouted, cracking his

whip. "It's an honor to worship Khaldi! You should be running to him! Unworthy! Worms!"

In this way the reluctant people were forced to stand before the tower. I watched in amazement, certain that most of the city gathered there. The crowd began at the foot of the black, glassy steps and stretched for blocks in every direction. I could smell fear emanating from the people even if I couldn't read it on their pale faces and wide, darting eyes.

A bell tolled from the bowels of the tower, shaking the steel buttresses. The crowd went still. Priests emerged from the dark to stand on the obsidian platform. At least a dozen of them came forward. Like the men with the whips, they too wore dark purple robes. In addition, streams of dark feathers decorated their backs and under their arms, so that when they stretched them out it looked like great, raven wings. Their faces were hidden behind raven masks. They raised their hands in unison and the great mass of people fell to their knees and prostrated with their foreheads to the ground.

"Hail Khaldi! Lord of the Sky!" the priests cried out.

"Khaldi forever!" the people answered in unison.

"Hail Khaldi, wise and magnificent king!" the priests intoned.

"Khaldi forever!"

"Hail Khaldi, Keeper of the Nine Realms, Master of Andiri, Beloved of the Dragon, Blessed One!"

'Khaldi forever, forever. Amen!"

Then, as one the voices recited yet another litany to the Raven King.

"To Khaldi we entrust our lives. To Khaldi we entrust our deaths. By the wing of the raven are we delivered. Our souls we lift up to you. Our hearts we lift up to you. Our praise and devotion we give to Khaldi as one. Khaldi forever. Amen."

As the people and the priests went through this ritual I could feel a shift in the air around me. It was a singular and altogether unique sensation. The best way I can describe it is to liken it to standing in a rough current. I could feel movement, mass movement, but neither water nor air.

What I felt was power and devotion moving out of the people and towards the tower. It was the soul-fire Canta had told me about. The life essence of the people, the very heat and light of their souls drained from them and into the tower as they performed their worship.

It made me sick to feel it. So much power, the essence of life itself, wasted. The people grew less. I could see it. Whatever dark power waited in that tower swelled as it fed it's ravenous appetite.

A shudder sounded from the depths of the tower complex, like the pounding of drums. I caught movement in the shadows, then the air exploded as thousands of ravens poured out of the tower and filled the already dark sky.

The mass of birds split up and formed into six, tight groups and dove towards the crowd. Screams of terror rose up but the congregation remained still, mired in fear and conditioned by the cruelty of their overseers.

Each smaller flock broke away and dove towards a person in the crowd, as if selecting them. They flocked and fluttered around them, covered them, making it clear that they had been chosen. Perhaps chosen at random, or by some unknown sentience.

The Overseers move towards the six people cursed enough to have attracted the attention of the ravens. Amid futile resistance they were dragged from the crowd and pushed toward the steps of the tower.

Only one of them put up any fight. A girl, no more than twelve years old, was elected by the flutter of ravens about her. When the Overseers grabbed at her she kicked and flailed, all the while crying out for her mother, reaching for help. Desperation and fear marked clearly on her face. Tears streaked her dirty face as blond hair, clumped in neglect and filth, whipped around by the violent motions of the girl's head.

She slapped and clawed at her captors who seemed not to notice or feel the girl's resistance.

The woman who knelt beside the girl didn't move either. Her head stayed fixed to the ground as if deaf to the pleas of the child who called to her in wailing desperation. The tears fell in vain and the girl was carried into the shadows of the tower, still reaching out her arms towards the only help she knew.

"The chosen ones of the Raven," the priests intoned as the girl's screams still echoed in the night.

"Blessed be the Raven forever," the people responded.

Still watching in horror, I felt the presence of the pale man exert itself near me.

"Behold what is to come," he told me what I already suspected.

"Does this have to be?" I asked, knowing I would do anything to avoid this fate. The city, though not beloved of me, inspired affection at seeing what dark fate awaited. No one deserved to be held under the sway of that shadow.

"If the Tree fails, then the Dark Lord will rise, and this city has been claimed as his," the pale man said. "Already the Raven gnaws at the root and his servants claw at the bark. His prison must hold or this doom awaits."

"What can I do?" I cried out as the vision darkened and I felt myself slipping away.

It was too soon to leave. I needed answers.

"The strength of the seal is in the heart of the people," the pale man said while full dark folded over me. "As the spirit of man fails, so the Tree fails."

A few days after the vision I received a letter from Erin. It was slid under the door, my name written in her precise and eloquent script. A small card waited inside. The brief note read:

I REALLY WANT YOU TO SEE MY NEW PLACE.
ALBION APARTMENTS, ROOM 514
SATURDAY, 4 PM. DON'T BE LATE.

I wasn't late. I was disappointed.

Albion Apartments, despite its lofty name, showed none of that ancient glory. The faded, red brick edifice rose some twenty stories high. A tattered, green awning covered the front entrance. Window air conditioner units stuck out of almost every third window. A fire escape rusted off the side of the building, hanging crooked and looking more dangerous than a fire. A kid on a tricycle with broken petals stared lazily up at me.

The inside fared no better. The linoleum floors had yellowed and cracked. Dim, florescent lights flickered through the narrow hallways. I didn't attempt the groaning elevator, opting instead for the poorly lit stairwell that smelled of old damp and urine.

Upon seeing Erin, the place took on a new glow. She seemed happy to see me. Her face lit up when she opened the door, and she wrapped me up in a fierce hug.

For a second she pulled back, searching me while her arm still hung about my neck. Tentatively, almost experimentally, she leaned in to kiss me. Without hesitation I kissed her in return until I felt something pull out of me.

We both gasped at the same time, breaking away from each other. She laughed and covered her mouth, looking down.

"Don't worry," she said, touching my arm. "I was just...trying it out. I would never take anything from you."

"You've learned how to feed then?" I asked, not sure how I felt about what she had just done. I felt the fire move out of me as I had before with Mesulina and Eladora. And just like those other times, an even greater surge of passion followed. Whatever they had taken from me, the loss was quickly replaced. Even so, the parasitic nature of the act left me

257

feeling ill at ease.

"You say it like I'm a vampire," Erin said. A crimson blush darkened her cheeks, belying the shame she felt.

"Feeding is what the others do," she told me. "Danileoth and his others. We just glean. And you know it actually increases the energy in a soul. Kind of like clearing ashes from a fire. Lets the soul burn better."

"I know," I admitted. "I could tell. It's just...a little strange, that's all."

Erin laughed. "Tell me about it. I don't know if I'll ever get used to it. I'm still learning and I didn't think you would mind. Besides, they said you were different."

I nodded, unsure of what to say.

"They really are good, you know," she said. "Canta and the others. We're not like Danileoth. Him and the others. They are shachat."

"They're what?"

"Shachat. Rotten. They've gone rotten. I'm told they used to not be like that. At the worst, they would play some bad natured tricks from time to time. A few went shachat, but that was rare. Not like this."

"Well, the place looks great," I said, steering the talk to something else.

Erin shot me a wry smile.

"It might be the ugliest place in the city," she said. "I feel like I'm in a halfway house."

"Not bad for a halfway house," I said, looking around at the brightly painted walls and the esoteric decorations. "You've done pretty good considering what you had to work with."

"The outside has to look inconspicuous," she told me. "Something that says, 'nothing magical here,' you know. Nothing to see here."

"So how many others like you live here?"

"There's about a dozen of us in this building. The Folk

own it, like all the others they use. But we don't concentrate in numbers. Try to blend in. You know, act like people. Get jobs and all that."

"So what do you do now?"

"Paralegal."

"Nice," I remarked. "Still doing research."

"Of course," she smiled. "And quickly being recognized as the best. As you know, there's nothing I can't find. The pay isn't great, but the gratitude is amazing."

"Hey, it's paying for all this," I stretched out my hands to indicate in mock grandeur the little space.

"Don't be deceived," Erin told me. "It might look like crap on the outside, but the courtyard is amazing."

I followed her downstairs to find the courtyard anything but amazing. It looked as drab as the rest. Situated in the center of the building, the sun barely ever reached the ground. Overgrown and neglected shrubs scattered about, brown under the winter snow. I could see trash strewn among the tangled vegetation. An empty and cracked fountain stuck out of the snow, a lonely symbol of long forgotten beauty.

"Yes, it's quite lovely," I said sarcastically, pulling in my arms against the cold.

"Look again," Erin prodded me.

Looking around in the quickly fading light I tried to see what she saw. At first, it was just a dirty and neglected courtyard. I looked deeper and something pulled at me.

On the far wall I saw it – an archway that had been bricked up. It reminded me of the woods behind my house.

"A gateway," I said, nodding to the mismatched bricks.

"I don't spend a lot of time in the apartment," she said. "As you can probably understand.

"Come on, let me show you something."

She grabbed my hand and started to pull me towards the arch. I pulled back, shaking my head.

"Not a good idea," I told her. "My last trip to the other side

257

didn't go so well."

I told her then about my visit to the building site. There was nothing I held back, recounting my capture by Danileoth and subsequent escape. As I spoke, her brow furrowed in worried concentration.

"Let's go back to my room," she said when I finished. "I need to tell you something."

"I haven't forgotten about the project you gave me," Erin said when we returned to her apartment. She put a kettle on the stove and sat across from me in her cramped kitchen.

"Erin," I chided. "Forget about that. You're here to stay safe, not get involved in all that stuff again."

"When I start researching something I can't stop until the job is done," she said. "It's a part of my nature. A part of the gift. Besides, the resources I have at my disposal now are amazing. Not to mention access to people who are really in the know. And what I found out..."

She sighed and took my hand. A serious and somewhat mournful expression took over her face. The kettle whistled in the background.

"I don't know what can be done about it," she said. "But I'll tell you what I know."

"I've put a lot of it together," I told her. "I think I have a pretty good handle on who is the real power in the world these days. I know they're building this tower, and it has something to do with the Raven King. And I know that if it's built, we pretty much have nothing but dark days ahead. I just don't know why. Why now? What are they really up to?"

"This isn't the first time they've built a tower like this," Erin said. "A long time ago, at a place called Shinar, they built another one. Or almost did. A different tower, but for the same purpose."

"What purpose?" I asked. "What is it they want? Is it to free the Raven King? Why would they do that? He is their enemy as much as ours."

Erin turned from me and picked up the kettle. She seemed to be gathering herself for an answer. She poured two cups of the hot water and handed one to me.

"Do you know the story of the first tower?" she asked me. "It's in the Bible, you know."

I shrugged, knowing lamentably very little of what was in the Bible. "I've never heard of a tower in Shinar. I've never even heard of Shinar."

"The tower is known by another name," Erin said. "It was called the Tower of Babel."

A chill ran through me. That story I knew.

"Wasn't that the tower that God tore down or something?" I said as much as I remembered. "Men tried to build a tower to Heaven so God tore it down."

"Pretty much how the story goes," Erin said. She blew into her teacup and took a tentative sip.

"Except they leave out all the important stuff," she continued. "As the story goes it was a bunch of people who wanted to build a tower that reached to Heaven. It was supposedly an act of great hubris, man wanting to be God and all that. In reality it was the Fae that instigated the building, that drove men to their labors. And it wasn't the heavens they were trying to reach."

"Why else would they build a tower so tall?"

"Oh they needed it high, but that was to channel the power for its real job, for what the tower was really supposed to do."

"And what was the tower really for?" I asked with a tremor in my voice.

She looked off in the distance, a pensive look crossing her face. "No one knows," she said, though I wasn't sure I could believe her. "It rose up high to channel the powers of heaven, so that it might... I don't know what it might do. Something dark and awful, something almost too terrible for words. Whatever it was, it meant the subjugation of the entire human race. It would channel the power of heaven, but somehow it would allow the Fae to feed off of mankind, grant them the life spark they so desire to consume. All human life... it would be awful. Humanity would become worse than slaves. They would become cattle. They would exist only to feed the Fae and their insatiable hunger. Imagine it, the entire human race raised up only to be fattened for slaughter, their souls gorged on by beings pretending to be gods. All human existence, all we do, and all we are, reduced to being food."

Strange, I felt no sense of shock when she told me; the absolute enslavement and subjugation of mankind. It made too much sense to shock me. Instead, it terrified me. Everything I saw in that last vision had said as much. It wasn't just my city that would be given over to the Raven King, the whole world would be cast under the domain of these frail and angry gods.

"What about the Raven King?" I asked. "What is his part in all of this?"

"I can only speculate about that," Erin shrugged. "From what you said they struck some sort of bargain. They aid in the Raven King's escape, allow him to rule, and his master helps the Children in their designs."

"Master?" I questioned. The figure in the crimson robe, hovering over the dark pit and accepting the bodies of children as sacrifice, surfaced in my mind. The stench of unspeakable evil filled my nostrils even then.

"He's not spoken of, not even by the Good Folk," Erin said darkly. "A malice ancient beyond counting, the enemy of all that is good and alive."

I nodded with uncertainty, thinking for a moment that it would have been better had I never awoken to such a terrifying world.

"Didn't God stop them the last time?" I asked. "Didn't he tear the tower down and scatter the people who built it."

"Yes and no," Erin nodded. "The Keepers of the Flame were the ones that brought it down. They fought the Fae and their servants and destroyed the tower. And when the tower came down the tongues of men were confused. No one spoke the same language all of a sudden. They couldn't understand one another. Slowly, the city was abandoned and the tower never was tried again. Until now."

"Because now there are no Keepers," I said.

"There are no Keepers," Erin echoed. "And there are very few men who would even make good candidates. That's what they've been doing all this time, for hundreds of years now. Little by little they have infiltrated the institutions of man; his universities, businesses, governments, all the powers that rule the world. Even the church has been a large part of it. And they changed life, changed how men live, how they view themselves and the world around them. And slowly, one generation at a time, the spirit of man has dwindled, has starved, until today he is but a shadow of himself. The soul-fire that used to be the bright star of the world has dwindled until it can hardly warm a single mind. So this time, when the tower goes up, who can be rallied to the fight? Who is there to stand up to them? Who has the strength, the courage, or even the desire?"

The ominous words stung. Every bit was true. Who among us could stand up to the Fae? Even if they aren't gods, we are certainly less than men. I raged inside at all of it. We should have seen it, should have known. Some did, and they warned us. They warned us that man had lost the path of life and chased after vain desires as he grew fat and lazy, a slave to the market, a dupe to popular culture and a dependent to the institutions that took away our liberties and our initiatives as they promised an easier and safer life. Until now, here we are, helpless before the predators that have stalked in shadow while we grow weaker and weaker.

"Except this couldn't have been their idea," Erin said.

At first her words didn't register. My mind was lost in the misery that had become human civilization, the cruelty that our own weakening, the very mechanics of our own undoing we hailed as the pinnacle of our culture.

"Wait. What?" I said, shaking out of my reverie.

"This, the whole plot," Erin said. "This couldn't be the work of the Fae. Danileoth couldn't have come up with this."

"How can you be certain?" I asked. "Didn't you say they did this before? When they built the Tower of Babel?"

"Not the tower," Erin clarified. "Much of that is necessity. I'm talking about the long plot to weaken mankind. This conspiracy that has been playing out for hundreds of years, this slow chipping away at his strength, his virtue, his vitality. The imagination has been starved, wonder has gone out of man's hearts. Courage has been undermined. Truth is relative. Life watered down."

She paused and looked into her cup. I stared out the window, feeling every word she spoke a nail in the coffin of humanity.

"This whole operation is too creative," she went on to say. "You have to possess a different sort of consciousness to come up with something like this."

"I don't think I follow you."

"I've had to learn a lot of hard truths over the last few weeks," Erin said with a sigh. She got up and turned away from me, moving to the window and staring out at the winter night.

"One of them is accepting what it means to not be completely human."

"Don't believe that for a second," I interrupted. "You're more than human. Your half god, Erin. You can do things we can only dream about."

"That's not true," Erin said softly. "We may have talents, some knacks. Maybe a little bit of magic too. But humanity is truly gifted. There is a magic that belongs to you that is more powerful than anything the Elihoud, or even the Fae could hope to possess. You have freedom and passion and creativity and...and a lot more besides."

"But you're human too, Erin," I insisted. "I don't care what anyone says, you're human."

"Not fully human," she said, turning around to face me. Tears welled in her eyes. My heart ached to see her in this pain, yet I felt it may be too deep to touch.

"I have enough humanity to know what I'm missing," she explained. "Part of my will is bound, so I can never be totally free. I will never be artistic or inspired. I will never fully know that swell of passion that drives humanity. I will never know what it's like to have God's own spirit within me."

"That can't be true," I said, standing up and moving to her. "The Fae have music all the time. And the dancing they do, and the tower. There's lots of creative things they do."

"We have a lot of talent and can pick up any craft with very little instruction," Erin explained. "But any music we play is stuff we've heard before. Same with the stories and the dancing. We can imitate. We can even perfect to some degree. What we can't do is create, truly create. Why do you think poets and writers and musicians have always been the favorite of the Fae? They create what we cannot."

"What about the Muses?" I asked. "Mythology is full of supernatural beings that inspire artists."

"Inspire, yes, but never create," Erin answered. "Inspiring man was one of the tasks of the original Watchers. We were made to be catalysts for man's creative spirit, to help him become more creative, greater. But it is to the children of men alone that this greatness belongs. It's something I will never know."

I tried to take her in my arms but she held out a hand to keep me away.

"I've come to terms with it," she said. "Mostly."

"So all this means that whoever wants to rebuild the tower is not one of the Fae."

"The Fae definitely want the tower built," Erin said. "But

all this planning that's going into it, the scheme itself is just way too innovative to come from one of the Fae. The level of creativity involved here is staggering, even for the human mind. For us, it is completely impossible."

A chill passed through me as her words sunk in.

"So what you're saying is a human is behind this."

"Not just a human," Erin said, looking up at me. "This is a man of rare and incredible intelligence."

"A genius?"

"Super genius," Erin said. "This is the kind of guy that would make a regular genius look stupid."

"Why would any man do that?" I asked. "Why would anyone betray humanity like that?"

"Why does man do anything?" She shrugged. "It's common for men to serve the Fae. They've done so since time began. But for one with this level of intelligence to do so is rare. He has to be receiving some enormous benefit for his cooperation. All we know is based on speculation, though."

This new information brushed aside any brief satisfaction I had felt. Things appeared worse than I originally thought. Not only were we embroiled in a scheme to enslave humanity that has been unfolding for hundreds of years and involved divine entities – as if that weren't bad enough. We had to contend with a super genius that lay behind it all. The weight, the impossibility of it, cast over me a shadow of despair. I tried to push it away. It pushed back, more confident than I.

"You're human too," Erin said, reading on my face the doom I felt. "You can do things clever and innovative and creative. You've just awakened and haven't yet realized the extent of your power."

"I'm no super genius," I answered her. "Heck, I'm not even smart on my good days."

"But you're good," Erin said, taking my hand and tracing shapes in the palm. "And good people do things that bad ones can never imagine anyone doing. That's your real power, you know, the real gift of freedom – the choices you make to be good."

That sorrow welled in her again. I could feel it radiating from her body. She still looked down at my hand, as if she were frightened to meet my eyes.

I tried to draw her to me again.

"We can't," she said, pushing me away. "Okay? We can't."

"Why not?" I asked.

"It's different now," she told me. At the same time her resistance wavered and I wrapped her in my arms.

"Are you going to eat me like a black widow?"

She laughed despite herself. "It's more true than you know."

"Yes, but whatever you take from me you leave more behind," I reminded her.

"Not if this goes much further," she warned.

"How bad can it be?"

"Things are different now," Erin said, remaining in my embrace. "If this were to be...consummated, you would be giving me a large share of your soul-fire. It's the most potent amount a man can possibly give, and one not easily replaced. It's designed to fuel life, you see, to be the foundation of a living soul, just like yours, bearing the image of God in its transmission."

"Will it kill me?" I asked.

Erin paused, as if carefully choosing her next words.

"No," she said. "But because of who I am I will take more than a human woman. I fear what it might do to you. What it might do to me."

"To you?"

"A man's essence is like nothing else we can ever feel," Erin explained. "It's exhilarating and dangerous all at once, like an opiate, powerful and addictive. Some of the Elihoud are said to keep harems of mortal men, use it to fuel them until the men wither into nothing."

"You wouldn't do that to me," I said confidently.

She pulled away to look me in the eyes. "I've never been under the influence of that power, at least like I am now. I don't know what I would do."

I leaned in to kiss her. She turned her head away, but slowly, reluctantly. I could feel her trembling in my embrace. Was it hunger or desire? Is there any difference? Whatever it was wore her resistance thin.

"I want to give you this," I whispered to her.

A moan escaped her lips as her fingers dug into me. Her lips found mine and kissed me fiercely. The unmistakable sensation of fire passing from me attended her affection. But as soon as the heat passed, it flared again, stronger, and again drawn from me. I could tell Erin felt it also as the intensity of her passion grew with mine.

"Not here," she said, pulling away from me. A fierceness blazed in her eyes, part hunger and part excitement. Her smile was devilish and tempting.

Somewhere in my mind, the reasonable part of myself warned me that this might be dangerous. Already Erin looked different. The hunger had transformed her in a way that gave her a predatory look. I was unsure I could resist her as prey, but my own passion had been aroused to an intensity that could not be ignored. Perhaps a part of myself remained free. If so, I disregarded it and allowed myself to be swept away.

Erin stopped to grab two small, glass bottles, like old perfume bottles, and took my hand. She led me out to the courtyard, covered in night snow, and towards the bricked-in archway. Together we stepped through and into that enchanted place the Fae call Annwyn.

We ran, hand in hand, to a hilltop, bathed in the light of a moon that loomed impossibly large in the sky. There, she pulled me down and opened herself to me and I to her. Every breath of air filled us with ecstasy.

I would not be so vulgar as to divulge the details of the

love we shared there. I will tell you that she did not devour me that night, though at moments I thought she might. When the fire passed from me, the emptying was absolute. Though attended with a pleasure I have never known before, it came also with the sensation that my very soul was being drawn out of me. And by the widening of Erin's eyes, the breathless gape of her mouth, like shock, I could see it filled her as something she had never felt before.

Within seconds, as Erin panted beneath me, exhaustion tore through my body. I was empty. Completely empty. The night felt intolerably cold and my eyelids possessed a weight impossible to resist.

I shivered in the warm air, all of my heat vanished. The last thing I saw as sleep crashed over me was Erin, tears coursing down her cheeks – tears of light, glowing gold under the mystical night of Annwyn's full moon.

The next thing I remembered was the sunlight filtering in through my eyes. I woke up groggy and alone in Erin's apartment. My whole body ached and my head throbbed as if I had a terrible hangover. Inside, I could feel an emptiness within me, one that still left a slight chill in its wake. Some of my heat had been restored, though I knew it would be some time before I would be back to full strength. It ended up taking a full three days before I felt myself again.

At that moment, even as horrible and drained as I felt, as I remembered what I shared with Erin I could not regret my decision. Unbelievably enough, the memory even aroused me. It felt strong enough to charge some of the lost fire in my veins. Truly, this is deep and powerful magic.

Erin was nowhere to be found. She left a note for me beside the bed and one of the perfume bottles she had taken with her last night. Inside, a golden liquid glowed with magical light.

"Fairy tears," the note said. "Use only in case of

emergency."

Another letter came to me three days later by courier. It contained one brief, but meaningful message.

THE KEEPER IS DYING.

A memory of my first vision flashed back to me. The ravens had said the same thing. This time, it was an invitation.

Gerard answered the door as I arrived at the Keeper's mansion. It was daylight, and the dusty and abandoned rooms didn't emanate such an ominous presence as they did at night. Still, as I followed Gerard through the opulent and unused rooms, the furniture covered in white sheets, I couldn't help but notice the poignant emptiness and the past glory that beckoned in the silent spaces.

"The Master's breathing has become more labored the last few days," Gerard explained as he led me through the wood-paneled hallway. "He has been quite distressed and didn't seem to calm down at all until I suggested that I summon you.

"Thank you for coming."

I nodded as Gerard pushed open the Keeper's door. Same as the last time I saw him, Sid lay reclined in a massive four-poster bed atop a sea of pillows. His mouth lay open as he slept and the raspy sounds of strained breath came from him. In the daylight I could tell how pale and ashen his skin had grown.

It took several tries before Gerard was able to wake Sid up. The old man took no time to regain himself. He looked up and motioned me over as he struggled to sit up.

"You came," he rasped, reaching for the cigarettes on his bedside table.

"Of course," I answered. "Why wouldn't I?"

"Because I'm an asshole," the Keeper said. He lit a cigarette and inhaled deeply, reveling in the smoke that exerted a noticeable calm upon him.

257

I didn't answer and the Keeper smiled weakly at me as he smoked.

"I'm sorry for what I said to you," Sid told me. "For how I treated you."

The beginning of a protest crept out of my mouth but the Keeper shut me off with a jerk of his cigarette.

"Don't bother," he said. "I don't have time for this, and I've wasted enough already. Death comes to me. I can feel her. She has cold arms, and they wrap around me. My breath fails me and...

"I've wasted enough time. Forgive me. I can't fix the past, but I can still change the future while there is breath in me.

"I was wrong to try and convince you that all is hopeless. It isn't. It's never hopeless. I used to believe that. Or maybe I didn't really. You see, hope is a strange thing. You never need it until it no longer makes any sense to have it. That's what I had forgotten. When things go well there is no need of hope. It's only when they all fall apart, it's only when the situation is hopeless, that hope is needed. Hope is the memory of light when darkness falls. You don't need that in the daytime. But I had forgotten."

A deep sigh rose out of Sid which fell quickly into a fit of coughing. His chest heaved and spasmed for several minutes until I believed it might not end. Then he fell back on the pillows, breathless and trembling.

"There's still something to be done," Sid said between labored breaths. "There's always something to be done."

"It's bigger than you might think," I told him, leaning in.

He barked out a croaking laugh. "Don't presume what I know or don't know. There is more strangeness to this world of ours than you can ever imagine. I know how deep it goes. More importantly, how deep it doesn't go."

"There are so many of them," I said. "And I'm only one person. Even if I had weapons there is no way I can even threaten them."

"Let me tell you something," he said, struggling to sit up. "Man gets this wrong. He always gets this wrong. He misunderstands the nature of victory and defeat. He thinks winning is about conquest and conquest is domination, and domination is the strength to inflict pain and death on another human being, and in doing so bend them to your will.

"But that's not so, at least not for real and enduring victory. Our strength is not measured by the ability to shed the blood of others. Strength is measured by the blood we shed of ourselves. Strength is in giving life, not taking it. This is especially true if the life you give is your own. Do you understand what I mean?"

A strange feeling came over me as the Keeper spoke. Something tugged at me, summoned my deepest heart. The moment slowed, then stopped, as a sense of weightlessness came over me. In that pause I felt one with the universe. For that fleeting second all of life felt right.

"Am I to be a martyr then?" I asked.

"Bah! Martyrs!" Sid spat with a dismissive wave. "The word has been corrupted. There is no gift in those lunatics with a bomb strapped to their chests. I'm talking about blood willfully given, not a life carelessly taken. A true martyr wants to live, and always leaves himself that opportunity. A suicide bomber has left himself only the option of death. He has given up on life. But a true martyr, even in risking his life, has made the greatest affirmation of life that there is."

Once again, his breath gave up and the Keeper panted on his bed. The color drained from his face and I noticed a tremble to his hands. It was clear that the conversation took much of the little strength he still possessed.

"I can't give you much," the Keeper continued as soon as he recovered. "But what I can offer you is a bit of hope."

He reached into the voluminous mound of pillows and produced a sheathed knife. After a longing look he reluctantly handed it towards me.

257

"A knife?" I questioned, looking at the unusual, but unremarkable instrument in my hand.

"It's more than it looks," Sid told me.

I turned it over in my hand, noticing the dark, red sheath, apparently made of some dried and hardened animal skin. The handle too was wrapped in skin, so the grip was both smooth and sure. Brandishing the blade, I saw nothing to indicate an extraordinary quality. It was made of a somewhat dull metal, sharpened on both sides and otherwise unmarked. The aroma of oil wafted subtly but unmistakably from it.

"I don't know who made it or how old it is," Sid remarked, nodding to the knife in my hand. "But what I do know is that it can hurt them."

"Them?" I questioned, though I knew who he meant. I wanted to hear it to be sure.

"The Elioud, the Fae," he told me. "Even the Dark Lords and the old gods."

Instantly, the blade took on a more glorious shine. I looked at it and marveled. A giddiness even crept into me. It didn't look like much more than a tribal weapon of some long forgotten aborigine. But if what Sid told me was true, then it may be the most valuable treasure in the world.

"Can it kill them?" I asked, waving the weapon experimentally.

"I suppose," the Keeper shrugged. "If any would hang around long enough to find out. I've only had the chance to nick one of them before the little bastard fled. Ha! They get a touch of mortality and become the biggest pussies in the world."

"You've stabbed one?" I asked in amazement. My admiration grew for the old figure in the bed.

"Ask Danileoth if he's been back to the Spanish Steps lately," Sid said with a chuckle.

I smiled at the remark. The thought of a wounded Danileoth delighted me. Any chink in his armor seemed a small victory for mankind.

"Hope," I said, admiring the gift.

"Dum Spiro Spero," Sid quoted. "As long as I breathe, I hope."

He reached out and clasped my hand. An intensity blazed in his eyes, shined with the strength of fading light. I saw it in him at that moment. Beyond the yellow age of his sclera, beyond the blue irises that once shone with youthful vigor; a fading fire. It flared one last time to impart that last gift to the world, to atone for the weight of one mighty wrong that burdened his soul to premature weariness. And yet the shine of that fire blazed stronger than any despair or wrong or guilt that weighed upon him.

"The Raven King must not be loosed on the world," the Keeper said in a voice powerful once again. "The prison must hold at all costs. The Tree must not fail."

"How can I keep his prison intact?" I asked. "The Tree is strengthened by the spirit of the people. If the spirit of man fails, so does the power of the Dark Lord's prison."

"That prison, the Tree, is a living thing," Sid explained. "It fails now because the spirit that upholds it is failing. The Spirit is life. That means man's spirit as well as the spirit of the whole universe. What the Tree needs is life, a show of life, an infusion of hope and faith, a burst of love and conviction and courage. You don't have to get the whole city to believe and be strong again. You're better off harvesting the tide. But the Tree cannot be allowed to die. And it lives by the power of men who are willing to do anything for the cause of truth and life. Don't you understand? We carry life in us. We are life. We strengthen the things around us, the things we make and even the earth itself. The Tree...you cannot let it die."

Just as quickly as it flared to life, the bright flash and the Keeper's eyes faded. The weariness returned, the weakness, the weight of years and years of guilt. The last Keeper of the Flame became a tired and despairing old man. He leaned back among his pillows. His eyes narrowed to slits and his breathing squeezed out harsh and ragged.

"Thank you," I said, reaching out to touch his hand.

"That was hard to part with," he answered softly. "It's been my security for years. The only way I can sleep at night."

"Do you need it?" I asked, reluctantly offering it back.

"No bother," the Keeper said with a weak wave of his hand. "I doubt my enemies care enough to go to the effort of hurting me. Besides, nature is about to do the job for them."

The eyes the Keeper closed completely and his breathing fell steady and regular. I watched him sleeping quietly as my own thoughts grew pensive. The stillness in the room was somehow full and potent, an electric atmosphere that told me I witnessed something monumental.

When I rose to leave, the Keeper didn't stir. It wasn't until I approached the threshold of his bedchamber that he called out to me one last time.

"As long as I breathe," the Keeper said as he raised a hand in farewell.

"I hope," I finished.

He smiled and his hand fell back to the bed.

It was the last time I would see him.

There is a tale out of Norse mythology about the god Odin, hanging three days from the World Tree, Yggdrasil. After paying this sacrifice, along with one of his eyes, he was given the power of the magic runes. It was ravens that had picked out his eye.

That image kept running through my head the days that followed my meeting with the Keeper. Except I hung from the tree instead of Odin. The ravens fed on me, picking at my flesh and only leaving my eyes. I even saw it in my dreams.

For days I moved about with a prickling fear that never quite left me. Anxiety attended my every step. Doom is one thing to consider when it exists as a distant possibility. As a present reality, as something that waits in the next days, that stalks in both dark and light, walking in your steps and breathing in your shadow; as it reaches out to take your hand, doom is a color that is leached uninvited into your picture of the world and bleeds into it and taints everything you touch.

It wasn't until the storm came that I found peace.

It was an unseasonable storm. For though we are known to have hard winters from time to time, a storm of this size and this late in the season never happens. We should have been feeling the touch of approaching spring. Already it had been widely remarked how winter seemed to keep its hold this year. The days should have been warming. Instead, just around the corner from the spring equinox and winter still relented none of its power.

No signs of approaching spring appeared. We saw no buds on the tree, no flowers struggling out of the snow. Cold and ice and snow remained fixed and unforgiving.

Though everyone remarked on what a long winter we had on hand, I was the only one that knew – that really knew. At some level the others could tell. I know they could. I could see it on their faces – the sense that something dark and terrible cast its shadow over us. Even the earth felt it. The seasons knew it. Spring could not come because the cold grew in power and a day darker than any man had ever known approached with the quickening hours.

Then came the storm. As if punctuating the irresistible grasp of winter, as if announcing that the days of warm and sun had ended forever, the storm barreled into the city.

Massive gray clouds billowed and gathered overhead. As they grew, the sense of impending doom grew in me, marshaling in my soul and feeding upon whatever happiness lingered.

I can't tell you what I felt, what I saw that night on the storm. The clouds dumped thirteen inches of thick, white snow. The winds howled over forty miles an hour. Visibility disappeared in the white out. All this you will remember. The news reported as much.

The real storm raged just beneath the surface of this one. Beneath it screamed the wrath of an evil imprisoned for thousands of years. It screamed with pent-up torment and visions of revenge nursed over long, buried hours. Bitterness decayed into corruption. Hate for all that is good and living rode on the wind. The earth trembled on the imminent eve. The people huddled safely indoors. Because of the storm they told themselves. The real reason, the one they would not admit to themselves, was the evil that came with the storm.

For many hours, I too huddled inside, thinking to ride this wicked night out. Though I did not have the luxury of shutting out the cries I heard beyond the wind. Something ancient and vile called out my name, promised me a death beyond death, and a fate that would make me curse my life and the day my mother and father met.

For many hours I tried to shut out those sounds. Then, with a courage born of anger, I grabbed the knife the Keeper gave me and stepped out into the storm.

"Here I am! Come and get me!" I screamed into the blanket of white that howled down on me. I slashed the knife back and forth as if I could cut back at the wind.

"Here I am! Here I am! Come out you coward! Show yourself and we will decide our fates right now!"

Laughter rumbled beneath the sound of the storm. Mocking laughter, arrogant and sure. I swiped at the wind again, knowing I only provoked more laughter.

I stopped my futile struggles then and let the snow cover me and the wind pierce through me. Voices continued to call and threaten and mock. Shapes materialized out of the swirling snow, shapes of ungodly things that sneered hatred at me then turned back into the roiling blizzard.

How could I fight this? How does one struggle against a storm? The weapon I held could hurt creatures of evil, but evil like this, of wind and darkness, what weapon can touch these untouchable horrors?

Victory is not bought with the blood we shed of others, but the blood we shed of ourselves. That is what Sid told me. It is not in the life taken, but the life given that true power is found.

Another phrase came to mind, one that I heard long ago, spoken long ago. No man has a greater love than this, that he would lay his life down for his friends.

And in that instant, I knew. All at once the thought and conviction came to me. I spread my arms wide and the storm howled and raged even fiercer than before. But behind its rage, I saw fear. For in that moment the storm saw what lay on my heart and it was afraid. It saw I held the one weapon it feared more than any other. It was not the knife. It was the conviction of my soul. In a stroke of instant inspiration it was given me. The one thing this evil feared flowed in me, filled me. In that moment I felt peace, one no meager storm could shake.

A blast of wind struck at me. Howls of fury sounded as the storm screamed in rage. A tree cracked and thundered to the ground, missing me only by a few feet. And yet, it didn't touch me and I didn't budge an inch.

Then the wind began to die and the snow fall subsided. I remained outside in the waning storm, waiting. A break opened up in the clouds and above me the stars shined fierce and bright in the clear, cold air. Rarely have I seen such a magnificent display of glory.

With the storm passed, the city rested in quiet solitude, covered in pristine, white snow. All the noise of the busy city had quieted, giving a peace that it rarely sees. I walked for long hours among its empty streets, down the middle of normally busy boulevards, through intersections glowing with the red and green of unheeded traffic lights. That peace, that indescribable peace, was my gift. I slept that night deep and undisturbed for the first time in months. In me, at least, the battle was over.

Only the hour remained, the hour when I must do what is required of me. And it remained not of my choosing. But it was close at hand. I knew it was. Soon, I would hear the call. The toll of the bell, the announcing of the hour, and then – death awaited.

Not the life we take, but the life we give.

The hour waited, for my work was not yet done. My record waited. I had this last bit to write down so the narration of all that had happened to me would be complete. Then, the ordering had to be done.

It is the common practice of dying men to put their affairs in order. The same impulse overtook me. I felt an irresistible sense that my life stood in an intolerable mess and that it would be a sin to leave it this way. Strangely though, the first order of business I felt pressing upon me was to return to work, to the office that I had spent years slaving away at papers and figures, wasting my life moment by moment.

It felt strange being in that building again, so much had changed in me. If before I felt the office to be a grim place, now it appeared to me mad and diabolical. I watched the people scramble about so desperate and anxious. It looked like an ant colony after a child has crushed the pile with his foot. They rushed so madly about building their stack of sand, oblivious and uncaring of the world around them. Nothing is made, nothing is gained. Life hurdles on heedless of their efforts.

Another man occupied my old cubicle. He looked every bit like me with a different face; hunched over the computer, clicking loyally away at the mouse. White, pressed shirt, yellow tie and a stain of coffee on his cuff marked him as a wage slave of the mighty skyscraper. I noticed the coffee stain the most, as if it were the mark of his master. It said everything about him: how he tried to look perfect, and how he needed the caffeine to make up for his lack of motivation, how he hurried, always one step behind, and always would be.

Pity swelled in me for this man, as one who shared a common prison. I wanted to reach out to him. But what would I say? I could no more force him out of his stupor than I could grow wings and fly. And it may even be that he believes himself happy, that he walks the road to the good life. What I offer might very well horrify them, seem a fate worse than death. Who am I to force men to awareness and liberty? They must find their own path as I have found mine. I can be a guide, a herald, a compass pointing to the mountaintop, to the vale of freedom, but that is all. Every man must choose for himself whether he desires safety in bondage or the peril of freedom.

Upstairs, my old office was locked. The desk Erin first occupied stood empty. Nothing lost there. For that office I lacked even the repulsive sentiment I felt for my old cubicle.

When I turned to go I found Janice blocking my way. She glared at me, a sneer twisting her face. We stood for a moment, facing off, a battle of wills sparking between us.

"What do you want?" she finally spat, making no effort to mask her contempt. Her iron gray hair pulled tight into a bun and the same tightness of her aged face carved an austere look upon her.

"Why Janice," I answered. "I came to see you." I tried to put on a winning smile which had no visible effect on her. Not that I expected any.

"You have no business here," she snapped. "You've been long fired. We have no use for ingrates like yourself and that whore for a secretary."

"Unlike the first one you sent me," I said, indicating Sierra, deliberately put there to seduce me.

"You think you're clever, don't you?" Janice asked as she paced toward me. "You're a fool. You know that? You have no idea who it is you stand against, how hopeless your cause is."

"The gods?" I asked, eliciting a look of surprise on Janice's rusted face. "Or at least what you call gods. Tell me, why would you betray humanity for them? You know they mean us harm."

"It is as you said," she told me. "They are gods. They are glorious and beautiful, eternally young and happy. I am privileged to serve them. To die for them would be a joy. Do you know what they even look like? Have you seen their radiance? We are worms, nothing but worms."

Emotion shook her voice as she spoke. Or rather, fanatical devotion. Her emotion was the passion of the zealot. Her face tightened even more intensely and her eyes pooled with tears. A moment longer and she would have fallen to pure hysteria.

"And yet for all their glory, it is a mere man that commands them," I said.

Janice threw her head back and laughed. I heard no strain or artifice in it. It was a sound of pure incredulity.

"No, you are a mere man," Janice corrected. "The Professor stands as a titan among you."

"The Professor?" I asked.

"You didn't get anything out of me, boy," she said. "That's who he is and that is all he will remain to you. Your days are numbered. Surely even you know that."

"My days are exactly as they should be," I answered with every bit of conviction as her.

I noted a hesitation in her, a wariness. She regarded me with grave suspicion, as if I had said something completely unexpected, or even dangerous. Or perhaps, my conviction shook her own resolve.

"Good for you then," she spat. "What is it you want? What are you doing here?"

In truth, I didn't know the answer to that. Some impulse had drawn me back to my old workplace as if I had some

257

unfinished business there. But what that was I couldn't say.

"As you said, my days are numbered," I answered, unable to think of any other reply.

"Finish what you came for and go," she said and scowled.

Strange, I hadn't given her an answer, or at least one that made any sense, and yet she seemed to understand. Was this the privilege of a dying man?

I walked past Janice and continued on my circuit of the building, seeing the places I had spent much of my life. The break room, pale in florescent light, and white, linoleum floors looked the same as I remembered. How many hours had I spent there absently chewing my lunch?

I asked myself again why I came, but I felt I knew the answer. There is something to visiting the significant places of your life, even if the place holds no fond memory for you. We leave pieces of ourselves everywhere we go. The longer we stay, the more of ourselves we leave behind. Places where we experience powerful events, good or bad, triumph or tragedy, we leave behind greater shares of our self.

I had come to collect. Of course, I could not go everywhere I had ever been. I only go to where I had left the greater shares of my soul. Now it was time to gather them back. I know that now. Perhaps that is all closure ever is – the gathering of the bits of ourselves that we had left behind, like breadcrumbs sprinkled over the path of life.

From the office I wandered the city streets, gathering the miles I had trudged through those crowded thoroughfares. My self was so meager then, I left so little behind. It didn't matter. It was me.

Perhaps the only place where I had left any great share of soul was the bar where I first met Eladora. I sat for a moment in the same seat, though the place was emptier now, just beginning to fill with its lunch crowd. I could still smell her smoke there and feel the thrill that coursed through me when she first walked in, like something from my dreams.

Whatever we leave of ourselves in the places we go, it doesn't compare to what we leave with the people in our lives. From them, we can never fully gather back what we gave. That is the whole point in relationships. With every person we meet we leave a touch of ourselves with them, and they leave a trace with us. That is how we become more, adding to ourselves, adding ourselves to others. The bricks of our being go up, made up of diverse pieces, colors of all we have done and been.

Most of my years belonged to my wife. My visit with her was awkward and forced. I don't think she believed me when I said I just wanted to see her. We talked for a moment in strained conversation. She checked her phone three times, eventually scrolling through something while we talked, her eyes not meeting mine.

It pained me to know how those many years meant so little. That was the piece I had left with her, wasted hours and regret.

With my children, the situation fared better. Our reconnected relationship helped. I took them to lunch and we talked long and intimately. I noticed this time I took nothing back of myself, but gave something more. Perhaps that is how we achieve closure with people. We give them that last piece of ourselves.

Along with that, I gave my daughter the pearls I had gathered on my dive with the Fae. To my son I gave the knife I pried the oysters open with.

They could both tell the gifts were unusual, beyond their apparent nature. My son looked at the knife in wonder. My daughter's eyes filled with tears, gazing at the handful of rare pearls. She reached across the table and squeezed my hand. A part of her, I believe, knew what this was all about.

Other people I had known, friends, acquaintances and associates, I dropped by to visit under some vague pretense.

We shared a last moment, or an awkward moment, and in unspoken ways I said my goodbye to them.

The last people I went to see were the ones I felt would understand what was happening. Gareth welcomed me with a nod and indicated a seat at the bar.

"It's on the house tonight," he said, pulling out a bottle of fine bourbon.

I stayed there much longer than planned. Gareth regaled me with stories. The whole bar stayed fixed on his every word and gesture. I laughed with them, sharing drinks and good wishes in that particular type of intimacy that only strangers can share.

"So what are they saying?" I asked Gareth when it was just the two of us left at the bar. I was drunk enough to dispense with any pretense.

"Not much," he said with a shrug. "We just hear that things are getting tense. And when they get that way they usually break soon after."

"So why all this?" I half-slurred, indicating the empty cups and bottles. "Why the good sendoff?"

"You have the look of a man who has made a final decision," Gareth answered, a warm hand on my shoulder. "Whatever you have decided, may the blessings of fortune smile upon you."

"Thank you, Gareth. You were a friend when I needed it the most."

My visit to Dr. Canta had to be delayed for a day. It took that long to nurse away the farewell Gareth gave me. His was more to the point.

"There's quite a buzz going on about you," Canta said as I sat across from him in one of the ER sick bays.

"I'm sure it's all good things," I remarked.

"You'd be surprised. Word is that Danileoth tried to kill you and you got away."

I shrugged in mock humility, as if the feat were nothing.

"You've come into some power," Canta pointed out. "You will only grow stronger. And we both know Danileoth won't abide by that."

"I know," I nodded.

"There's a storm coming," Canta said. "We can all feel the power gathering.

"Do you know what you're going to do?"

"I think so," I said. "I don't know the details, but I have an idea."

Canta nodded in approval. "Those are usually the best plans. It's better to be guided by what you want to happen rather than how it must happen."

He regarded me for a moment as if deciding what to do. Then he reached out and took my head in both his hands. Leaning close, he whispered over me in a language I did not know. It had an ancient feel. When spoken, it rose up from under shifting sands, out of the caverns of long buried pharaohs, from barrows of Celtic princes and the graves of forgotten heroes, from abandoned cities and broken monuments of past glory. Energy flowed from those words and into me, infusing my cells with a rippling power.

"Go in peace, Awakened One," Canta finished his benediction. "And may God go with you."

Finally, there was Erin. Erin, my light in the darkness, my ray of warm sunshine in the cold of winter. How could I say goodbye to Erin? At my lowest and most lonely, she was there as my only friend. What words were there to express the ache in my heart? What could I gather from her, or what could I leave with her that would be enough?

As it turned out, words were unneeded. Erin opened her apartment door and wrapped me in her arms. After holding her for a moment I tried to pull away and say something. I'm not sure what I wanted to say. But she put a hand on my lips, staying me.

"We're not going to talk about it," she said as her eyes pooled with tears. I could see the radiance in them like drops of liquid gold on her face. "Just stay with me today."

So I stayed. We spent the day together as if it were a normal day. We watched TV, walked together, ate, kissed, and laughed. At night we walked under the bricked archway of the apartment's courtyard and into Annwyn.

We lied down in a clearing atop a rise in the forest. Stars no mortal eye sees blazed above us. Meteors streaked the dark. The moon rose a thin sliver and tracked a slow course over the sky. And Erin and I lay side-by-side, our figures entwined, silently watching the night.

At some point, small creatures began to flit around us, their bodies glowing a soft white. They circled and lighted upon me until my body was outlined in dozens of small lights.

"They honor you," Erin said, turning on her side to look at the glowing points all over my body. "The Lux shun the presence of men, and they never tolerate to be touched by one."

"Why not?" I asked, lifting one of the shining figures on my finger. I could for a brief second make out some semi-substantial figure that looked like a miniature infant. The figure was absorbed into the light and I saw nothing but the glow.

"It is said they are the souls of infants who die in the womb," Erin told me. "Some were miscarried, but most were destroyed willfully. So they have a natural distrust and fear of humans, suffering such violence at the hands of their own mothers."

"Why would they honor me?" I asked, amazed and humbled at such a simple and profound gesture.

"They feel in you what was always denied them," Erin told me. "The love that brings life. Your soul-fire is different now. Anyone with eyes can see that."

"I'm no different from any other man," I was quick to

257

point out.

"But you're more," Erin said, wrapping me in her arms and pulling me close.

After some time she fell asleep. I pulled gently away from her and stood up to leave. The Lux floated around me, their own brand of farewell, and flew away.

I looked down at Erin for long moments, relishing the pain of our parting. Finally, I kissed her sleeping lips. My eyes took in her slumbering form, more beautiful by far at night, that I might engrave upon my mind every detail of her face. Satisfied that I could not remember her any better, I left her for the last time.

And so there is nothing left to do. My will is simple. All that I own I give to my children. My body will be laid on the altar of humanity. My soul, I give to God.

There's nothing left to do but await the call. I have no doubt I will know it when it comes. I only pray I may be equal to that fateful hour.

It has been a week, and still I wait. I have spent this time alone, having said all my goodbyes. I feel like a monk, secluded in his cloister, separated from the world. Alone, I wait.

Doubt assails me now and again. Maybe I've gone mad. Maybe this is all a delusion. Perhaps I've dreamt all this up, fabricated this whole fantastic conspiracy to rescue my aching soul from the banal drudgery of life.

But no, all I have to do is look out my window, at all the ravens gathered there. Every tree is thick with them. Contrasted to the white snow they stand out like ink blots across clean paper.

Though they mean great evil to me, they remind me that I am not mad. Strange friends they have turned out to be. They desire my flesh, to feed on my organs. But they remind me I am not mad.

I dreamt last night that the city was stripped and desolate. Darkness lay over its empty streets, full of ash and dust. The skyscrapers were gutted and half torn down. A hot wind howled through the narrow ways.

There, I walked alone in the tortured wilderness. I saw no green or any other sign of life. The howling screech of wind and my empty steps echoed alone.

Then, amidst ash and dust, I saw a rose growing up through the cracked asphalt. A vibrant red blazed from one, single blossom. It stared triumphantly at the darkness that did not mar her beauty. Instead, the beauty of that rose was magnified, not diminished, by the desolation that surrounded it.

I understood.

By the strange power of perception we possess in dreams, I understood that the desolation was powerless to harm the rose. Whatever destroyed everything else around me, it could not harm the flower.

This is the very heart of truth and beauty, I thought. I could not grasp it, but I knew.

This rose, in desolation, told me all I needed to know.

As I awoke this morning, a thought entered my head, and I do not think it was from me.

There are footprints we make on the beaches of time that can never be erased.

It felt good to think this. So I will keep the thought with me.

The call came. It was not what I expected. I don't know why, but I had thought it would be an angel voice that would call me. A siren song, perhaps, that I would hear and be led to my destiny.

It was nothing like that.

I had just sat down to supper, a fork poised in the air before my open mouth. A scream, though not a noise that could be heard by ears, tore through the night. It filled my house, my mind. It shook the air, and I think the whole world paused, aware and unaware alike, knowing that something good suffered.

It was an ungodly noise if ever an ungodly noise pierced the air. Suffering and pain concentrated in the sound. It was the sound of murder and brutal rape all at once. It was the sound of tearing, of life violated by death.

The call did not come by the voice of God or his angels. The Tree called to me. In pain and fear and desperation she called.

I fell to the floor as her scream convulsed and wracked me, body and soul.

When the sound faded, still shaking, I forced myself to my feet and took hold of the knife the Keeper had given me. In the moment there was no hesitation. Before I walked out, I grabbed this book and a pen. On impulse, I also grabbed the vial of fairy tears. They still glowed, and I stuffed them in my pocket and rushed to whatever waited.

Any fear that in the moment I would act a coward was destroyed by the deep and terrible need I heard in that cry. Hearing such pain I could not harbor a thought for myself.

This too, was meant to be.

One last pause, and all will be done. I think of that time, when a teenager, I stood on the edge of a lake, over a great drop looking into the water below. My friends had already jumped in and I was the last one to go. The fear and tension tore through me then, threatened to tear me apart. But when I finally jumped, that terror broke open to pure ecstasy.

I feel like that now, as if I stand again on that cliff, terrified of the jump below. I know somehow a great thrill awaits me –

something greater even.

Right now I sit on a little wall that surrounds a mostly empty lot in the heart of the city. Inside, the Tree stands besieged. Signs of early disease threaten it. Snow covers its empty branches. These are nothing compared to the ravens that choke every branch and cover the ground beneath it.

When I came near they stirred in anger. Their wings fluttered and I could hear the protest in them. The air shook as the mass of birds took flight and swarmed the Tree.

"You do not belong!" they yelled in the thrum of wings. "We will gouge out your eyes! We will feast on your tongue! Begone! Begone!"

The birds coalesced, tried to form the shape of a man. The mass of violet feathers shuddered and broke apart.

He is near.

The ravens returned to the Tree and they stare at me with murder in their eyes. It is quite unsettling to have a thousand birds fix their dumb gaze upon you. They hate me. They fear me too. Every so often they swarm the sky again and try to take shape, try to combine and become the shape of a man, take the form of their master. Each time it seems the outline grows clearer, the form more definite.

Even besieged as it is, the Tree possesses a rare and powerful beauty. To think, this grew from the Tree of Life. It has stood in the midst of the city here for as long as men and longer. I have passed it by unnoticed more times than I can count. How could I have not noticed?

Even as it dies, I can feel the power of the Tree. What must the mother look like, the one from which this was cultivated? As it perishes it still speaks. Perhaps its voice is clearer in death than in life. Is not the song of the dying swan the most beautiful?

If nothing else, the Tree reminds me how beautiful life is. How beautiful it can be. How beautiful it thrives despite the enemies and powers amassed against it.

There is such potential all around us. Even in the stillness, in the cold of snow, I feel it. It emanates from the earth, from the air, from the vault of heaven above where blaze the thousand eyes of hero and angel alike.

But we have lost so much. We have exchanged passion for safety, glory for wealth, virtue for the petty pleasures that we buy at bargain close out. We have sold our souls to purchase comfort, and there exchanged the greatest treasure of the earth for mediocre, machine-made, mass existence.

Ah, why do I prattle on? Enough of that. Let my last words be those of the goodness and wonder that still surrounds me.

It would be wrong to say that life is full of potential. Life is potential. When we exist as living things we exist as potentialities in a universe that waits in breathless anticipation for what we might do next.

For we can do anything. Might do anything. We can be great. We can be heroes. Or we can be the most depraved villains in all creation.

It is not right that we fix our ambition to be divine. We were not made to be gods or angels. Mankind is our destiny, a much more thrilling and terrifying endeavor. All that lies dormant within us longs to mature into a glory that is fit for us. Passion, freedom, beauty, creativity, faith, hope, courage, determination, and most of all, love; this is what makes us human. These are the compositions of that strange and magical essence which is humanity. We should cultivate all of them within us.

As we grow, we should not become less, but more than we already are. Our potential should increase, not decrease as it does, moment by moment, resigned choice by resigned choice. We were all destined to be more than gears in a machine that wear us down with use and the passage of years, and when worn away and useless, tossed aside and replaced.

When the world was young, before the will of man scarred the earth and polluted the pristine oceans, before life had

257

become mere existence, ruled by countless processes, laws and institutions; man looked on the face of God and reached out his infant hands to take hold of the glory reserved just for him.

Man was capable of so much. His life was full of depth and character. His love was fierce. His friendship was fast. His word was his honor and his honor was life. He filled the world with legendary deeds and history with his heroic work.

The scholar today scoffs at such extraordinary exploits. They say such things are impossible, embellishments of a superstitious and ignorant people, naïve and unlearned. Stories of heroes and legends of old they dismiss as fantasy, convinced that no man could live 900 years, or build an ark to hold two of every animal, or heal with the word, or slay giants and dragons, or be suckled by a shewolf, or slay a legion of men with the jawbone of a donkey. Such things never happened, they tell us. They are mere stories, told by an ignorant past.

What I think is that man's spirit and imagination has grown so weak and feeble that he cannot even conceive that such things are possible, much less do them himself.

The Age of Legends may be passed, but it still waits in us. Greatness still longs to nest in the soul of man. The magic that once blazed from our eyes flickers deep within us. It needs only nourishment, to be fed and cultured to life again. We can be legends again, we can.

There is a voice of doubt within me, that insists on knowing some good reason for why I do this. Why, it asks, do I risk my life for no real gain? No one will ever know what I do. It won't matter, it won't make a difference. Just go home, this voice of reason insists, and let this ungrateful generation rot in the mire they have fashioned out of the good world.

I almost give in. I am tempted. Then I remind myself that what I do, I do in memory of a lost world. I do this to honor the blood of heroes. I do this that every other great life that was lived before me will not have been lived in vain. I do this so that all who have sacrificed their lives, what they sacrificed their lives for, will not end because of my cowardice, and will not perish because this generation cannot recognize a true hero.

I understand the rose now. The flower in my dream, immune to the desolation around it, thrives of its own power. Death and evil cannot touch it, not truly. Even if you were to destroy the rose in one form, it returns in another. Death has no power over life. Evil has no power over good.

Trample the rose, and it only increases in life. Slaughter the man, one who has reached out to his true humanity, and he only grows more powerful. That is the mystery and wonder of life.

It is not the blood that we shed of others that gives us the victory, but the blood we shed of ourselves.

As long as I breathe, I hope.

I know that my hope cannot be stopped by anyone but me. I know my life remains unconquered, even in death. Especially in death. I know that death is not the end of life, it is the crown of life.

I have done all I could. I went to the church, and even at this late hour a priest was there. I didn't ask, but I know his heart was moved by the cry of the Tree, and his faith brought him into the sanctuary. He heard my confession in the dark church, lit only by the candles of the faithful, lights in the darkness. He blessed me and I rose ready.

Now I wait, sitting on the wall as the ravens coalesce, very nearly into a humanlike form, though perversely inhuman at the same time. The time is upon me.

Moments ago Danileoth appeared. He stared angrily down at me, and for a moment I thought he would approach. I pulled out my knife and there was only the shadows of the trees moving in the wind.

I turned and looked the other way and saw Eladora. Her look was one of sadness and regret. She smiled weakly and blew a kiss towards me, her lips forming a perfect rosebud. Then she was gone too, disappearing on the breath of night, leaving only the memory of beauty.

I am alone now. It is just me and the Tree and the ravens swarming in vicious anger. They coalesce again, and for a moment the shape holds before breaking apart. I thought I could see dark eyes staring out from the rush of feathers. Hungry, they stared at victory and defeat all at once in lost eons of impotent rage. Soon, very soon, and it will be too late.

I gird myself with the love that all have given me, and the hours of their affection and trust. I pray, oh Lord, that you remember me, and look upon your servant in mercy. May what I do here not be in vain. And may the footprints I leave in this hour upon the shore of eternity remain beside that unbound ocean, so Heaven may not forget what transpires this day. And may it be a path that leads us all to new life.

Epilogue
Written by the Finder of This Journal

As soon as I finished this story, this tale too incredible to be believed, I rushed out to the place where I found it. The tree, if it really is the Tree, looked so different to me all of a sudden. I could see the green buds bursting out through the snow as the tree glowed with a power I find difficult to even describe.

But it was what lay scattered about it that I really came to see. Raven feathers lay everywhere. It must have been hundreds of birds that dropped them, even thousands, but I couldn't see a single corpse among them.

I stepped over the wall to get a closer look when I saw something move in the shadows beyond. A tall man, appearing to be middle aged, though he could have been much older or much younger, stepped closer and into the light of the street lamps.

I felt cold all of a sudden, thinking this must be the pale man. Then, I noticed his eyes were not blue, and he held a dagger sheathed in a cover of red animal skin. Another name from the journal came to mind.

"Gerard?" I asked, feeling foolish the instant the name escaped my lips.

Unbelievably, he nodded and smiled.

"He's not here," the butler said.

"I figured because I..." I held up the book as if that said everything. "I read about him."

"Where did you find that?" Gerard asked.

"It was sitting on this wall," I told him. "Do you need it? Do you need it for something? Will it help?"

The man shook his head. "No, if you found it, then it must be because you were meant to."

He nodded at me again and turned to leave.

"What happened?" I called out to ask. "Is he still...? Did he die?"

"The Tree is alive again." Gerard turned and answered me. "The prison holds."

"What happens now?" I asked.

He thought for a moment before nodding towards the book.

"You will go and do whatever that leads you to do. I go and await the Keeper."

"He is still alive then?"

Gerard nodded his head. "The Keeper still lives as we wait for another to be appointed. There will always be another."

"Then we are not lost?" I asked. "God has not forsaken us."

"We are never completely lost, and God will never forsake us. Remember that. As long as I breathe..."

"I hope."

Gerard nodded, then turned and faded into the shadows again.

I began to step away when I saw something glint in the snow beneath me. I stooped and picked up a little bottle, like an antique perfume bottle. It was mostly empty, only a drop remained of what was once inside. But that little drop glowed like liquid gold.

For some reason, that made me smile. It made me think that maybe, for whoever braved all these unholy things, at the end, all went well for him. Maybe there is new life. For him and for us all.

I know something is different now. I can feel it. The long winter is over, a winter that has lasted longer than any of us know. All because of one man. Because one man believed that it is not in the life we take, but the life we give.

I can feel it. Even on the cold air. On the wind it comes, on a breeze full of rich promise and expectation.

Tomorrow. It brings tomorrow.

A<small>ND WITH IT COMES THE SPRING.</small>